WATER
Dragon
THE BRIDE HUNT BOOK 2

CHARLENE HARTNADY

DEDICATION

To Siggly Wiggly, this one is for you my boy.
For all the years of joy you gave me. For being the best dog a girl
could ask for. I will miss your soft fur and big, brown eyes. I will
miss the sound of your claws on the tiles, as you followed behind me,
and the sound of your breathing as you slept at my feet.

I will remember you with fondness. The way you couldn't run
without wagging your tail. The way you barked loudly at dinner
time because I could never make your food quick enough.
I will miss you forever . . .

"THE GREATNESS OF A NATION
CAN BE JUDGED BY THE WAY
ITS ANIMALS ARE TREATED."

Mahatma Gandhi

CHAPTER 1

Ellis made a snorting sound as he blew out a breath. He looked away for a moment, clearly annoyed. Then he turned back to her and his eyes widened, a look of shock took the place of the annoyed one.

The guy was a complete asshole! "You're acting like this is news to you. How many times have I warned you? You obviously haven't been listening to me." Candy put her hands on her hips, keeping her gaze on his.

"I heard you just fine." He rolled his eyes. She couldn't believe that she had actually liked him once upon a time. That she had believed that he had her best interests at heart. Ellis only cared about number one. End of story. She was finally old enough and wise enough to realize it. He frowned. "You don't mean it. The money is amazing. How can you just walk away?"

"Easily and I couldn't be more serious if I tried. I've warned you and warned you. School starts in two weeks. I've enrolled."

"Candy." He spoke using soft tones. "Get in the car." He tapped the soft top of his convertible. "We'll talk about this later. You're going to be late for your first—"

Candy folded her arms and sighed heavily. "I told you that I'm not meeting any new clients. What part of—*I want out*—don't you understand?" She spoke softly and clearly, not that it would help.

Ellis clenched his jaw, when he turned his eyes back on her, they had hardened up. "Don't do this, Candy. I'm counting on you. You would've been in a gutter somewhere if it weren't for me."

Here we go again. Ellis was about to play the guilt card. She'd had enough of him and his bullshit. "I told you plenty of times. I explained things very carefully. When I agreed to our terms it was under the strict condition that it was a short term thing. I can't do this anymore."

"Why the hell not? Do you know how many women would love to be in your shoes? They would kill. Look at you." He waved his hand in front of her. "Designer digs . . . the best tits money can buy . . . you drive a—"

"None of it matters."

"Come on, Candy." He sounded exasperated. "You have two clients." He held up two fingers. "Two, god dammit. One of them can't get it up and the other would prefer to have you on his arm than on the end of his dick, you get money for jam."

"It's soul destroying. I wasn't put on this earth to entertain wealthy men . . . even if they are good guys . . . I have a greater purpose." She wasn't sure exactly what that purpose was but getting a degree would be a good start.

Ellis laughed. It was a nasty sneer, devoid of any type

of humor. "You are a fine piece of ass that can suck dick like—"

Candy didn't know what came over her. She hit him across the face. There was a cracking sound as her palm hit his cheek. It felt good.

Damn him.

She'd had enough of Ellis and his remarks. He pretended to respect her but the truth was that he said what he had to, to keep her happy. His eyes narrowed, his face flushed from anger. It was times like this when his true colors were revealed and they were selfish and nasty.

Candy wanted nothing more to do with him or his escort agency. She had enough money saved to survive, frugally, for the next few years. Hopefully it would be enough to see her through medical school. Even if she had to get a job waiting tables or cleaning toilets. She didn't care what it took. She would stand on her own two feet and make a go at life.

The slap was hard enough to sting and she fought the urge to rub her hands together. Ellis didn't move a muscle for a half a second. In that moment, she was tempted to apologize. She bit the inside of her cheek to keep from doing it. He deserved it. She wasn't taking it back even though she knew there would be repercussions.

"Fuck, Candy! You are a whore. Do you hear me? Nothing more than a fucking whore." He put his hands around her throat and pushed her up against his car. His grip was tight, but he did it carefully so as not to damage his paint job or to leave marks on her. "If I tell you that you are going to see a new client then you damn well do as I say. You only get to leave the business when I say you can and not a moment sooner. I've always been good to you." His voice softened. "I've never hurt you or pumped you full of drugs. I've never sampled the goods myself." His fingers tightened ever so slightly, making it a little hard to breathe. "All that can change, little Candy. I think someone has forgotten their place."

One of his hands unfurled from around her neck and closed on one of her breasts. He squeezed her flesh while making a moaning noise. "I'll pump you full of heroine. I'll get you so addicted that you'll be begging to suck any cock I put in front of you for a hit. Is that what you want?" He moved closer to her, his hot breath all over her face.

Ellis wasn't a bad looking guy. He was tall and built, covered in tattoos. The guy could pretty much crook his finger and women would come running. Candy had never been attracted to him. In recent months she'd gone from thinking of him as her boss, someone who had helped her when she really needed it, to hating his guts.

"So tell me. Do you want to be a crack whore, Candy?" He squeezed her breast, harder this time.

"No," she managed to push out. It was barely a whisper.

"I don't want that either." He released her. "You would have to service at least ten guys a day and you still wouldn't make half of what you do now. In short . . ." He fixed the lapels on her jacket and straightened out her pearl necklace. "You are worth way more to me now. One more client. That brings the total up to three. One or two dates each a week. Your new client is much younger, he's a prominent figure."

He said it like it would change her mind. She was done in this business. It wasn't something she'd ever been comfortable with. Candy hadn't had an actual boyfriend or been on a real date since working at Kitty's. She wanted her life back. She wanted to be able to look at herself in the mirror again.

In this moment though, she wasn't sure what to do. She was shaking like a leaf. Her heels felt wobbly against the asphalt. What the hell was she going to do? How was she going to get out of this? She was fooling herself by thinking that Ellis would ever let her go.

When she didn't say anything, her asshole boss obviously took it as consent because he smiled and cupped her cheek. It took everything in her to keep from pulling away. That hard look was still there. His shoulders were tense. Self preservation kicked in and she didn't move a muscle. "That's my girl." He narrowed his eyes, looking at her lips. He'd never looked at her sexually before. His rules were not to sample the merchandise. He had a lot of such sayings. She should have known that he was a ginormous douchebag by the way he insisted on talking about women like they were retail stock.

He pulled away from her, staying within her personal space. "His identification must remain strictly confidential. It's important that you know that he's insisted on an exclusive fuck. He insisted on you, Candy."

Candy felt herself flinch at his crass words. She had to be just about the most timid call girl in the business.

"As far as the senator is concerned, you are going to be servicing him and him alone. He knows you date those two old farts, but he must never know that Charles actually gets it up on the odd occasion."

"The senator as in, William Lawson?" Her voice was a little high pitched.

"One and the same." There was a glint in Ellis' eyes. "He asked for you by name. My best, and I'm giving it to him."

It. Like she was some kind of commodity.

Ellis cocked his head. "He's willing to pay double your going rate, which equates to a small fucking fortune."

"No damned way." The words were out before she could stop them. "Senator Lawson is married."

"Unhappily."

"I don't care," she blurted. "You know my terms. I won't *date* . . ." She forced the word out. They both knew that this wouldn't just be a freaking date. Confidentiality. This wasn't about being arm candy for an elderly gentleman. The senator was in his late forties, young compared to Charles and Harold. What he wanted would take place strictly behind closed doors. It turned her stomach and had bile rising in her throat.

"You are going to meet with the senator. I'm getting sick of repeating myself. Get in the car and quit mouthing off. If we don't leave right fucking now we're going to be late."

His face had turned red again and his hands were fisted at his sides.

"He's married," she mumbled.

"You sound like a god damned stuck fucking record. Quit your whining and get in the car."

Candy grit her teeth to keep herself from calling him a couple of choice names that might help her feel better but wouldn't get her out of this situation. She needed to buy herself some time so she could think. "I'll get in on one condition." Ellis still needed her. There was an edge of desperation in his actions and tone.

He rolled his eyes and sighed dramatically. "What?" he spat.

"I'm not having sex with him today. I'll meet with him and talk to—"

Ellis cut her off with a laugh. He turned his eyes to the sky and pinched the bridge of his nose. "The senator doesn't want to meet with you to discuss the weather or politics." He laughed at his own stupid joke. "He wants a set of perfect tits and an ass that just won't fucking quit. He wants to fuck, Candy." He just stood there looking at her, blinking his eyes like a moron. "If a fuck is what the good senator wants, then a fuck is what he will get."

She shook her head. "I didn't sign up for this. This wasn't a part of our agreem—" She didn't get to finish her sentence because Ellis backhanded her. It was hard enough to make her stagger. Hard enough that she could taste the metallic tang of blood in her mouth but not so hard as to leave a mark or a bruise. Her lipstick would still be perfect. She didn't even have to check. Ellis was a pro at roughing up a woman without leaving a mark.

"You listen and you listen good. I'm sick of your whining. My girlfriend puts out more than you do. You're taking this gig with the senator and you will keep seeing your granddaddy dates. More importantly, you're going to pretend to love every second."

"All I'm asking is to be given an opportunity to meet with him first."

"What for? You're a hooker. You might get paid more than most but that's what you are. A cheap, fucking whore. It's about time you realized that."

Not by choice. She screamed it inside her head.

Ellis pointed at her, his finger only inches from her face. "You are getting in this car and putting out. Whatever Senator Lawson wants, he gets. I don't care if you have to suck dick or take it up the ass. I will stand outside that fucking hotel room door and I want to hear him having the time of his life. When you walk out of there, so fucking help me, he had better be a satisfied man or . . ."

There was a gust of air and his eyes widened. One minute Ellis was standing in front of her and the next he was gone. No, not gone. He was sprawled on the ground about ten feet away. *How did that happen?* What the hell . . . His arm was at a strange angle and he wasn't moving. Not even an inch.

The hairs on her whole body stood on end and everything in her told her to look up. Yet, at the same time, that same voice screamed for her not to look but rather to run instead. Icy tendrils of fear crept up and down her spine. *Oh god!* Her eyes slowly lifted.

What the hell!

It was large and scaly with golden eyes. Its wings spanned at least twenty feet.

A dragon? No fucking way? Had Ellis knocked her unconscious? That had to be it. This was a dream.

It was a nightmare! The thing swooped down, grabbing her in it's giant talons. It wrapped those huge claws around her in a vice-like grip and rocketed to the sky so quickly that the air was pulled from her lungs, taking her blood curdling scream along with it. It sure as hell felt real. The wind in her face, the scales against her skin, the adrenaline in her veins. Lord help her. She had just been taken by a dragon. The scream finally made it from her lungs and once she started, she struggled to stop.

CHAPTER 2

The next day . . .

Water filled her throat and nostrils. She was going to drown. If she wasn't so busy fighting for her next breath, she would have laughed at the irony. Less than twenty-four hours ago she didn't think that things could get worse. Yesterday she had two choices, agree to a third escort—a prominent senator who wanted to screw her brains out—or become a crack whore. Neither decision had seemed appealing at the time. Go figure!

At least she'd had a choice in the matter though. Right now her only option was to run.

Run.

Run.

Run.

Make that . . . drown. Her only consolation was that she was moving fast down stream. The current that threatened to take her life, was also saving it. Another hilarious irony. The relentless current was taking her farther and farther away from the dragon shifters. Those huge SOB's that were intent on raping her.

Candy managed to break to the surface, she gulped in air. She had given up trying to swim to the edge. It was no use, the current was just too strong. She felt like a leaf in a shit-storm.

Her dress was thin, it didn't weigh her down, but it was up around her arms and her hair was in her face. She was too busy trying to gulp down her next breath to care.

Those monsters that were after them had to have been almost seven feet tall. Their chests were bare and roped with layer upon layer of muscles. She prayed that the other four women were okay. All of them had been abducted by dragons for a barbaric pastime. Fun for the dragon men. Terrifying for them.

The hunt.

Panic welled up in her and she kicked harder even though there was a small part of her that told her it might be better to give up. To stop trying to survive. To let the river take her. It would be better than what those assholes would do if they got their hands on her.

"No." She sobbed as she broke to the surface, quickly sucking in a ragged breath. Water churned around her. Candy was so cold she could barely feel her limbs. She was a fighter, a survivor. There was no way she was giving up now.

No way in hell.

Despite the freezing cold and her quivering muscles, she continued to kick. Continued to fight for that next breath and then the next. Whether she had been in the water for minutes, for an hour, or more, was hard to tell.

Candy slammed into something with her shoulder. Pain blossomed, shooting down her arm. The current pulled at her legs, pulling her under even though the solid object was in front of her.

It must have been on instinct that her arms wrapped around whatever the big solid thing was. By some miracle she managed to pull herself up so that her head came out of the water. Candy filled her lungs, she coughed and spluttered for about a half a minute before she was able to get enough oxygen into her air starved body that she could think clearly.

Had to get out.

Had. To.

She was going to die otherwise.

It was a massive tree that must have fallen into the water. Half of it's bulk lay in the water and the other other half straddled the shore. Candy had her arms wrapped around the trunk. There was no way she could pull herself out like this. She was afraid to let go with the bottom hand because the river might pull her under if she did. She couldn't stay in the water like this indefinitely though. The warmth inside her was slowly being sapped from her body. Her teeth were clattering so hard that she thought they might crack at any moment. She was panting hard.

Gripping as tightly as she could with the hand on the top of the trunk, she released the hand on the bottom. For a second she thought she was a goner. The currents were terrifyingly powerful. The river was strong and deep. If it took her again she probably wouldn't survive. If she didn't get out soon though . . . Candy slapped her other hand on top of the trunk. Using all of her waning strength, she pulled with all her might. It felt like she weighed a freaking ton. Like her legs had been carved from lead.

She somehow managed to get a knee onto the trunk. For a moment it felt like she was going to be sucked back. Her arms shook. Her whole damned body shook. With a mighty pull, she got her belly onto the rough tree trunk. Candy cried out as she pulled herself further out of the water. Unfortunately, that's where her energy reserves dried up. Then again, she could count herself lucky. She was out of the water. Mostly out of the water. Her feet still dangled in the cold on either side.

Then she blacked out.

The sound of her own moaning brought her back to her senses. Her legs hurt. Everything hurt. She needed to get out of the water and needed to get dry. If only she could get her body to work.

She moaned again, this time in frustration. Shit! Hands closed on her waist and pulled her up. It was one of them. She tried to scream but a whimper escaped. She was in worse shape than she had thought. Her legs felt like useless pieces of dangling meat. How long had she been in that water?

The huge shifter pulled her against his body.

You'll be torn to pieces. The words of the woman dragon shifter returned to her. These guys planned on using them in the worst of ways. She might have been a high-priced call girl. One with a list of terms as long as one arm, but she wasn't ever going to allow herself to be degraded in that way. Candy began to squirm, she tried to get away from the big son of a bitch even though she knew that it would probably mean falling back into the river and to certain death.

Such small frail beings. Our males will hunt you and fight for you. The successors will get to keep you. To rut with you. The tall, dragon shifter woman with the red hair had been clear about what their fates would be. She seemed to enjoy telling them in detail what was waiting for them if they were captured by the much stronger shifters. You are to be mated and impregnated. I doubt you will survive the mating let alone the pregnancy.

Her lip quivered, this time more from fear than cold. Candy struggled harder. Her legs prickled with pins and needles as the blood flow returned to her limbs. Had to escape. She had to get away.

Run.

Run.

Run.

"Stay still," the monster growled, he tightened his grip on her.

His voice was rough and commanding. He said it with such an air of authority. Like he expected her to just give up. Bastard! Candy squirmed harder.

"Stop that or I will throw you back." There was something in his tone that told her that he meant it.

Yes! No! She would die if he threw her back in and she

didn't want to die. She was too young. Candy sighed. All of the tension left her battered, exhausted body and she slumped against him. "Don't hurt me," a mere whisper. She hated begging but what choice did she have?

A soft gasp of shock escaped as he deposited her on the bank. For a moment it looked like he was going to leave her there. Candy couldn't believe her luck. Maybe she was going to survive this after all.

The dark eyed monster with the gruff voice leaned in next to her and swept the hair from her face. Shit! He wasn't leaving. She moaned, terrified and sickened just thinking about what was going to happen to her next.

His eyes moved to hers as the ground vibrated with heavy footfalls. They weren't alone. Oh god! There were more of them. Maybe she would get lucky and they would kill each other. She forced her gaze away from the terrifying man at her side and her heart stuttered in her chest.

The beast that approached was bigger than the dark one. Way meaner looking. He moved quicker than she thought possible. His eyes were a pale blue, the color of a glacier on a winter's day and just as hard and cold. His features were set in a hard grimace. A shiver ran up her spine.

He didn't even glance in their direction. Those hard orbs were fixed on the path ahead. He frowned, there was a look of determination edged onto his features. His ridiculously large hands were fisted at his sides. His arms were like massive tree trunks. They were corded and knotted with muscle. Her mouth fell open with the sheer shock of seeing a specimen like him. Thank god he didn't seem interested.

Wait a minute!

That didn't bode well for her. She needed them to hurt each other. To focus on one another and forget about her. Feeling was slowly coming back to her limbs. If given a few precious minutes, she might be able to crawl out of harms way. Her energy reserves were almost on empty, but she needed to try.

Another soft roar sounded from somewhere behind the pale eyed monster. Oh hell! There were more of them coming. Though the sound was coming from a distance, it was still unmistakable. There were a lot more of them out there. Her body shook with fatigue. Her teeth clattered. She ached all over. Candy was foolish to think that she could escape. She was fucked. Well and truly fucked.

Torrent wanted the dark haired beauty. It had nothing to do with her coloring. Such things were of little importance to him. He wanted a strong female. One capable of carrying his heir. He was the water king after all. A royal. The strongest of his kind. Nothing less than the best would do.

It needed to be that one. The dark haired one. A voluptuous female with a bit of meat on her bones. She was one such female. Even though they wore shapeless dresses, as was customary during the hunt, he could tell that she was the strongest of the humans.

Not that humans could be termed strong. They were small and fragile. He knew that this would change once they were mated. They would draw strength from their much stronger mate. They would grow even stronger as their bellies swelled with child.

An heir.

Adrenaline rushed through him and he had to suppress a growl. He could not wait to fully claim his future mate. The dark-haired one. The sturdy one. It was important to have a good foundation. The other two remaining humans were scrawny, little things. Especially the one with hair like the sun. Her arms were mere sticks. She lay sprawled on the ground like a drowned rat. He was shocked to see the fire prince tend to her. Torrent was convinced that they had been after the same female. He had seen how the male's eyes had locked with the dark-haired one. He hadn't looked in the least bit interested in this one until now.

Maybe the male had changed his mind. The sun-haired one did have an enticing scent. Maybe that was what had drawn Coal to her. It was fruity and exotic. She moaned, reminding him of her weakness. Coal pushed hair from her face. The male was going to claim her now if he hadn't done so already.

Torrent suppressed a smile. He chose to focus on his prize instead. One second, he was on his way to claim the female and the next, he was biting the dirt . . . hard. It was an error in judgement that could end up costing him dearly. A lesser warrior roared in the distance. The female moaned again.

Torrent shook his head to try and clear it. His ears were ringing. His prize . . . he had to stay focused on his prize.

"The dark-haired one is mine," Coal barked as Torrent leapt to his feet.

Like hell. "I want her," he growled. His ears still rang from the fall. His shoulder felt stiff and his jaw ached. Torrent was so irritated and frustrated with himself that he could roar. Anger coursed through him. Who did this little prick think he was? Unfortunately, they were evenly matched. The male was a fire dragon. That gave him the advantage. More heat energy coursed through a fire dragon's veins, making it a simple fact. Fire versus water.

Torrent's mind was reeling. He felt dizzy. The fall had been hard, as he was moving quickly. Coal had used his momentum against him. Fuck! Coal's closed fist came at him from out of nowhere. There was nothing Torrent could do to avoid the blow completely. He took a step back to circumvent the worst of the force.

Torrent could hear footfalls behind them. It was of no concern to him. The approaching male would take the sun-haired female. It would buy him time to defeat the fire prince.

Perfect.

Torrent decided to give Coal one chance at surrender. "That female is mine," he snarled, his eyes locked with the prince's. "You may as well give up now. Take this one." He said in the most commanding tone he could muster, his eyes stayed on Coal's. A non royal would cower and drop to their knees. Coal flinched.

Good!

The little prick huffed out a breath. His shoulders slumped and any sign of fight fled from him. "Fine." His gaze dropped to the downed female.

Good. At least he knew his place. Insolent little fucker. Torrent began to move towards his human. He had to stop himself from shaking his head. Coal might be fire but he was merely a prince and Torrent—a king. How easy the prick had allowed himself to . . . ?

Torrent heard his trachea crunch beneath the male's fist in a move he didn't even see coming. Next, the male gripped his neck in what felt like a vice. There was only one prick in this situation. Torrent himself! What the fuck had he been thinking? He hadn't. Not one bit. He had been too damned eager to win a human. Suddenly all those weeks he had abstained from sex seemed stupid. He'd convinced himself that it was in preparation for the hunt. His thinking had been that it would make him hone his skills and make him hungrier for a female, a mate. In the end, it had made him think with his little head instead of his big one. Make that, he hadn't been thinking at all.

Zero air passed through his damaged throat and Coal maintained his hold. His lungs burned and pain consumed his trachea like a wildfire. Torrent could feel his eyes bug out from his skull.

Thank fuck, the male finally released him. Not that it helped much. Air still would not find it's way down his throat. The pain went from grossly unbearable to plain unbearable. A slight improvement. He'd take it!

Torrent could hear the sounds of battle over the roar of his heartbeat in his ears. Coal was fighting the approaching male. What? Why? Why didn't he just go and claim his prize? It would take a few minutes for his throat to heal enough to get air to move through it. The extra time would have put Coal well ahead.

Instead, he was choosing to waste his time by taking out the lesser. There was a crunching noise as the fire prince punched the other male's face. Over and over. He pulverized the poor male. Torrent couldn't help but feel a begrudging respect for the bastard. Fast, strong and clever. The male was also a prick, and if there were even an ounce of strength left in him, he would fight him.

The poor bastard finally fell into a heap and Coal walked back to Torrent. It was only when he had to look up to maintain eye contact with Coal that he realized that he had fallen onto one knee. He managed to draw the tiniest wheezing breath. Thank claw. The dark patches in his vision cleared, but only marginally.

"The others are a few minutes behind." Coal glanced to the horizon and Torrent could barely make out the grunts and growls that gave credence to his words. There was a large group approaching at a speed. "You still have time to claim her." The male glanced at the human who was just a few feet away from him.

Her eyes were wide and filled with fear. Something in him clenched. A need to protect rose up in him. She was so small and fragile. Not the female that he wanted but she would do. What did it matter anyway? The female was fertile. Their kind had watched a group of females for months before making final decisions about who they were going to take. The females needed to meet various criteria. Amongst other things, they needed to be destitute, not easily missed by loved ones and fertile. That meant that she would have gone into heat at least once while they observed her.

Coal was going to get the dark-haired one, whether he liked it or not. It was take this one or wait for the next hunt.

The fire prince narrowed his eyes on Torrent. "Take her," he said. It might be another trap, though to what end? Torrent was still pretty much fucked. At least he could get some air through his broken windpipe. It wouldn't be long and he would be back on his feet. Right now, he was no threat.

The human whimpered. "Don't come near me," her voice shook. It was filled with fear and panic, but there was also a hint of anger there. Good! At least she had some fire in her human veins.

"Do it." Coal urged as he turned and ran.

The sounds of approaching males were growing louder. Boisterous grunts and groans. He only had two or three minutes at best. Torrent needed to claim her right now. He forced air through his throat. Fuck! It hurt like a ballbag to an open flame. He rose to shaky legs and took a staggering step towards her.

The female's lips trembled and even though she looked as if she was weak as a new born lamb, she began to crawl away from him anyway. Her fingers dug into the earth and her legs didn't work very well, leaving deep grooves. The small grunts she was making spoke of determination. Maybe she would do after all.

CHAPTER 3

Oh God!
Oh God!

He was coming for her. She could hear him wheezing behind her. Could hear his uneven footfalls as he staggered closer. The guy was an animal. A straight up animal. He should be dead. Why wasn't he dead?

She'd watched what the other one had done to him. How he'd pulverized his windpipe. Pulverized! She'd heard the revolting crunching sound. Just thinking about it turned her stomach.

Her legs still prickled but at least they were moving. There was no way she could stand or even crawl very well but she would damn well drag herself along. There was no way in hell she was making this easy on the asshole.

Her only small consolation was that he was hurt. She'd seen the look of pain in his eyes. Maybe he couldn't force himself on her if he was hurt.

The footfalls grew more even and faster. He was right behind her. She moaned in both anger and frustration, her hand closed on a rock. On impulse, Candy turned and hurled the thing at him, surprised when it hit him in the chest. He was closer than she realized.

His eyes widened and he made somewhere between a huffing and a groaning noise as the air was forced from his lungs. He fell to his knees. The wheezing noise grew louder as he struggled to get air into his lungs.

Within a second or two, he was back on his feet and towering over her with a menacing look on his face.

One hand went to his throat and he grimaced. Candy wasn't waiting around, she rolled back onto her belly and clawed the ground. She forced her legs to obey and managed to half pull, half crawl forwards. It felt like she was hardly moving. Tears of frustration coursed down her face. Wet hair clung to her cheeks.

Big hands closed around her waist and pulled her over onto her back. It happened with zero effort. His legs were on either side of her. Veritable tree trunks. Did his mother put steroids in his milk as a baby?

If only she had strength. If only her body would listen to her because she'd kick his balls so hard they'd fly right out of his asshole mouth. She'd flatten them to the point where he'd never think about sex again. She bit down on her lip to keep from moaning or whimpering, mostly though to keep herself from begging for mercy.

His pale eyes were devoid of any so why bother? He slumped over her, putting his whole weight on her. His breathing was choppy. He still wheezed, but it wasn't as bad as before.

Lucky asshole. At least he could breathe. She couldn't move. Definitely couldn't breathe. The only thing that would end up flat at this rate, was her.

Then he pulled most of his weight off of her as he leaned onto his elbows. Relieved, Candy sucked in a deep breath. She tried to move the lower half of her body to kick him. To do something, anything, but he was pinning her down with his big-ass body.

She was making noises. Little grunts and moans that showed how hard she was trying. "Off. Me." She managed to grunt. "Now," she ground out.

His breath was hot against her ear. "No."

She got an arm free and hit his back with her closed fist. The action hurt. *Her.* Certainly not him. She may as well be hitting a brick wall.

"I need to kiss you now." He rasped directly into her ear. It caused her to shiver . . . from the revulsion.

"No!" she half shouted.

"Yes," a rough rasp.

Candy hit him some more. She tried to squirm out from under him.

He was still panting. "Stop," a low vibration.

For a second she was tempted to obey his commanding tone. What the? She even stopped fighting but soon managed to shake it off and picked up where she had left off. This time, with even more vigor. Asshole!

"Stop," he repeated. "Listen." He pulled back a smidgen and cocked his head.

Again, she did as he commanded. Why the hell was she even listening to him let alone . . .

Wait just a minute.

Growls. Roars and snarls. The sounds were still soft but

growing louder by the second.

"Let me kiss you and you will be mine." His voice sounded fractured and pained. Good!

"You can go to hell. I'm nobody's. Do you hear me? I want to go home." Her voice shook.

"I am a king. I have much to offer you."

Another rich bastard that thought he could buy her. Fuck that! She heard many feet thumping against the hard ground. Her heart rate went into overdrive and she whimpered. "Please," she whispered. "I don't want to be raped." She said it more to herself than to him.

"I will protect you. I will ensure that no harm comes to you." He pulled his head back, staring her deep in the eyes.

"Please don't force yourself on me." She was appalled at how her voice trembled. "Please don't let them . . ." A sobbing noise was torn from her at the thought of being passed around . . . torn to pieces.

The large group of shifters was right there now. Seconds away.

The beast of a man cupped her cheek. His touch was soft and careful. *What?* It shocked her to her core. "Trust me and do as I say, do everything I tell you and you will be safe. Do we have a deal?"

"Yes." She blurted as one of the shifters roared. It sounded like a battle cry.

"Kiss me now," he growled.

His lips were a only a few millimeters away. What choice did she have but to kiss him? To trust him?

None.

Zip.

Zero.

She was out of options. Candy reached up and touched her lips to his. They were warm and soft. So soft. Surprisingly soft. Her eyes were open, so she watched as his drifted shut. His lashes fanned his cheeks.

She made a noise of surprise as he pushed his tongue into her mouth. Shit! His hand tightened ever so slightly on her jaw, he tilted her head and plundered her mouth.

Oh god!

This monster could kiss. He could seriously freaking kiss. Not that she was enjoying herself. Forget that. She only prayed that he had told her the truth, that he would protect her from the rest of them. Although she struggled to understand how he would get that right. There was a whole group of them and only one of him.

There was no way he could keep his promise. Candy turned her head, breaking the kiss. He stayed just above her like that for a few seconds, his eyes still closed. His chest rising and falling against hers. Then his eyes opened. Those unnaturally pale orbs locked with hers. His eyes narrowed, like he was trying to tell her something. A warning perhaps.

There was a sound of feet shuffling. Of breathing. She slowly turned her head. It was a group of about twenty of them. Twenty more of these huge giants. The bastards stared down at them. They looked pissed. Each and every one of them looked beyond angry. The one closest to them snarled, his lips curled away from his teeth which looked abnormally sharp.

Candy turned her head and buried it into his chest, which was as soft as it was hard. His skin was soft and hairless. The muscles underneath made it hard. She noticed how his tattoo was a bright golden color. It had flecks of turquoise green intermingled in the gold. All of the others' chests had silver markings. Maybe he wasn't full of BS when he told her he was a king. It seemed significant somehow. Not that it mattered to her. His promise mattered and that was it.

"She is mine." The warrior king on top of her rasped. His voice barely a whisper. His throat seemed much better though. The guy didn't seem interested in moving off of her. She almost didn't want him to. She felt safer sheltered underneath him like this.

The closest guy with the long teeth actually flinched as the king-guy spoke, and took a small step back before his features hardened with determination. "I challenge you for her then." His hands curled into fists.

"Why bother? This female has chosen me as her mate." He turned his attention back to her and her mouth dried up in an instant.

What the?

What was this big ape on about? She started to shake her head but he covered her mouth with his before she could speak. It was a quick blistering kiss that caused her practically lame toes to curl. They wouldn't move when she needed them to earlier, but right now, she could almost be termed a ballerina. It was because she was sickened by his touch. Yes, that was it.

He pulled back and gave her a ghost of a smile. She sighed . . . with relief. "Don't play coy, human. The sooner you tell them that you have chosen me, the sooner they will leave us in peace." He sniffed at her. Sniffed.

Shit! These beast men weren't normal. *Duhhh Candy, they are dragon shifters.* Normal didn't factor at all anymore.

"Um." She kept her eyes on his for a moment before turning to face the group.

Oh shit! The guy looked even more pissed. His eyes looked weird. Scary!

"Yes," she mumbled.

"Yes . . . what, human? Speak up." The scary one asked. He narrowed his slitted eyes at her. That was it, his eyes looked distinctly reptilian. A shiver ran up her spine. It felt like someone had just played hopscotch on her grave.

She looked back up at the shifter on top of her. His pale eyes narrowed and his jaw clenched.

Shit.

Her choice was, take her chances with the likes of him or . . . she looked back towards the throng. They grew more restless by the second. She didn't really have a choice, did she?

"I have chosen him. He's telling the truth." She tried to sound confidant. Like she really meant it but failed dismally. Her voice came out as a soft, shaky whisper. Was she making a mistake? Please let her not be making a mistake.

Please.

The big brute gave her a cocky smile and nodded his head in approval. "I will keep my promise." He winked at her. Winked. This had to be some terrible dream. At least he seemed to genuinely have her best interests at heart.

The big shifter turned his head to the crowd. "You heard the female. She is mine. I command you all to leave right now so that I can fully claim her."

The other guy's shoulders slumped in defeat and several of the men looked like they were grumbling. One even cursed loudly. Most of them moved away. All but one or two stragglers.

The big beasts pale gaze was on the remaining men. "Suit yourself." He growled, it was a terrifying sound that caused his chest to vibrate against hers. "You can stay and watch. See if I care."

Then he did something at total odds with their agreement. He hoisted her legs up around his hips.

Candy whimpered. Her gaze was still on the shifters. Their eyes widened and they turned. "What? Wait? What?" She sounded like an incoherent idiot.

"Don't argue." He whispered as he pulled up her dress. All the way up, till it bunched around her hips. She wasn't wearing underwear.

Candy began to hyperventilate from the shock. "Oh god!" She yelled as he settled over her. She could feel something massive, something rock hard against her and had a good idea of what that something was. Thank god he was still wearing his pants. There was a thin barrier of material between them. It wouldn't take much for him to free himself.

She should've known that this was too damned good to be true. Humiliation rose up in her. If he expected her to just lie there and take it, he was sadly mistaken. She knew that there was very little she could do. She was so weak, so tired. The last of the adrenaline was leaving her system, her body too exhausted to make any more.

She sucked in a breath to scream 'no.' To call him a couple of choice names but he slipped a hand over her mouth. The dickhead gave a small shake of the head. His jaw was clenched. She was breathing hard through her nose. The whole length of his body held her down. She could feel him there. Throbbing against her. Any second he was going to rip into her. Claim and take and destroy.

She moaned against his hand, hearing the air as it moved in and out through her nose. So quickly. She could hear the sound of her own heart thudding in her ears. The man on top of her blinked in and out of focus.

No.

She was losing it. She was about to faint. All those hours of running, all that time she had spent in the freezing cold water, it was catching up to her. *No! Not now. No.* Maybe it was a blessing. Maybe he wouldn't hurt her as much if she was unconscious. No! She couldn't live with not knowing exactly what had happened. Her vision became even more blurred. There was nothing she could do to stop it. Bright lights winked and then everything went dark.

CHAPTER 4

Candy sat upright.
No.
Stop.
Don't.

She could hear someone screaming and quickly realized that it was her. She tried to make herself stop but couldn't. It was only when she felt the sheet crumpled in her fisted hands that she realized where she was.

A large airy room that looked like it had been carved from rock. Her chest heaved as she sucked in a lungful of air, trying to calm down. She looked up, she looked down, then left and right, trying to make sense of what she was seeing. She was on a double king size, four poster bed on crisp white linen. The room was sparse but tastefully decorated with a delicate orchid in a gold container on the bedside table. There was a couch and a coffee table. In the far corner was an ornate, antique looking desk. At the center of the high ceiling, cavernous was probably a better word, there was an enormous crystal chandelier. It was beautiful and delicate looking, depicting the bottom of the ocean in wisps of seaweed, shells and starfish.

That wasn't the most amazing thing though. The thing that stole her breath and made her eyes widen was the view. Deep blue ocean for as far as the eye could see. To the left, the water was cut by a long coastline with chalk white cliffs. It was . . .

Oh god!

As beautiful as it all was, she was suddenly reminded of her ordeal. Her shoulder felt stiff. Her body still ached.

Oh god!

Candy looked down. She was wearing a thin white cotton and lace gown that looked like it might reach her ankles if she were standing.

Oh god!

No!

How the hell did she get here? Who had changed her? Cleaned her? What the hell had happened to her? She pulled up the hem of her nightgown and clasped herself between her legs expecting pain. She felt fine. She pushed a little more firmly. No tearing, no bruising, no pain whatsoever. Candy frowned. Next she opened her legs and inspected her inner thighs looking for bruises from his big hands.

She had scratches on her knees and she had a gash on her hip but that was from dragging herself. There were a couple of bruises but they didn't look like hand prints and they were on her shins. Probably from running and hitting into the odd rock in the water.

"Is everything okay?" A strong, feminine voice.

Candy shrieked and grabbed her chest. She straightened out her dress and flashed her gaze to the entrance of the room. An extremely tall woman stood in front of the closed door. She smiled at Candy, concern shone in her eyes. "Are you in pain? I hadn't thought to check your pussy." She frowned. "Although I don't know why that would be sore."

Say what?

Candy made a squeaking noise. She cleared her throat and gave her head a quick shake. "Who are you?" She pulled the sheet around herself.

"Oh, I'm sorry." She laughed. It was then that Candy noticed the tray in her hands. Her stomach growled despite the circumstance.

The woman's eyes shone. "My name is Sky." Her hair was dark but her eyes were a deep blue, reminding her— cliché time—of the sky on a cloudless day. "I'm an air dragon."

Oh boy.

She was one of them. Candy should have realized. The woman was so incredibly tall and built like an athlete. She wore one of those dresses, only it actually fit on her larger frame instead of looking like a sack.

The other woman laughed. "This is the part where you're supposed to tell me your name."

Candy closed her gaping mouth and nodded once. At first glance, she liked the shifter woman. Her face was open and friendly. It was a huge contrast to the two she had met after she had first been abducted. "I'm Candy.

I'm sorry, it's just, this has all been a big shock." Her lip wobbled. She'd always rated herself a strong woman. She'd had to be from an early age. Life had tossed her some doozies and she'd always managed to end up on top.

The shifter, Sky, made a noise of concern and walked over to the bed. "Oh, honey." She shook her head. "I'm sure it was an ordeal. Especially for such a weak human like yourself. The hunt is supposed to be fun and exciting."

"How can you say that?" This woman was sweet but she was also clueless.

Sky set the tray down on the side table. "It should be fun. It's probably because you're not a shifter female. You don't fully understand our traditions."

Candy snorted. "Forgive me if I don't like the idea of being hunted by a group of horny guys and then having them fight each other for an opportunity to rape me."

"Rape?" Sky frowned.

She really was clueless. "Yes, rape as in force themselves on me. Forced sex." She added when the woman's frown deepened.

"Who forced you?" Then she gasped. "Is that why you were checking yourself . . . down there?" she frowned. "That can't be right," she mumbled to herself.

"That bastard." Candy's voice shook. All the details were coming back to her now. "He promised." A tear rolled down her cheek but she wiped it away with an angry swipe of her hand.

"Who promised?" Sky sat down on the edge of the bed.

"What did they promise? Speak to me. What happened to you? If one of those males forced themselves on you." She shook her head. Her eyes blazed with anger, which quickly morphed to confusion. "Although I find it hard to believe that any of them would. Dragon shifters are honor-bound." She sighed. "Then again, they are desperate. Maybe . . . Who was it? I will have his dick removed."

What?

Really?

"You're joking, right?" Candy swallowed hard. She leaned forward.

"No, I'm not joking. Unless you would prefer for the male to be put to death. If it were me, I would insist on it."

"He would be killed?" As much as she hated that animal, she found that she didn't like the thought of him being killed. "I would prefer it if his dick was removed please."

"Would you be able to point him out?" before she could answer, the shifter carried on. "Describe him to me? Let's start with the exact color of his markings"

"They were golden with—"

"What?" Her whole body tensed and she jumped up as if an electrical current had ripped through the bed. She frowned. "That can't be."

"He had very light blond hair and blue eyes with a golden tattoo on his chest." She gasped. "Oh yes and there were turquoise green flecks mixed in with the gold."

Sky shook her head. She practically vibrated with anger.

"I thought that humans were sweet and kind. At least, that's what I was told by our males. I can see that it isn't true. Then again, maybe it's just you. A bad apple."

What?

"I just told you that—"

"There is no way in hell that the water king forced himself on you. I find it utterly ridiculous and laughable that you would suggest such a thing." Then she leaned over Candy and sniffed her.

"What are you doing? How can you be so sure? You weren't even there." She added, feeling more alone than she had ever felt before and that was saying something. It seemed like she had been wrong about the woman.

Sky made a low growling noise and huffed out a breath. "He never rutted you. None of the males did."

"What's wrong with you?" Candy's voice was a little shrill. "There is no way that you would know a thing like that."

Sky touched her nose. "I'm a shifter. I can scent it. Although Torrent touched you, he didn't rut you. You are a liar." She narrowed her eyes.

"Are you sure?" Maybe this woman was right. She prayed she was right. "Do you promise me that you're telling the truth?"

"He didn't rut you, female. He barely touched you." Then she stared out the window for a half a minute. "You genuinely seemed relieved. Did you really believe that he had raped you?"

Candy swallowed hard. She nodded once, feeling her

eyes prickle. "I didn't feel sore . . . done there." She glanced between her legs. "So I hoped not, but . . ." She made a noise of frustration. "He told those other guys that he was claiming me fully and then he pulled up my dress." Her lip quivered. "Unfortunately I can't be sure what happened after that because I blacked out. It was a terrible ordeal, my body shut down."

The shifter had her hands on her hips. She was difficult to read. Candy wasn't sure why she even cared what the other woman thought about her but she did. "I swear to god, I thought he had raped me. You can't blame me for thinking it. Not after what those other shifter women said."

Sky narrowed her eyes. "What women? What did they say?" Her stance softened, just a little.

"Their names were . . ." She had to think about it. It felt like forever ago. "Scarlet and Ash. They said that we would be hunted and rutted. That the shifter men would tear us apart. We would be used and"—she paused as she thought of the exact words—"mated and impregnated, if we could survive the hunt, that is. You've just told me that your men are honor-bound, that they don't force women. Something isn't adding up."

Sky grit her teeth and shook her head. She walked away.

"I swear I'm telling the truth. We were petrified, and when"—she swallowed—"Torrent, is his name Torrent?"

Sky turned sharply and gave a nod of the head before putting a palm to her forehead. Her jaw was set.

"He grabbed me and pushed my dress up . . . I thought

the worst."

"He must have had his reasons for doing it. You will need to talk with him about it. The only thing I can tell you is that he didn't hurt you in that way. Our males are . . . they don't do things like you just described."

"Why am I here then?" she whispered.

Sky glanced at the tray. "You need to eat. I think it would be best if your . . . if Torrent explained things to you. He sure as claw has a few things he needs to explain to me." She said the last under her breath.

"Just tell me."

Sky shook her head. "It is not my place. I'm sorry you were misled in that way. Torrent might be . . ." She looked around before locking eyes with Candy. She gave a small smile. "A bit arrogant—he's the king so he can't help himself sometimes." She spoke softly like someone might be listening. "He is a good male. If he made a promise to you, he will keep it. Give him a chance."

Candy tried to talk but Sky removed the lid of the tray. "Eat. Get your strength back."

Why did she need her strength? Why the hell was she here? If Candy knew anything, it was that a lie was very often just a step away from the truth. Those dragon women had lied but it didn't seem too far from the truth. She had been brought here for a reason. One she had a feeling she wasn't going to like.

Two days later . . .

"With all due respect, my lord." The air princess smoothed her dress with her hand. "You need to speak to the human. You can't leave her in her room like that indefinitely."

"Has anyone else been in to see her?" Torrent couldn't help the growl in his voice. "Did you say anything to anyone about my . . . situation?"

"No, my lord." She sucked in a breath. "On both counts."

He felt a portion of his stress evaporate. "What about to your mate? Did you tell Lake?"

She shook her head. "I haven't said anything to your brother but you can't expect me to keep your secret for much longer. With all due respect, my lord, you've allowed this to get out of control."

Torrent squeezed his eyes shut for a few moments. "I've been waiting for her to heal. I will fix it." It was true. What was the point of visiting with the female if he couldn't rut her?

"She was fine from day one. A little scraped up and bruised. Maybe a bit tired, but—"

"Okay, okay. I get it." He held up a hand. He needed to be sure. The last thing he wanted was her whining. He might change his mind about her and then what?

"Anything you would like to talk about, my lord." She quickly added, and her eyes flashed away as he turned towards her.

"No . . . thank you," Torrent ground out. Sky was a good female. She meant well even if her concern was misguided. "It is between the human and I. Just keep things quiet . . . for now."

"You can't keep her hidden. Explain things to her. I'm sure that she will be willing to . . ."

"Humans are very different. They do not see things like we do. A dragon shifter female would understand. I fear that the human will not." He paused. "Candy." He let her name roll off of his tongue. "It is a strange name. I have never heard one like it. I wonder about the significance." Dragon shifters had names that meant something. Names that had been passed down from mothers to daughters, grandmothers to granddaughters and uncles to nephews. Their names were just as much a reflection of their tribe, as the colorings of their markings.

Candy, a sweet confection. A treat.

If her scent was anything to go by, the female was sweet indeed. Maybe he should obtain some of these confectionaries to plump her up. He shook his head. It didn't matter. Torrent had been with many human females, granted all of them had been more substantial than her, but he had yet to break one of them. Harm them in any way. She would do.

"I will go to her today," he announced.

"I look forward to your mating ceremony." Sky smiled.

"Any sign of your heat?" He refrained from sniffing her.

Sky's face fell and he felt like a prick for a brief second.

Tough luck. He was the king. They needed royal births. The more the better. A sense of urgency suddenly struck him. He needed to get the human with child as soon as possible.

His sister by mating shook her head. "I fear that I am months from my next heat." She shrugged. "Although you never know. These things are erratic."

Torrent felt himself frown. "Let me know if anything changes. It is one of those things that is out of our control."

Sky smiled. "Yeah, if only we were like humans. One or two heats a year is nowhere near enough. Is it true that they come into heat every month?" She raised her brows.

"Yes." His balls ached.

Sky's eye widened and she averted her gaze. "Go and visit your female, my lord . . . I mean . . . if it pleases you, my lord."

"It does." His voice had turned husky with longing. Torrent turned and strode from the room.

His need increased all the more. All this talk of a female in heat. It made him think of losing his seed into the female. Of making her writhe with pleasure. Of filling her belly with his young. Even if she wasn't entirely to his liking, just thinking of getting her with child was aphrodisiac enough.

He paused midstride. The human was timid. She had no understanding of their ways. None whatsoever. She had initially thought that he had planned to force her. That if he rutted her, she would be ripped apart and unable to take his size.

Bullshit!

Torrent understood that she had been misled. He got it. This situation was as fucked up as they came. He picked up his stride but stopped outside her door. Shit! He was still hard. The human thought the worst of him. He needed to convince her otherwise. It would be impossible with a hard-on—the size of a large battering ram—in his pants.

He was tempted to find one of the few available dragon shifter females to slake his need. It had been far too long since he was with a female. Nah, he was here, might as well get this over with. Hopefully she would be willing once he explained things. Hopefully she would come into heat soon. This line of thought was not helping his painfully hard situation.

Torrent pictured his grandmother's kind face. The way the corner of her eyes wrinkled when she smiled. The way she scolded him for bringing back an unconscious female. His grandmother had scolded him even more for snarling at everyone to stay away from her. They had all assumed that his protective skills were in overdrive, and strangely enough that was true. Which was warranted, but moreover, he didn't want anyone getting close enough to scent her properly.

Fuck!

When he looked down, his dick was at half mast. It was working. He thought of the worst day of his life. The day his father died. His dick shriveled like a sea cucumber in the sun.

Torrent knocked twice.

"Come in," she called. Candy. Her voice was bright and sunny. He liked hearing it.

Torrent walked in and stopped dead in his tracks. What was she doing?

Whatever it was, he needed her to stop doing it and right fucking now. She was bent over, her feet slightly parted. She touched the ground with her finger tips, then came up a bit and then reached back down.

She was wearing tight black pants that molded her ass. Torrent suppressed a groan. Her butt wasn't plump. Not at all. It was small. Two tiny orbs. It was tight as fuck. Seeing that she had such a small ass wasn't a shock. He had carried her back to his lair yesterday. The female weighed nothing. What he hadn't expected, was to like such a small ass, but he did. Dammit, he liked it a whole hell of a lot.

His dick paid attention as well. Think about other things, thing about other things.

She was talking. "What excuse did the jerk give this time? Why isn't he here?" An exasperated sigh as she continued to bop up and down . . . up and down . . . Torrent was forced to turn away.

"I'm fine. One hundred percent. I mean look at me . . ." He could hear that she was still doing her ridiculous movements. He didn't have to look to know that she was fine indeed. Do not look!

Think of other things.

She huffed out a breath. "I'm even working out again. I like being in shape."

In shape . . . yeah . . . that's what she was.

"Why the silent treatment, Sky? Cat got your dragon tongue?" He could hear that she had stopped moving. Then she gasped.

Torrent lifted his gaze and looked straight into the eye of the storm.

"You," she pushed out, putting her hands on her hips. "About freaking time wouldn't you say?"

Torrent couldn't respond because his tongue was currently stuck to the roof of his mouth. He might never be able to get it unstuck.

Beneath all of that grime and mud was a beautiful female with high cheekbones and delicate feature. Her lips were like rubies, her cheeks were flushed. Her eyes were as blue as the deepest ocean. Her breasts . . . lord help him.

Torrent couldn't help but growl softly as he eyeballed the fuck out of her. Such big, plump mammary glands on such a tiny wisp of a female. How was it even possible?

She crossed her arms over her chest, blocking his view. "Eyes up here, asshole. You men are all the bloody same."

He made a groaning, growling noise. It ended on a soft whine. He sounded like a human pet. A dog. He sounded just like a begging dog. Next thing, he'd wag his tail and start drooling. Except it wouldn't be a tail he would wag. Oh no! There was another far more interesting thing that wanted to wag. Woof! Woof!

This female was tiny. She was scrawny. Sticks for arms.

It didn't change anything. She was fucking exquisite. Beneath all that dirt was a treasure.

"What the hell is wrong with you?" She cupped her mammary glands with her hands. Although he couldn't see her pink nipples outlined through the t-shirt anymore, the way she held her breasts accentuated them even further.

"You should put on more clothes if you don't want me to look." His voice was gruff. The statement was utter bullshit. As a shifter, nudity was not a big deal. He'd seen every dragon shifter female across the the four kingdoms naked. He'd seen many human women naked. Whether she was clothed or not should not have been of any consequence.

She pursed her lips. Lips he had sampled. Delicious, succulent, decadent. He could think of a hundred more such terms to describe them. Candy narrowed her eyes on him. "First off, I wasn't expecting you and secondly, no one bothered to supply me with under garments. It's not my fault I'm not wearing a bra, you asshole."

"You gave me permission to enter and I entered."

"I didn't know it was you. How the hell was I supposed to know that? Turn around. Do it now." She widened her eyes.

Torrent frowned. It should bug him that she was throwing commands at him. It didn't.

"Turn around so that I can go and put some more clothes on." She made a noise of frustration. "Why aren't you at least looking away?"

"I've already seen you, so what is the point? Besides . . ." he paused. "I'm going to be seeing a lot more of you, so you can relax." He smiled at her. "You don't need to cover up."

Her eyes bugged out of her skull and she made a spluttery effort to talk. Then she sucked in a deep breath and looked at the ceiling for half a beat before turning her eyes back on him. "If you are telling me that you have seen me without my clothes on, I'm going to have to gouge your eyes out of your head." She tapped her foot. "While we're on the subject, why did you . . ." She looked away. Her eyes clouded with . . . hurt.

What the hell?

Candy bit down on her lower lip for a second and then turned her gaze back to him. "Why did you pull my dress up and . . . what happened after I passed out?" She held up a hand. "I know nothing actually happened. At least, Sky assured me that we didn't . . . you know, but . . ." She didn't say anything more. She looked stricken.

Torrent hated the way that made him feel. "We didn't," he said. "You were injured and afraid. You passed out. There is no way in hell I would rut a female in that state."

Her whole stance relaxed. She nodded once. "I needed to hear it from you."

"I didn't take advantage." He shook his head.

She huffed out a breath and seemed to relax a smidgen.

"As to why I pulled your dress up, it was to—"

"Turn around. I need to put more clothes on and then we can talk."

Torrent shook his head. "It is unnecessary."

"Humor me."

"Fine." He growled as he turned to face the other way. "I'm going to see you naked by the end of today anyway so I'm not sure what the big deal is."

CHAPTER 5

H is ass was just as yummy as his . . . not going there. His back was just as beautifully sculpted as his front. Hard meaty glutes encased in those thin pants. They looked to be made from cotton. Loose fitting. Black. The color contrasted with his bronzed skin and light hair.

Damn.

The guy was hot, as in smoking. He also had a colossal ego. Sky wasn't wrong on that one.

"I'm going to see you naked by the end of today anyway so I'm not sure what the big deal is." And there you go, that same arrogance. Evenly dealt. He completely believed what he was saying.

Candy didn't answer immediately, she pulled a sweater out of the closet and pulled it over her head. It was miles too big. The sleeves came over her hands by a few inches and the bottom hung to mid thigh. "You are delusional if you think that is even a remote possibility."

She turned and came almost face to face with all seven foot of him. At least, he seemed that tall. It was almost laughable. Candy came up to his chest. She was like a child next to the huge beast of a man. A sexy beast though, if she said so herself.

No!

It didn't matter. His looks had nothing to do with it. She'd never met a man with hair that color though. The most sun-kissed blond, it was practically white. His eyes didn't seem as pale, not nearly as hard. Fanned by thick, black lashes which contrasted with his coloring. They were intense and seemed to look right into her soul.

Even the stubble on his masculine jaw was light. His cheekbones were prominent. His mouth . . . oh that mouth. It didn't help that she knew he could kiss like a cupid-possessed demon.

His mouth quirked into a half smile and he raised a brow. "I think you may be the one who is delusional. I could hear that you were finished dressing, I wasn't sneaking a look. Though, by the way . . ." He sucked in a breath. "We are mated so it is my right as a male to claim my . . . what is it you humans call it . . . ? Ah yes . . ." He paused and raised both brows. "My bride."

She choked on nothing. Maybe it was spit. Either way, her throat closed and her lungs seized and she had a coughing fit that forced her to cover her mouth with one hand, and to bend over her middle.

When she finally managed to gain a semblance of control, she raised her gaze to meet his. His expression had morphed to one of concern. Torrent took a step towards her, his arm outstretched, he stopped just short of touching her. "Are you okay? I can understand why you are having a hard time with coming to grips with everything that has happened in a short amount of time."

"Oh, can you now?" Her voice was low. "I take it you've been abducted, chased and manhandled. Thrown in a room . . ." She looked around her. "May as well be a jail cell," she whispered more to herself. "And then told that you're married . . . mated . . . whatever . . . to a complete stranger. One that is not even your species."

Torrent flinched. Good. Let him have some sort of an idea of what she had been through. "Can we sit? Maybe have some tea?" he asked.

"Tea. You want tea?" What the hell was wrong with this guy? "You want to sit and sip tea at a time like this. Pinky up too I suppose."

He frowned for a beat. "No." He lifted his arm and this time he did touch her on the side of the arm. It was a light brush of the fingers. Everywhere he touched, those cells seemed to spring to life. Her skin warmed. A moan hovered on her lips.

"Don't." She shook her head, looking pointedly at his hand.

Torrent dropped his arm back to his side. "I think we are highly compatible. It is a good thing." He nodded, looking pleased with himself. "I think that going through the motions of making tea will calm you down."

"Nothing will calm me down. The only thing that would help is if you took me home."

He shook his head. His jaw tightened. "No can do. I think I will make us some tea now. Would you mind?" He gestured towards the kitchen area, which was situated to the one side of the big open area. It was modern, with gleaming surfaces and stainless steel appliances. It contrasted with the rest of the space but somehow worked.

She shrugged. "Go right ahead." She choked out a laugh. "I can't believe you are actually asking my permission."

He had already begun to make his way towards the kitchen and turned. "I gave you a choice from the word go."

"Except for the part where I was abducted." She folded her arms.

"Except for that part." He put the kettle on and grabbed some mugs. "Can I make you a cup?"

She shrugged. A hot drink sounded good but she didn't know if she wanted one from him.

He smiled. Good lord, he was even more good looking when he smiled. He was like those models on the covers of men's magazines about health and exercise only more good looking. It irritated her that she was attracted to him.

Torrent ran a hand through his hair. "I'll go ahead and make you one." He threw another teabag into a teapot. Then he turned and folded his arms.

Biceps aside, his forearms were huge. His shoulders were broad and . . . nope. She wasn't looking. Candy turned to face the beautiful view. The one that was outside, not inside.

"I'm sorry you were abducted and that you suffered at

the hands of those she-dragons. Please know that I have reported the matter to the fire king and the females will be punished."

"Punished?" She turned back to Torrent.

There was a loud clicking noise as the kettle switched off. He poured some of the steaming liquid into the pot, stirred and closed the lid. "Yeah, I am not sure what he will do to them." He looked thoughtful for a second. "You must realize that we have very few females. They have always been held in high regard. Revered and cherished. None of the kings has ever punished a female before. Blaze is not sure how to proceed. If it were a male that pulled such a move, he would be lashed with a silver tipped whip or put in the cages, or both."

Shit! She tried not to react. It was on the tip of her tongue to ask about 'the cages' but she bit back the question.

He put the pot, cups and spoons onto a tray and gestured for the sitting area. "If the crime is bad enough, he might be put to death."

"That seems pretty over the top. Are you telling me that there's no trial?" She took a seat, choosing a wingback chair.

He smiled. The guy had one hell of a smile and one hell of a body. Muscles galore. Apparently he'd carried her the whole way back to his lair. It took the entire night but he'd done it. Candy couldn't remember much. She'd been warm and more tired then she'd ever been before. There were a couple of times where she'd tried to wake up but couldn't.

Torrent sat on the couch opposite her, choosing to sit in the seat closest to her. "There is a trial of sorts. We are an honest society. Questions are asked and answered and fates decided. It is simple and it works. It has been many centuries since someone was put to death."

"What type of crime would warrant that?"

He poured tea into each of the cups. "Sugar?"

She shook her head.

He handed her one of the cups. Candy nearly dropped it. "Shit, that's hot."

"Sorry." He smiled and she felt herself smiling back. "I'll put it down here for you." He placed the mug on the table in front of her. "If a male were to kill another male and it is found to be on purpose, with ill intent."

"Murder?"

He nodded. "Yes. Another serious crime is if a male forces himself on a female. In most cases that male would be killed." Torrent took a sip of his tea. His knee was almost touching hers.

"Or castrated." She shivered. "I think it's fitting."

"There has only ever been one such case that I am aware of. We do not force females."

"I thought you said that females . . . women are in short supply."

"They are. We go into one of the neighboring human towns twice a year to . . . let off steam."

"Oh." So they were familiar with humans. That's why Sky knew with certainty that dragons and humans could be together . . . sexually. "I wouldn't be ripped apart then?" Her eyes widened and she dropped her gaze to her lap. Shit! Why had she said that? She didn't plan on having sex with him, with any of them.

"No." His voice was deep and husky. "Any notion you have of sex would be ripped apart. It would be that good." He threw her a casual smile.

"Arrogant much?"

Torrent shook his head. "It is a fact. I have been with many human females, we are better endowed and far more in tune with a female's body."

She snorted. "Yeah right. Whatever." Her body hummed at his words.

"It's true. Our senses are far more developed. We can hear every heartbeat, every hitch of the breath. We can see even the tiniest goosebumps and dilation of the pupils. Our sense of touch is second to none." He leaned forward in his chair. "I would find your g-spot in seconds. I would feel for that bundle of nerves. I could make you come in less than a minute and with just my dick."

What the? Holy hell! "Too much information." Her voice came out high pitched. "We don't even know one another. It's rude to speak about things like that."

He gave a small shrug of one shoulder and took a sip of his tea. "I can scent that you are aroused by my words. I can tell that you are attracted to me. I am greatly attracted to you as well." He looked confused. Why would such a thing confuse him?

Then she remembered that he had originally been after

the brunette. What was her name? Julie. They were polar opposites. The brunette was tall for a human. She was curvy with boobs, buns and thighs, where Candy had more of a slim, athletic build. Okay, fine, she was pretty skinny. The only thing that was curvy were her boobs and only because they were fake. Men seemed to love her figure. Human men. She'd heard that the non-human guys preferred curvier women.

Torrent had practically been forced to take her. He hadn't been the least bit interested. Why did that make her feel . . . ? She wasn't sure how she felt. She was attracted to him. What woman in her right mind wouldn't be? It didn't mean that she liked him. "If you say so." She finally blurted. He had wanted Julie. It didn't matter. Why was she even wasting her time thinking about this? "This whole marriage mating thing, it ain't happening. I want to go home."

To Ellis?

To her old life?

She'd learned a few hard truths in the last while. School started in less than two weeks. She needed to get back before then. Once she got to her house, she'd pack a bag and find somewhere new to live. Maybe she could find a roommate closer to campus. She'd put her old life behind her. A fissure of fear caused her throat to tighten. Ellis wasn't going to just let her walk away. Then she remembered his motionless body. She didn't feel sorry for him but at the same time, she didn't wish him dead either. Not even Ellis deserved that.

Torrent shifted in his chair. "Too late. The whole marriage thing has already happened."

"Well, we need to undo it then. I want a divorce. Hold up." She made a snorting noise. "I didn't say 'I do' so technically . . ."

"Yes, you did."

"You're crazy." She huffed.

"I have many witnesses. You publicly chose me and I you."

"You're talking about when you were on top of me and all those guys were getting ready to . . . I thought I was about to be raped, torn apart. You took advantage of that."

"I didn't know all of the bullshit stories you had been fed. It was my understanding that you were fully briefed. It is done, we are mated."

"Just like that?" She felt panicked and confused. "No damned way." She could recall that there was talk of being mates. She had admitted to having chosen him and he her but that was all . . ."I just said that to make the others go away. I didn't mean it."

"It does not matter. Your words are binding. I pulled up your dress to make them think that I was claiming you and I would have done so too"—his jaw clenched—"with your full consent, but you were in such bad shape. The point being, the others believe that we are mated. It is only a matter of time before word spreads. The water dragons already know."

"I don't care." She reached for her tea and took a small

sip, keeping the mug in her hand, which shook slightly. "I thought that they planned on raping me. I thought I needed your protection. It turns out I didn't. You just told me that forcing a woman is punishable by death."

He nodded.

"You lied to me by withholding information."

"I had no idea you weren't aware of the rules. You begged me to choose you, to help you. I assumed that you wanted me."

"You were wrong. All I wanted . . . all I still want is to go home."

"It's too late for that." His voice was deep and menacing. "We are mated and I will need to make that official as a matter of urgency."

"Official?" She raised her brows and took a sip of tea.

"Official, as in we need to rut."

Candy choked—again—tea came squirting from her mouth and even out of her nose. She put a hand over her lips and coughed.

"You look shocked." He looked amused. "Rutting, it is what mated couples do."

She still had her hands over her mouth. There was tea everywhere.

"I want to get to know you. Everything about you. We can start with your likes . . . in bed . . . or, we could use the tub or the floor, or up against the wall. You tell me how you want it." His hand tightened over the mug. "Once we have both relieved our tension, we will be in a better position to get to know each other in other ways."

She used the sleeve of her sweatshirt to wipe her face and watery eyes. She tried hard to get her breathing back under control. It was the choking that had winded her, not his words.

Torrent licked his lips. "I want to know what drives you crazy. The things that make you writhe and scream. I want your pussy on my mouth and . . ."

Candy made a noise that expressed her shock. She was shocked at what he was saying but also at how her body reacted to his words.

No damned way, Candy.

Thankfully he stopped talking. She'd spent so long making others happy. Sex was never about her. It was about her clients. She hadn't had sex with many men since becoming an escort but it was always about them. Always. Hearing his words made her mouth dry and other places soaking wet.

Torrent sniffed. "You seem to like the thought of my mouth on you."

"I don't."

"Your body sure as hell does."

"My body doesn't have a say in the matter. I can't help . . ." She let the sentence die. Candy wasn't about to admit to being attracted to him. His ego was big enough as it was.

"You don't want to admit to your urges. The fact that you're attracted to me."

She made a noise of indifference. "You're not bad." She lied through her teeth. "Whatever." She added, knowing that she sounded like an idiot.

"Human females find me irresistible. *All* females want me. You are no exception."

"You might have some attributes that are appealing but your whole *'look at me,' 'I'm the greatest'* thing you have going is nauseating. It's not attractive in the least." *All true.*

Torrent stood, towering above her. His eyes were stormy and his whole stance tensed. "I am a king. The purest royal blood runs through my veins." He fisted his hands and raised them. "You should feel privileged that I chose you to be my mate. Privileged that I am here—"

"Screw you! I don't even know you. I didn't ask to be here. I don't know your stupid dragon rules. Further more, you're an asshole. Just so you know, it's a rule of mine, I don't have sex with assholes."

He tried to talk but she cut him off.

"I want to go home." Candy rose to her feet as well.

"Forget about going home." He said it on a snarl that had her stepping back. Her ass hit the window. "We are mated, Candy." Much softer this time. "I'm not letting you go."

"Why not? We don't even know each other." There was a desperate edge to her voice

"You are mine. I don't give up on what is mine." He clenched his jaw.

She shook her head and made a snorting noise. This guy was too much. "I'm not *yours.* You can get that right out of your mind."

His whole stance became even more tense. His body

seemed to vibrate raw energy. Torrent made a growling noise, low in his throat. He turned and headed for the door.

"Where are you going?" *Why had she asked him that?* It was good that he was leaving. Fantastic! Besides, she didn't care.

"I will come back when you are in a better mood. A more agreeable mood."

"In that case, don't bother coming back." She shook her head.

"I'll be back, *mate.*" Torrent put emphasis on the word mate.

"Don't call me that."

"It's what you are." He stopped abruptly and turned, closing the distance between them in an instant. Torrent gripped her hips gently in his big hands and pulled her towards him. He covered her mouth with his, forcing his tongue between her lips.

Candy made a sound that was laced with shock. Her eyes widened and she put a hand against his chest, intent on pushing him away. Bastard!

Torrent stroked his fingers through her hair and cupped the side of her face. He pushed her up against the window with his big body. He adjusted the angle of his head and stole the air from her lungs, the sanity from her brain.

Next thing, her one hand was wrapped around his neck, the other one was curled around his bicep. Her breasts were plastered against his chest. She whimpered into his mouth as she kissed him back. Giving just as much as she was getting. He moaned. It was a delicious sound that reverberated right through her.

Torrent broke the kiss and put her down. They were both breathing hard. Wait a minute! He put her down. As in, her feet had been off the floor. That was so hot!

No it wasn't.

How could she even think that? She should never have kissed him back. It sent the wrong message. The big asshole had blindsided her though. "That was rude," a whisper.

He licked his lips. "That was amazing. It was also nothing in comparison to what I have planned for you. Get some rest. You're going to need it." He kissed her forehead and walked out of the room. She heard the lock click back into place, reminding her that despite the fact that her clit throbbed and her nipples were as hard as stones, she was still a prisoner.

CHAPTER 6

Torrent practically vibrated as he walked down the hallway towards his chamber. His whole body felt tense. His balls ached.

There were only two options right now, take a shower and relieve some of the tension himself, or expel some of the energy in his dragon form. He was going for the latter. Torrent planned on spreading his wings and flying and flying until he dropped. Then he might take a refreshing dive into the ocean. If that didn't cure the longing coursing through his veins, then nothing would.

First he needed to lose the hard-on . . . again. Shifting with a dick the size of a tree trunk was difficult, to say the least. It was also painful.

A female dragon turned the corner up ahead and picked up her pace as soon as she spotted him. "My lord." She dropped her gaze for a few seconds in a show of respect.

"Ocean." Torrent nodded his head. Her eyes were the most beautiful green. She was one of his favorite females and a regular bed partner. Or at least, she had been until recently.

The she-dragon giggled and pointed at his erection. "Is your mate still unwell?"

Torrent nodded his head. "Human females are timid. They are easily damaged and take a long time to heal." He sighed. That was the story he was telling and for now he would stick to it. Surely he could convince Candy to accept his advances. The female was attracted to him whether she liked it or not. If the others found out that he hadn't fully claimed the human yet, he would be a laughing stock. Not only within his kingdom, but across the four kingdoms. Torrent had not been over exaggerating, he had never had a problem with securing a female. He wasn't about to start now. His mate would come to her senses and she would do it soon.

Ocean nodded. Her long black hair hung loosely about her shoulders. She was tall, only a head shorter than him. Her body was well muscled, her breasts full. She smiled up at him. "Yes, I have heard that they can be timid. Did you break her when you rutted her for the first time?" Her smile widened. "I know how wild and enthusiastic you can be." The female winked at him.

"Of course I didn't harm her. I'm not some kind of animal." His voice was a low growl.

She laughed. "I beg to differ." She raised her brows when his frown deepened. "I'm only joking, my lord." Then she ran her hand down the side of his arm. It made him feel uncomfortable. "I could help you with that." She looked down at his dick.

Torrent felt himself frown. "I'm mated." He wanted to

keep on walking but she blocked his way.

Ocean shrugged. "Your mate is unwell. You are the king." She put her hand on his chest and proceeded to stroke him with the tips of her fingers, trailing her way down. "It would be perfectly acceptable if . . ."

He gripped her hand as it was about to push below the elastic of his pants. "I am mated. What kind of a male would I be if I rutted another female?"

She looked down at her hand and he realized he was squeezing her fingers. Torrent released her.

"Your mate can't be very nice if she expects you to remain celibate while she is healing. A she-dragon would never require that of the king."

"Do not speak of your queen in that way. Candy is just about as sweet as they come." His mouth twitched with the need to smile. *Sweet.* Not by a long damn shot but it was none of this female's business. "For the record, my mate has not demanded anything of me." *Unfortunately.* He could think of a whole list of demands he would love to hear fall from her lips. "I do not wish to be with any other females. I have one already. That is all, you can go now."

She gave a curtesy. "As you wish, my lord." She stepped to the side and he moved past her. "Please don't hesitate if you change your mind." She called after him.

Not likely.

Torrent picked up the pace and turned the corner that led to his chamber. Fuck! What now?

Tide leaned up against the wall next to his door. "Your little plaything was waiting outside your chamber."

"Let me guess, you offered to take my place?" Torrent opened his door and stepped back to let his brother in.

"Of course, seeing as you're a taken male and all. Ocean is meeting me later." Tide chuckled. He stopped and sniffed the air. "So, your female is still not well? She didn't seem that injured when she arrived."

"She is much improved but we have decided to take things slowly."

Tide burst out laughing.

Torrent felt his blood heat. "What? She is human. Humans are different to she-dragons. They need more time to—"

"I heard that all of the other humans are rutting like rabbits on . . . what's the name of that human drug that keeps the males hard for extended periods?"

"I can't remember," Torrent grumbled.

Tide waved his hand around in irritation. "It doesn't matter. They're all rutting up a storm. As far as I know, none of them are mated yet." He laughed again. "You have mated the female already, yet no sex. You?" He shook his head. "The one male I know that can crook his finger at any human and she'll come running."

"I can't wait until you win a human female of your own. Then you'll understand. Candy is not some quick fuck. She's not just any human. She's my mate, I need to treat her with respect and to get to know her better. I'm not putting her under any pressure. I need to be more than sure that she is well, that she is ready."

Tide frowned. "You've already rutted her, you're acting

like you're still trying to win her."

I am.

Fuck!

He was. Torrent had never had to win a female before. He wasn't sure how to go about it.

Tide waved his hand in front of Torrent's face.

"Stop that," Torrent said.

"You disappeared there for a moment. Lost in thought?" He smirked.

"Like I said, I can't wait until you go through this. I'm going to take great joy out of watching you beg and crawl."

"Forget that! My female will be all over me, like white on rice. Like green on scale. Like—"

"Enough. You're giving me a damned headache." Torrent removed his pants, throwing them over the back of a chair. He opened the large, sliding door and stepped out onto the balcony. Tide followed him.

"I expect you to win a female at the next hunt." Torrent said.

"I was this close." Tide held his fingers a millimeter apart. "This fucking close. That bastard Coal beat me to her by seconds. Shit!" His eyes glazed over. "That human was so sexy. So damned hot I still have wet dreams about her. All that dark hair and lush . . ."

"Enough." Torrent expected to feel something at the mention of the dark beauty. She had been his first choice and the type of female he always went for but there was nothing. Just like with Ocean, nothing. It seemed that he wanted Candy. His mate. Although she wasn't officially his mate, not yet anyway.

Soon.

"Forget about that human. She is gone. By now claimed." He took in a deep breath and moved to the railing. The air was thick with salt and humidity. It invigorated him. The water looked inviting. The open skies looked just as appealing. He turned his head back to where Tide was standing. "Be ready for the next hunt. Train hard. As the first prince and next in line for the throne, I expect you to win a mate."

"With Coal out of the way, that should be easy."

Torrent had to smile. His brother was strong and intelligent but he was also naïve. Not that Torrent had much of a leg to stand on himself. Not after falling for everything that Coal had pulled.

"What?" Tide narrowed his eyes.

"Blaze will also be taking part."

Tide pulled a face like he had a screw loose. "The male didn't even feature. He doesn't want a human mate. It was clear. Blaze will not be a problem."

Torrent choked out a laugh as he unlatched the gate that formed a part of the railing and stepped onto the very edge. "It doesn't matter what Blaze wants. He is the fire king. The male has to take a human mate. He needs heirs. Mark my words, he will be major competition and so will Thunder."

Tide's expression became stormy. "I had forgotten about the air king."

Torrent nodded. "Thunder will take part. Blaze won't

be able to stop him a second time." Thunder had made a pact with the fire king, one of the fertile air princesses in return for Blaze's sister, the fire princess, who was also one of the last fertile she-dragons.

Blaze's sister mated a vampire, forcing him to break the agreement. In a moment of rage, Thunder had given his sisters to the second prince's of the water and earth kingdoms. It was how Sky had come to them.

Tide had obviously been thinking about the whole affair as well. "I still think it's unfair that Lake got to mate Sky. I would give anything for a fertile female of my own."

"I tried to get Thunder to agree to allowing his sister to mate with you but it would have strengthened our kingdom too much to have a she-dragon mate with the first prince."

Tide gave a one shouldered shrug. "Oh well." He grinned. "I prefer human females anyways. After seeing them, being up close to them." His eyes glazed over and he made a humming sound. "I want one. I want one real bad. I only wish I had gotten a better look at your mate."

The bastard's grin grew wider. "My interest has been further piqued because you seem to be hiding her away. The only thing I could see was that she looked like a tiny thing."

It was true, Candy was tiny. The need to protect her rose up in him. It was an irrational emotion, brought on by his need to claim her. He almost turned and ran back to her chamber. It was wrong that they were separated. It was something that would be rectified as soon as he blew off some steam. The female was going to sleep with him from here on out whether she liked it or not. Let her try and resist him, he could be very persuasive if need be.

Tide chuckled. "Maybe Ocean was right. Did you break her? Is that why you can't rut?"

Torrent growled. The sound low but a deadly warning all the same. "Stop talking about my mate. You will not look at her too closely. You will not talk about her. You will stay far away or so help me."

Tide put up his hands. "Hey. Calm down. I didn't mean anything by it. I'm seeing Ocean later, remember, I don't need your female. I'll win my own in the next hunt."

Cocky bastard.

"You'd better."

"I will."

Torrent looked out ahead of him. "Good," he said, as he dropped from the edge of the balcony. He felt his body crack, pull and strengthen as he morphed into his dragon form. It took him a few seconds longer than normal. The ground rose up towards him as he unfolded his wings.

It was too close for comfort. He needed to bring his strength levels up, he needed to rut. He also needed to follow his own advice, which was the exact opposite of trying to get into Candy's pants. He would have to give her space and show her respect. Torrent flapped his wings, feeling himself lift. Not being able to rut her was a dilemma. One he had never experienced before.

CHAPTER 7

C andy paced her room. The sun was going down over the ocean. It was the most beautiful thing she had ever seen. A view she would never grow tired of and yet, she sighed. The problem was, there wasn't anything to do. No books to read, no magazines to page through, no TV to watch. Not that she did much of the aforementioned anyway but when a person was stuck between four walls. Okay, three walls and a large window, any type of distraction would do.

What she wanted most of all was to walk along the beach, to take a dip in the ocean. She wanted to go outside and to be a part of that view.

There was a knock at the door.

Candy turned to face it. Was it him? Her heart beat faster at the prospect.

"Just a minute." She grabbed the sweater and pulled it over her head. It wouldn't do to have him looking at her like he had earlier. It was an eye fucking if she'd ever seen one, and it had made her uncomfortable.

The way his gaze had lingered on her boobs. Men loved

her breasts. Loved that they were so full. Particularly since, she was so petite. Sometimes she wished she never had them done. People mistakenly assumed that she was some dumb blonde. Ellis had talked her into it. Although, that wasn't entirely true. She'd always been a little shy about her smaller chest, so, after much deliberation, she'd gone ahead and done them. She ultimately did them for herself, for the way they made her feel. So feminine and sexy. She liked that she filled out a bathing suit and that she didn't have to wear those extra padded bras anymore. When men glued their eyes to her chest though, she sometimes had doubts.

Torrent had practically drooled. When she'd looked at herself later in the mirror she could understand why. A tight white tee and no bra. *Hello!* Her nipples were everywhere. She had to chew on her lower lip to stop herself from smiling. With him, it hadn't felt so intimidating. He'd had such a goofy look on his face. At least she knew she wasn't alone, he was also attracted to her. There was some kind of comfort in that.

No wait! Maybe that wasn't a good thing. The guy was a dragon shifter. He had a colossal ego and he was her mate.

Mate.

She felt her heartrate pick up. There had to be a way out of it. There just had to. She planned on fighting her attraction to him, which shouldn't be too hard since he was an asshole. Once he realized that it was never going to happen between them, he would have to let her go and then it would be all smooth sailing from there.

No sweat!

There was another knock. Oh shit! "Come in!" She shouted, her voice a little high pitched.

A key turned in the lock and Sky walked in. Candy huffed out a breath.

"You look like you just saw a ghost." Sky smiled at her. "You also look relieved. The whole look you have going on there is a strange combination."

"I'm relieved." Candy felt her whole body relax. "I thought you were someone else."

"You thought I was Torrent." Sky raised her brows. "What happened between you two earlier? The male went for a four-hour flight after visiting with you. He came back completely exhausted and is mumbling one syllable answers to everything. He's in an awful mood."

"He thought he could just waltz in here and jump into bed with me." She shrugged. "I set him straight."

Sky shook her head. "But you are his mate. Our king . . ."

"I don't even know him."

"You will get to know him." She said it so matter-a-factly.

"That's not how humans go about it. We first get to know someone and then we have sex with them. It can take months . . . years to get to a point where we marry a person. It's a really big step, one not taken lightly so you'll excuse me if I'm a bit weirded out by the whole thing."

Sky frowned, she looked confused. "Mmmmm. That's

not what I've been led to believe." She paused. "The males often talk about the stag runs."

"What are stag runs?" After having talked with Torrent, she could guess.

"As you know, there are very few she-dragons. Our males have needs."

"Oh." Needs! Yup, as an escort she knew all about men's needs.

"They go into town every—"

"Yup!" Candy laughed. "Torrent told me all about it. He didn't name the whole expedition by name. A stag run." She couldn't help but smile. "What a fitting tag."

"Well . . ." Sky continued. "I have heard our males talk after coming home from the stag runs. Human females throw themselves at the males. They never have a shortage of bed partners."

Candy could only imagine. The shifter guys were all tall and buff. They were pretty darned attractive. During the hunt they had seemed scary and aggressive but thinking back, now that she could think straight, they had all been really sexy. Her thoughts drifted to Torrent, to his wide shoulders, to that whole V thing he had going on just above his pants. Aside from a banging body, he was really attractive. The two didn't always go hand in hand. Those pale blue eyes, his full lips, he was rugged and handsome. All the guys she had seen were. Even that dark beast of a guy that had saved her.

"Are you even listening to me, Candy?" Sky put her hands on her hips.

"Sorry, I missed what you said, would you mind repeating it?"

Sky looked at Candy like she had grown horns. "You just told me that humans take ages to get to know someone before having sex with them. We just established that it's not true. These females have plenty of sex with our males. They are willing participants." She added, still clearly a little pissed that Candy had even suggested that any of the dragon shifters would force a woman. "Our males get one night twice a year and they have plenty of sex. There is no time to win a female over. It's the females that are often the aggressors and rut our males even though our males are clear that there is no future for them together. It's . . . what is it you humans call it . . . oh yes, a one-night stand." She raised her brows.

"Okay." Candy huffed out a breath. "You're right. Women will have sex with guys for the sake of having sex. A one-night stand, a booty call. There are plenty of names for it." Candy had never been one of those women. It was quite comical considering she had sex for a living.

"Well then."

"It's a bit different when it's a potential relationship, when it's two people who might just have a future. Things are generally more complicated. This whole situation is complicated." Candy scratched the back of her neck.

Sky frowned. "There are always plenty of females that beg the males to leave their contact details. Some of them beg to go with the males, they want a future, even though it was agreed up front that the relationship would be short-term and just sex. A booty call." She smiled. "They want more and this, after just one night together. Human females are quite capable of developing feelings for a male quickly and easily. You are overcomplicating things."

Candy nodded. "I'm sure it happens regularly. Women are wired to want more, for that matter, I think everyone is wired to want more, especially after giving themselves physically. It's part of the reason why sex can complicate things. In order to want a relationship with someone you have to, at least, get along with them and I'm not sure I even like Torrent."

Sky's jaw dropped, as in her mouth gaped. It took a few seconds for her to regain her composure. "You don't mean that."

"I don't really know him, but from what I can tell, he's just so full of himself. He can be a real jerk. You even told me yourself. Maybe not in so many words but . . ."

"He is a king. He is used to everyone catering to his every need and obeying his every whim. I don't think anyone has ever told him 'no' before and that includes the females he encounters on the stag runs."

I'll bet! Candy snorted. "There's a first for everything." She folded her arms.

"It has put him off balance. Just so that you are aware, Torrent is well within his rights to seek another female if you withhold sex from him."

It was Candy's turn to gape. These shifters were sick. Not that she cared what Torrent did. She didn't even know the guy. "Whatever," she muttered. "I don't even consider us to be married or mated. He can do whatever he wants. I won't stop him."

Sky walked to the other side of the room. She just stood there looking out the window. Candy could see that she wasn't really staring out the window. The other woman was deep in thought. She felt like this room was too small, like the walls were closing in. She needed to go home. This had never been a part of her plan.

"Torrent turned down a female today." Sky finally said, her gaze still on the outside view. "Ocean is one of his favorites and he turned her down flat. It is a compliment to you."

Candy choked out a laugh. "If you say so." She paused. "What kind of a name is Ocean anyway?"

"I do say so," Sky said. "Ocean is a perfectly acceptable name for a water she-dragon, just as Sky is a normal name for an air dragon."

"I didn't mean anything by it." Candy quickly added. *Shit!* Talk about putting her foot in it. She was acting like a bitch. She wasn't normally like this but then again, she'd never been in a situation like this before. "I think that Sky is a beautiful name. I'm sorry. I just wish I could get out of this room. I'm feeling claustrophobic and it's making me cranky."

"That's fine." Sky gave her the ghost of a smile. "You are jealous. It is understandable. I would suggest sex but easing your male will also work fine, for the moment. Have him ease you as well."

"Ease." She held up her hands. "I'm not even going to

ask. Torrent can forget it."

"That's a pity because it seems that he doesn't want any other female. He wants you, his mate."

Candy had to suppress a sigh. She didn't want Sky to think that she was relieved because she wasn't. "Well, he's going to have to wait a really long time because I'm not interested. I told him I want to go home and I stand by that."

Sky raised her brows. "Torrent is used to getting plenty of sex."

Candy made a squeaking noise. Why did Sky insist on talking about this to her? It was too much information. There was a part of her that wanted to interrupt the other woman to tell her just that, but she bit her tongue. If it made Sky feel better, then she would listen. The she-dragon had been nothing but nice to her since she arrived there. She'd gone out of her way to take care of Candy. Bottom line, she was good people. Candy nodded once.

"The lesser males are used to being starved of sex and of operating on lower energy levels. They know no different. Torrent on the other hand will find it increasingly difficult to function at optimum level. It's going to start becoming obvious." She paused and licked her lips.

Candy shuffled from one foot to the other.

When she didn't say anything, Sky carried on. "The idiot male decided to turn down sex in the weeks leading up to the hunt. He had this hair-brained scheme that it would hone his senses and make him hungrier for a female. It is going to backfire on him soon. You need to be aware that he cannot go without sex indefinitely, without recourse. He's going to be forced to take another female soon. It won't be a choice."

Candy didn't know what to say or to think. There was a part of her that felt sorry for him but it didn't mean she was going to just roll over and accept him into her bed.

"On a lighter note." Sky smiled. "You mentioned wanting to get out of this room."

Candy nodded. She practically held her breath. Had Torrent agreed to her going out? Maybe he was letting her go home. It was a pipe dream, but a girl could hope.

"Pack your bags because you're . . ."

Could it be, was Torrent letting her go. Please. Please. Please.

" . . . Torrent wants you to move into his chamber."

"What?" *No, no, no.* "What?" She repeated, like a complete idiot.

Sky tilted her head. "I'm here to help you pack and to escort you there."

"Um, please tell him thanks but no thanks." Candy had never lived with a guy. She planned on waiting until she was married. Ironic considering her profession but totally true. Then again, Torrent was technically her . . . husband . . . mate . . . no he wasn't. He'd somehow married her by accident. It didn't really count. Did it?

Sky's mouth fell open in another gape. "I can't tell him that."

She shook her head. "I'm not moving in with him." Oh

god, he would probably expect to share a bed. The thought made her shake her head harder.

"You must."

"I won't."

"You have to." Sky looked appalled. "It is the king's wish. You are his mate, your place is by his side, in his bed."

Oh god! Flip! Candy swallowed hard. "That's what I was afraid of. I think that it's best that I stay here. That whole thing about needing a change of scenery, forget it!"

"Please. Torrent is a good male. Once you see below that"—she nodded and smiled—"slightly arrogant exterior, he's a wonderful and caring male. He also has a—"

"I'm sure he's awesome and wonderful and dynamite in bed but I can't just move in with someone I only just met." It was Candy's turn to pace across the room. She clasped her hands together tightly.

Sky took a few steps towards her. "Give it a chance. Torrent is a male of honor, he will respect your wishes regardless of how weak he is. You will be able to get to know him if you move in with him, perhaps you will be pleasantly surprised."

No way. Candy shook her head. "Does he have a separate room in his . . . chamber?"

Sky shook her head. "The layout is similar to this."

"Only one bed?" Candy already knew the answer.

"Yes, of course. Torrent is your mate . . ."

"I'm afraid that I have to decline. Please thank him for

his kind offer."

Sky's eyes widened, making them look huge in her head. It was almost comical. "But . . ."

"No buts, I've made up my mind."

After a few moments of deliberation, Sky nodded her head. She pushed out a deep breath. "I'd better go and inform the king." She began to walk towards the door. "He won't be happy."

CHAPTER 8

U nderstatement of the century.

Not happy. Hah! More like completely pissed.

There was a hard, bone jarring knock at the door. One single bang. After about three seconds the key turned in the lock and the door was flung open. The hinges were practically torn out and the wood creaked with the force of the impact as it crashed into the wall.

The door was bigger than a regular one, yet Torrent took up the entire space with his huge body. His whole stance reminded her of a bull about to charge. He even huffed out a breath, making his nostrils flare. His eyes were an even more vivid blue. They were narrowed in on her. His mouth was set, his jaw tense.

Her first reaction, on instinct, was to run, to hide, to get away. Candy had to force herself to stand her ground. She would stand up to him. She still had rights.

The big man advanced, taking enormous strides. His movements were fluid, graceful even considering his enormous bulk. His intense gaze bore into her and for the second time since meeting him she felt like he was the hunter and she the prey.

It became even more difficult to keep her feet rooted to the spot. Candy held up a hand. "Wait. You can't just . . ."

Torrent ignored her and closed the small remaining distance between them. He picked her up and tossed her over his shoulder like she was a sack of goods. She made a noise that spoke of shock. He was essentially manhandling her so she was well within her rights. "Put me down." Her voice sounded relatively calm. *Way to go, Candy.* "Now." A little more panicked.

Torrent had turned and was walking towards the door.

"Put me down." All out panicked. She dangled halfway down his back. His ass was even more sculpted up close. His glutes shifted and clenched with each long stride. She wasn't just checking him out, was she? What was wrong with her? "Put me down." She shouted and began to beat her fists on his lower back and on his ass. Damn him and his ass and his pecs and abs and . . . just damn him.

"Stop that." A low growl that vibrated against her thighs, which were on his chest.

"Screw you!" she yelled.

"Stop! Or I will be forced to punish you." He slapped her ass, hard. It stung. The patch immediately warmed up. She'd have a red hand mark for sure.

Candy made a yelping noise.

Torrent rubbed on the spot, almost tenderly. It made her squirm. It made her . . . uncomfortable. It felt good.

What was wrong with her? Tears stung her eyes but she wasn't about to cry.

He pushed open a door. It was at least twice the size of the one he'd almost broken. He slammed it shut, not as hard as before. It wasn't easy being upside down but she tried to take in the space. Her head felt swollen from all her blood rushing to it.

The chamber was huge. It had a similar design and layout, only there was more of everything. More couches, a bigger kitchen, a huge tub and a huge . . . bed. There were feminine touches, yet it came together as masculine.

The bed was humungous, probably one and a half times a regular king size bed. It was a four poster bed carved from a dark wood. The sheets were black and looked like they might be silk. The room was designed in dark, masculine colors. Blues, greys and black dominated, as did big motifs and rich fabrics like velvet and . . .

She landed on the bed and bounced once. Candy turned, her eyes immediately locking with his as he got onto the bed as well. "What do you . . . ?"

"Be quiet and don't move."

"Like hell I . . ."

He smiled, it was predatory. "I enjoyed spanking that sexy ass of yours and would like nothing more than to put you over my knee and make you scream out with every hard whack."

Shit! What the! She wanted to retaliate just to see if he would follow up on his threats but by the look in his eyes she knew he was deadly serious. The biggest problem was that the thought of him spanking her wasn't nearly as horrible as it should've been. She was oddly turned on by his words. Candy didn't move a muscle.

"That's better." Torrent kept his eyes on her as he moved closer to her.

What was he planning? She plastered herself against the sheets, which were indeed smooth, cool silk. Every muscle inside of her tensed.

He straddled her, putting his hands on either side of her head. He was so damned close that she could feel his heat and yet, he didn't touch her. Not even one hair on her body. "Do I have your attention?"

Candy swallowed hard and nodded.

"Good." He leaned forward and the air froze inside her. She couldn't breathe, couldn't move, she couldn't think. His chest was heaving. Then again, so was hers. Why did he have to smell so good? This was crazy. She should be terrified, or angry, or something. The problem was that despite everything that had happened, she trusted him. Torrent was not about to hurt her in any way. He was different from human guys. God, like chalk and cheese. He had a gruff exterior and could act like a colossal jerk but she sensed that he was good deep down. She could see it. She also trusted Sky and respected the woman's opinion. The newfound knowledge should've had her relaxing under his close scrutiny. It didn't.

His face was a couple of inches away from her. His eyes moved to her mouth and he licked his lips. Was he going to kiss her again? Then he lifted his gaze to meet hers.

"You're staying here, with me." A deep rasp that had goosebumps forming on her skin.

She sucked in a breath, intent on arguing but he covered her mouth with his fingers. The guy could move really quickly. She couldn't help but swallow again. "This isn't a discussion. You're staying here. We are mated, mated couples live together." His gaze moved to the right of her, focusing on the mattress for a few beats before returning to lock with hers. "I am a reasonable male."

Yeah right! His fingers were still resting on her lips so she couldn't say it.

His eyes flared with humor. "I can see by the look in your eyes that you don't believe me."

Candy narrowed her eyes for a moment. She didn't believe it for a second.

Torrent removed his hand. "I won't try to rut you. I won't so much as touch you. No sexual behavior whatsoever." He removed the hand from her mouth.

"What would you call this?" She allowed her eyes to travel over his body for a few seconds before looking back up at his face. The guy had her caged in with his massive bulk. He was sporting an erection. The sight of it wasn't as scary as it had been before. She was becoming more used to seeing it. He might not be touching her anymore but everything about him screamed sex. Sex with a capital S and then some.

Torrent smiled. It wasn't fair. It only made him more attractive. His rugged good-looks turned a tad boyish. In short, he was devastatingly handsome. "This? This is nothing. Less than nothing. We are both fully clothed. Now, if we were to remove these barriers." His eyes darkened up a tad and he turned serious. "If I were to touch, stroke and caress you." His voice both lowered and deepened. "If I were to do so with my hands, my mouth and my cock . . . now that would be sexual. If I were to make your pussy weep with a need so great that—"

"Okay, I get it." Her voice shook just a little, which made his mouth twitch and his eyes crinkle a little at the edges. He found her reaction to his words humorous.

"Believe it or not, I want more than just sex. I want to get to know you. I want to be reasonable about this because, as my mate, you are my equal. I really want you to give this a chance. I'm willing to discuss it."

He'd turned down the advances of another woman. He was trying to be nice, well, sort of. She got the feeling that this was being nice for a guy like Torrent. "If that is true, then I want to negotiate one other thing aside from the no sex rule."

"It's not a rule." He frowned. "A rule would indicate that sex is off the table. I want us to rut. Ideally right now and in as many positions as possible." He swallowed, causing his throat to work.

Oh flip! Those crass words were affecting her. She felt overheated, her heart was beating out of her chest and her palms were sweaty.

"However . . ." A deep purr. "I understand that you need time and space. I gave it some thought. It would be best if you initiated sexual contact. I will avoid doing so.

You tell me what you want, when you want it and how you want it and I will oblige. It would be my pleasure and yours." His gaze moved back to her mouth and he inhaled deeply.

This was different. It was also not something she was used to. Normally her 'dates' dictated when and how *they* wanted it. This was new and refreshing. Not that she was going to actually take him up on it. "Okay . . . fine. We're mated, so even though I'm not fully onboard, I agree to give this thing a try. I agree to at least getting to know you a bit better but without the pressure of sex." What did she have to lose? It's not like there was much for her back home and Torrent intrigued her. He was multilayered, that was for sure.

He nodded and seemed to relax. Torrent moved off of her and went to sit on the edge of the bed, finally giving her some room to breathe.

Candy pulled herself into a sitting position, she smoothed down her sweatshirt and tucked her legs underneath herself.

Torrent twisted his body so that he was facing her. "You said that there is something you wish to negotiate."

Candy nodded.

Her big blue eyes were focused on him. She picked some lint off of her baggy sweatshirt. He wished he could rip the garment from her body.

Note to self, procure some proper fitting human clothing and as a matter of extreme urgency.

Her agreeing to stay with him was a major breakthrough. They were actually communicating. Excitement coursed through him. It was just a matter of time before she sought to have her needs met. He could scent that she was aroused even though he had barely touched her.

How bad could her requirements be? If it meant her staying with him, he would grant them in a heart beat. How bad could they possibly be?

She licked her lips and took a deep breath. Why was she stalling? He didn't like it. Candy finally looked him in the eyes. "It doesn't matter that we are . . . mated."

Yes, it did! He didn't say anything. He needed to give her an opportunity to talk first. She seemed to struggle with the notion. Although he had never spent any extended time with humans, he had plenty of experience with them. Those that wanted more after one night were normally running away from something. Most were happy with just the sex. There were also those that were somewhere in-between.

"I don't see us in that way. As mates." She licked her lips. "It's just too soon. I think it's too soon to live with you, even if the situation is temporary."

He growled softly at her words, he couldn't help it. *It's not temporary!* He grit his jaw to keep himself from saying it out loud.

"You might not like it but it's how I feel. I'm willing to meet you half way by staying here but I can't share a bed with you."

It was bad.

Really fucking bad.

Torrent squeezed his eyes shut and clutched the back of his neck, which felt like it had gone into instant spasm. He willed calm to come but it didn't. "You are my mate." He released his neck. "Mates should sleep together. I won't try anything." He held up his hands. "I swear." He never thought he would ever say such a thing but here it was.

"If you want me in your space then I need to sleep alone."

Fuck!

The question was how badly he wanted her here. He could sense that this would be a deal breaker. Candy had made up her mind. He couldn't move in a second bed because everyone would know that his mate didn't want him in their bed. The best he would be able to do was sneak in an extra blanket. It was a no brainer. He would deal. He had to. Torrent nodded. "Fine, but this is my private chamber. I need to feel comfortable and to be myself in this space. Do you agree to that?"

She widened her eyes, seeming to contemplate what he had just said. Then she frowned looking confused. Candy finally shrugged. "I suppose that's reasonable. So . . . let me get this straight . . . no sex."

"No sex initiated by me. You on the other hand . . ." He couldn't wait until that day came. It would be soon if he had anything to do with it.

Her pupils dilated. This female did want him whether she liked it or not. "Yeah, that." She breathed in and out a few times. "I get to sleep in the bed . . . alone," she quickly added.

"Lastly . . ." She smiled. This female was spectacular. "We need to make a concerted effort to get to know one another. Did I miss anything?"

Torrent shook his head. "That sounds about right."

"I would appreciate it if we could get out. I want to explore this place. I want to walk on the beach and swim and meet some of your people." She looked animated, excited even. He wished he could give her everything she asked for and more. It would certainly help them get to know each other. It was a pity it couldn't happen.

Dammit! He'd expected this to come up but not so soon. "Let's first concentrate on getting you settled. We'll enjoy an evening meal together here in my chamber and then, we'll see."

Candy nodded. "That's fair but we're going out tomorrow."

"It depends," he blurted. He needed to be completely honest with her and although he'd mentioned this in passing, it seemed, he needed to spell things out for her. Torrent couldn't allow himself to forget that she wasn't a she-dragon. They were very different.

She frowned. "What do you mean?"

"I told you that although we are mated, we still need to make it official." He raised his brows.

Her frown deepened. "I think I remember you saying something along those lines. I don't know what it means though."

"I pretended to fully claim you but I never actually did it."

She had no idea what he was talking about.

"I believe you humans call it to consummate the relationship." He registered shock on her face. He'd already come so far may as well go the whole hog. "In order for our mating to be binding, we need to rut."

Candy laughed. There was a whole lot of shock, mingled with humor. It registered on her face, clear as day. "Are you telling me that there is a way out of this, that we're not technically bound together?"

Torrent shook his head. "We are bound female. I told you that I consider you to be mine. All that is left is to claim you."

"What you are saying is that the whole ceremony hasn't been completed. It's not done yet. We can still back out."

Torrent felt anger course through him. The need to throw her down on the bed and to make her his rode him hard. He knew that he could have her begging him to take her and in no time, but he couldn't do such a thing. Candy would regret it. She would grow to hate him.

"We openly chose one another. According to our lores, the bond between us has begun to take hold. I know that you can feel it. It is only a matter of time before we can no longer resist one another." He had to smile. "A matter of time before you give in to me. You won't be able to help it. Even if I were to take you home, your body would crave mine, just as mine craves yours."

Her eyes darkened up for a second and she pulled her lower lip into her mouth. Then she snorted. "You're so full of it."

He couldn't understand her aversion to him or her statement for that matter. His words were true. It was that simple. "You are attracted to me and we are bonded. It is only a matter of time before things progress naturally."

"This changes things. If we're not already mated then take me home, I'll take my chances with the whole craving you thing."

He shook his head. "I can't do that. You need to give this a chance. You agreed."

"That was before I knew the facts."

"This doesn't change anything."

Her eyes widened and a look of horror appeared on her face. "It changes everything."

"You are staying right here. I agreed to your terms and you agreed to mine. You stay here, in this chamber until I have officially claimed you. I'm sorry but you cannot leave before then."

Her chest began to heave and her fists balled in her lap. "That's bullshit! You're essentially keeping me prisoner until I agree to have sex. That's wrong on so many levels. You realize that, don't you?" Her eyes glistened with unshed tears.

Shit! He hated to see her upset like this. This wasn't how he had planned for this to go. "You asked me to help you. You begged. I agreed. I helped you, Candy. I didn't know that you didn't know the rules. I wasn't aware that you hadn't been informed. I didn't have to choose you. I could've left you to the lesser males. I helped you. I bound myself to you in front of them. I was injured and may not have been able to fight all of them and win. It was the only option left to me, to us, at the time. I chose to help you and now I'm asking you to help me."

"It was convenient for you." The anger had left her voice. "You need a mate right? Someone to have your babies? You didn't do it to help me, you did it because you had to. You did it for you."

Torrent shook his head. "I didn't have to take you. There is another hunt in a few weeks." He shrugged. "I could've waited. Maybe I should've waited but I didn't, you begged me to help you. I did it."

A tear slid down her cheek. Hell! He was making this worse.

"So I'm a charity case." She swallowed hard. "Look, I know you actually wanted the other woman. That you and that other dark haired guy were fighting over her. Her name is Julie." Another tear slid free and she sniffed. It was as if she suddenly realized that she was crying because she wiped her face using both hands before looking back at him. "Let's just forget this. You don't really want me. Let's annul this thing and you can start over on the next hunt." Her lip wobbled like she hated the idea of him hunting for another female.

Torrent shook his head. "The fact of the matter is that I did help you. I wanted to help you. I am bound to you now just as you are bound to me."

Her big, beautiful eyes were tear soaked even though no more of them fell. Her eyelashes glinted. She held her lip between her teeth. She looked away, keeping her gaze on anything but him.

Torrent huffed out a pent up breath. "Shit, Candy." He moved over to her and she allowed him to cup her face with his hands. He turned her face, forcing her to meet his eyes. "I did initially want that dark haired female. I won't lie to you."

A tear escaped and her throat worked. It definitely hurt her to hear him say it. She did feel their bond despite everything she said to the contrary. She tried to pull away but he wouldn't let her. "I chose you, Candy. I didn't have to but I did anyway. I wanted to. It is important that you know that I am attracted to you in a big way. I haven't so much as given that other female a passing thought since bringing you here. I'm glad things ended up the way they did. Let's work on it. I really want us to give this a chance." He moved away from her and gave her some space.

"Thank you. I appreciate your honesty. I am still struggling to accept that I am stuck in this room . . ." She looked around her, her eyes widened here and there as they roamed. "As beautiful as it is. I'm essentially a prisoner here until you either let me go or I have sex with you. It's not an ideal situation. Why can't you just tell everyone that we're dating . . ." She pulled a face that spoke of panic and gripped her temples. "I haven't dated anyone in a very long time. This is so . . . unexpected." She huffed out a breath. "I don't understand why I need to be locked away. It's not like I can escape or anything. We're in the middle of nowhere."

They were moving forward. He needed to come clean about everything. "Everyone thinks that I have fully claimed you."

"What?"

"My people think that we are mated."

"That we had sex?" Her brows lifted.

Torrent nodded. "If you go out, they will know that it is not true. When we do rut . . . consummate our relationship, you will scent of me. It will be subtle but there."

"You had to"—she paused—"pretend to . . . you know . . . the whole dress lifting thing." She looked flustered. "Is that how they got the wrong idea about this?"

"Yeah, that. I made those males believe that I was claiming you. I had to. Some of them were water dragons. They came back here and spread the word that I had mated you."

Candy nodded. "I see."

"I obviously didn't really do it. You were already half unconscious and I could never . . ."

She waved her hands. "Yeah, yeah, I know. So everyone thinks we did the deed."

Torrent nodded. "I should've said something when we returned here. Set the record straight. It is acceptable to fool one's opponents but I felt a need to protect you. I was worried about you. You'd been out cold for a long time. There were short bouts where you opened your eyes but I could see that you weren't really awake. It scared me. Non-humans are still governed by instinct. It is my responsibility to protect you." He paused.

"Once we got back here, I snarled and growled if anyone tried to approach you. Based on the information they had already received and on my actions, they assumed I had fully claimed you. No one got close enough to scent that I hadn't actually done the deed. I allowed them to assume it. I guess I wasn't thinking clearly. I liked the idea of you as my mate and I didn't think it would take long to claim you anyway. So . . ."

"So . . . all your people think we're already mated, I mean, like, for real."

He nodded.

"Tell them you lied. Set the record straight."

"I'm their king. They need to be able to trust me. I don't know why I did it, all I know is that it's done. We are going to finish this so why cause unnecessary shit?"

"You're never going to let me go, are you?" Her lip wobbled.

Torrent clenched his teeth for a moment or two. He wanted to go to her, to put his arms around her and reassure her but he refrained. What would he say? That she was wrong? That she was right? Fuck! This was one hell of a mess. "Let's get to know one another. I concede that it's not an ideal situation. I fucked up. I might be a king but I make mistakes. I honestly thought that you would be in my bed as soon as you healed."

Candy laughed. "I actually completely believe you. You do realize that your arrogance and that oversized ego of yours is to blame, right?"

"Does your smile mean that you forgive me? That you'll work on it."

"You've been straight with me and I appreciate it. I . . ." She licked her lips and took in a breath which she held inside her for a beat or two. "I believe that you are attracted to me, that you see a future for us and that you want this to work. I guess it's my turn to be honest." She paused again, clearly struggling to find her words. "I am also attracted to you. Very much so. I also feel a pull to you, a bond, whatever you want to call it. I don't understand it. It scares me. This whole situation is . . . different. I don't know that it is enough to base a whole relationship on but I agree to giving it a try. It's the best I can do."

"Thank you." Torrent felt elated. "I will make sure that you don't regret it. I want you to be more comfortable. I need you to write down a list of things that you need. Anything, big or small. You can start with clothing. Make sure you add sizes." He felt everything in him soften as he looked at her. "It won't be so bad, I promise. I'm glad you are giving us a chance. I want it to be your choice though. If, in the end, you decide you still want out, I'll take you back."

Candy seemed to relax. "Do you mean that?"

He nodded. It killed him to say it but he couldn't be with a female that wasn't one hundred percent onboard. "Yes."

She gave a small nod. "Okay then."

CHAPTER 9

After knocking, Torrent walked inside a few beats later. He was carrying an enormous tray. The most wonderful smells wafted towards her.

Her stomach made a soft growling sound and she pressed her hand against it. She had since showered and changed into another pair of sweats. She'd rolled the sleeves and the pants around the waist. All of the clothes were too big.

Torrent smiled. "Hungry?"

How did he hear that? Oh yes, shifters had much better senses than humans. "You have no idea."

"Good." His smile widened. "I brought all of the foods that you said you liked."

"All of them?" She could hear the shock in her voice. "That's a ton of food."

He nodded. "Burgers and french fries, pizza, tacos and brownies."

Her stomach growled again, louder this time. "Yum." Not that the food up until then had been bad or anything. It was just all so healthy. Meat and salad. Although healthy was good, sometimes a little unhealthy was required and today was one of those days.

"My males will bring back sushi when they go to town tomorrow to pick up your supplies."

She felt her cheeks heat. "You're going to send a bunch of guys to buy the stuff for me?"

He nodded, a frown appeared on his forehead. "Is that a problem? Two males will go and get you your list of items."

"I put a couple of feminine things on the list. I guess I don't mind. I feel a bit sorry for them though." She giggled, putting her hand in front of her mouth. She could just imagine how it would look. A couple of big burly guys were going to have to buy her tampons and underwear. There were also a couple of steamy romance novel titles and a woman's magazine or two on the list. There were one or two others things on there that she suddenly wished she had left off. She could just picture how the checkout person's mouth would gape.

Torrent shrugged as he put the tray down on the table. He pulled a chair out and motioned for her to sit. "You require the items. They will collect them. There is nothing to be ashamed about. I had a look at the list myself."

Her cheeks went from hot to inferno. Candy took a seat across from him, she busied herself with dishing up her food.

Oh shit!

He'd looked at the list!

He was going to get the wrong idea. Arghhhhh!

When she finally looked up, she met Torrent's amused gaze. She looked down at her plate and lifted her fork.

"Hungry?" he asked.

Oh god, Candy had piled her plate high. A whole burger, two slices of pizza and a taco. There was just no way in hell she was eating all of this. No damned way.

Her mind was on other things. "Starving," she managed to eek out. All of a sudden her stomach felt wound into knots. She took a bite of the pizza anyway.

Torrent grabbed a plate and helped himself to one of the burgers and some fries. He put the food onto his plate and then paused. When she snuck a peek at him he was looking at her strangely, his head was cocked to the side.

"What's wrong?" She instantly regretted the question.

Torrent pushed his plate of food forward and folded his arms, leaning them on the table. "You're embarrassed that I looked at the list. I can tell by the way your heart is racing. Your cheeks are bright red and you won't look at me."

She shrugged. "I'm fine."

"You are embarrassed and greatly so . . ." He leaned back in his chair. "I can see it."

"I suppose I should have known that you would take a look. I guess I am a bit embarrassed." Make that hugely embarrassed. You would swear she was an inexperienced virgin.

"You shouldn't be." He paused. "Did I overstep the boundaries? I didn't think it would make you so uncomfortable or I would never . . ."

"It's fine." They were both adults. She managed to sort of smile and took another small bite of her pizza. "I'm okay with it." *Not at all!* Yes, she was. She was an adult, dammit. They both were.

"I'm glad you put condoms on there." His voice sounded a little husky. He looked deadly serious. Torrent licked his lips, she watched the slow glide of his tongue over his lower lip.

Then what he'd said registered. Oh god! *Ground swallow me whole.* Him looking at the list was one thing but she didn't exactly want to talk about it.

"There you go again. Your cheeks have turned seriously red." He gave a small shake of the head. "You have nothing to feel embarrassed about. You're making me repeat myself here." He gave her a half smile. The guy sure was sexy. Far too sexy. Torrent leaned forward, the smile disappeared and his eyes narrowed. "I'm fucking thrilled you put them on there. It means—"

"Don't get any ideas. It's just precautionary. I don't have sex without a condom especially since I can no longer get my pill prescription filled."

"You mean pills so that you can't become pregnant?" He didn't look happy.

"Look, just because I'm getting some condoms doesn't mean we'll be using them any time soon, and by the way, they work perfectly well at preventing pregnancy too."

He frowned, looking confused.

"I can see you're not happy that my pill prescription ran out. Like I said, condoms work just as well. In fact, they work better since they also prevent STD's."

"Firstly . . . I don't want you taking pills to prevent pregnancy. Secondly . . . I don't want to use condoms"—he put up his hand when she tried to talk—"but I would do so in a heartbeat if it would make you feel better. I want to fully claim you. I also want to start a family as soon as possible. We can't give each other any STD's and I can scent when you are in heat. Humans call it ovulating."

She dropped the pizza back onto her overfull plate, glad she wasn't swallowing because it would've made her choke. "Back up about a hundred miles, please. We're not even properly married . . . mated. I haven't even wrapped my head around that yet. Pregnancy and children?" She swallowed hard. "We need to get to know each other much better before we can take the whole mating step let alone to bring a helpless child into the world." She struggled to pull air into her lungs. It felt like someone was sitting on her chest. "I didn't have the best upbringing. My dad had a ton of affairs. My mom was . . . is an insecure wreck because of it."

Torrent clenched his fists and his jaw tightened. "That is when one of the mated pair ruts with someone else without their partner's consent?"

She nodded. "Yup. He finally ran off with one of the women. I was still very young. I never saw him again. After he left, my mom went through boyfriends like she did underwear. She had zero confidence and needed a partner to bolster her. She's far too clingy and chases guys away. I hated my father for leaving but I missed him just as fiercely. I do want kids of my own . . ."

Torrent seemed to breathe out a sigh of relief. He visibly relaxed, his attention on her. "I'm glad to hear that."

"Thing is . . ." She went on. "It's important that I be in a stable relationship. I want for there to be a father for my child. I want . . ."

Torrent reached across the table and grabbed her hand. "That's good." He smiled. "I want the same things. Dragons mate for life. There would be no divorce, no running away. I plan on being there for my children and supporting my mate. I would never leave you or our babies. It's as simple as that."

"I want love and that doesn't just happen, Torrent. We're attracted to one another but it takes time for those other emotions to develop. It would've been nice if we could've explored this a bit more before . . ."

"Before taking the plunge." He finished the sentence for her.

"Yeah."

"We are going to be just fine, Candy." He squeezed her hand. "Let's just forget about all the serious stuff and concentrate on getting to know one another." His face had become animated, filled with boyish charm. It was appealing. She was sure that he didn't show this side of himself often.

Her chest tightened and that sensation of having her chest compressed increased. "We can't have sex though." Why the hell had she said that? Why did she keep bringing it up? It was like she was trying to convince him . . . no to convince herself. No. Sex. With. Torrent. Not yet anyway.

He chuckled softly.

Candy pulled her hand from his. She had to stand up and reach in order to give him a light slap on the arm. "It's not funny. We're dating . . . no, make that living together. We're attracted to one another but we can't have sex because that would mean instant marriage. It's completely nuts. What if it happens by accident and we both regretted it?" She sucked deep breaths in and out, trying not to lose it.

"I wouldn't regret it." He looked so damned sure. "Not a chance." Oh god! He looked like he loved the idea of them being together . . . like that . . . forever. Her whole chest tightened all over again and this time in a different way.

No! This was all happening too quickly. "You can't know that."

"It's hard for you to comprehend but it's true. Look, if it will make you more comfortable, if we decide to have sex, we need to first take a cold shower, if we both still want to proceed after the shower then . . ."

She laughed. It bubbled up unexpectedly from inside her. It felt good. Really good. "You're serious? A cold shower."

Although he was smiling she could see that he meant it. "Yes. If we take a freezing cold shower, and trust me when I tell you that mountain water is fresh. If we shower and are still game, then nothing will happen without thinking it through first. We won't be able to regret anything."

"Deal." She felt a lot better and even picked up her burger and took a small bite.

"Deal." His gaze locked with hers. There was a lift to his mouth and a strange look in his eyes.

Candy swallowed and took another bite. It was juicy and really delicious, she tried to ignore the way that Torrent was looking at her.

"Just for the record." He took a sip of his water, that mischievous glint was still out in full force.

She made a humming noise to let him know that she was all ears.

"We don't have to rut in order to explore each other sexually."

Bring on the choking. Candy put her hand over her mouth. She coughed and spluttered and then coughed and spluttered some more.

"It's not something we need to talk about right now, but keep it in the back of your mind. Also, I will wait for you . . . I'm not making the first move."

Candy took a long drink of her water and nodded. "Okay." Her voice was high-pitched.

"Why were you abducted?"

That was an odd question. "What do you mean? You guys took me. You know why. To mate and impregnate me, I guess." She shivered.

"I keep forgetting that you were never briefed the way you should have been. I will follow up with Blaze. It seems he is reluctant to punish those she-dragons." Torrent grit his teeth, looking pissed for a moment or two. "We didn't just take anyone, human females were specially earmarked. There were several criteria that needed to be met, things like age, fertility, a female needed to be unmated and without young. I've told you some of this already." He paused. "There were also other reasons why the five of you were ultimately chosen, we looked for females in need of rescuing. We wanted to try and give you all a second chance. As much as we needed you, we wanted this to be mutually beneficial."

Their reasoning might be skewed but they weren't a bad bunch, these dragon shifters. When she didn't say anything, he leaned back in his chair. "Why did you need saving? What happened to you, Candy?"

Candy picked up her water and held it, she rested the glass on the table in front of her. "I didn't need saving"— she chewed on her bottom lip for a moment—"not really, I would've been fine."

"You can talk to me. Tell me about your old life." Torrent picked up his burger. "You wouldn't be here if everything was fine."

Candy swallowed hard. For whatever reason, she didn't feel comfortable talking to him about Ellis and what she did for a living. Not yet. If she was honest with herself, she felt ashamed. She was worried about how he would react. What would he think of her? She'd never been ashamed before. Why now?

"Okay." He must have sensed her reluctance. "Start with something simple. Tell me something about yourself."

She took a sip of the water and put the glass back down. "Well, you already know my favorite foods." She smiled widely. "I try and eat healthy though. I exercise every day. I love being outdoors . . ."

His whole demeanor stiffened. "I'm sorry you're stuck in here." He smiled. "Maybe I can take you out tomorrow. We would need to sneak out though, I don't want anyone following us, or accidentally catching your scent."

Out! No way! "That would be amazing. I would love to go to the beach." She had a thought. "Could you add a bathing suit to the list of items. I would love to go swimming."

Torrent's eyes darkened. "I could do that." He cleared his throat. "No problem." It didn't help, his voice came out sounding just as rough. "I would love to take you swimming. I might just be willing to kill to see you in a bathing suit." He said the last more to himself than to her. "What else?" His eyes snapped back to hers.

"My favorite color is"—she lifted her eyes in thought—"green. I'm a nature and an animal lover," she added. Most people liked blue or red. People hardly ever love green.

"Of course it is." He smirked and gave his chest a rub, smoothing his fingers over his golden tattoo. It had beautiful green swirls within the golden depths. It was truly beautiful. "I like that green is your favorite."

"A complete coincidence."

"Is it?" His gaze was intense and disarming. She could

drown in those eyes of his.

"I didn't know they could make tattoos that color. It's really amazing." The need to touch, rose up in her but she suppressed it.

Torrent smiled. "They don't. We're born with our markings. Royal dragons are born with gold. I'm a water dragon, that is why I have green markings within the gold."

"That's interesting. We've been told very little about your species. How long do you guys live?"

He smiled. "I think my answer would scare you." He took a bite of his burger.

"Why? Are you an old man beneath all of that muscled exterior?"

Torrent swallowed. "By human standards, I'd already be dead . . . a couple of times over."

She had to laugh even though she felt a little breathless at his statement. "I'm only twenty-four."

He shrugged. "Age is of no importance. You are mature." He wiped his hands on the napkin. "You will age much slower once we are properly mated. Your senses will improve and you will become stronger as well."

She nodded. What did she say to that? Yay! It was a serious bonus. "Are you trying to convince me?"

"I didn't think that such superficial things would be of importance to a female like you."

"They're not." Part of her felt like a fraud. Her boobs were fake. It wasn't important though. It didn't mean that she was hung up on superficial things. If they ended up in a real relationship, she would tell him. She'd only had one boyfriend and that was still when she was in high school. There had been no one since . . .

"Why do you look so deep in thought?"

"No reason." None she wanted to discuss.

He paused and for a moment it looked like he was going to argue, but then, thankfully, he nodded.

They finished eating and he helped her clean up. She washed, he dried and put the dishes away. It was weird to see such a strong guy—leader of his kind—happily drying dishes.

They talked about various things. She felt comfortable in his company. Torrent made her laugh, it made her realize how much she had been missing in her life. This all felt so crazy and yet, it also felt normal. It was nice.

Candy felt guilty when he threw a blanket onto the couch. The thing was far too small for his huge frame.

There was no way she was sleeping in the same bed with him though. No way. They took turns using the bathroom. She went first.

Candy removed her sweats once she was safely under the covers. She folded them and placed them in a neat pile right next to the bed. Easy to reach in the morning. She wore an extra large shirt.

Torrent made himself comfortable on the couch. His legs hung over the edge. Not looking! He had to lie on his side to fit on the narrow base. Not Looking! This was his choice, not hers.

"Would you mind if I removed my pants? I'm used to

sleeping naked." His deep voice seemed to fill the large space.

Really!

Yes, I mind. She didn't like the thought of him naked under that blanket. What if it fell off in the night? She felt like groaning out loud. "I . . . um . . . guess that's fine." She was already making him suffer, she couldn't force him to wear clothes to bed as well.

"Thank you. I don't think I could sleep otherwise." She heard a rustling noise as he removed the garment.

It was about ten minutes later when he spoke again. "Are you still awake?" His voice was low.

"I am now."

He chuckled softly, the sound moving right through her. "You weren't asleep."

"How do you know?" She could hear the smile in her own voice.

"I have superhuman hearing."

"Oh yeah." Still smiling. "Why did you ask me then?"

"I'm not sure. I need to say something but I didn't want to bother you." More serious.

"You're not bothering me."

"I took the lube off of the list."

Oh god! Despite the dark, she covered her face with her hands.

Torrent breathed out. "You don't need it, not with me."

Oh shit!

She rolled over and squeezed her thighs together. "If

you say so." She managed to somehow squeak out.

"I do, Candy." So deep and without a trace of humor. "I most definitely do."

She believed every word.

CHAPTER 10

The next day . . .

Torrent was on the floor. The blanket covered him from about mid calf to mid chest. He was sleeping soundly even though the floor in question was hard and cold.

His bed was soft and comfortable. Candy felt another momentary spark of guilt. She pushed it down. It was his own damned fault. She carefully dressed, sure to keep the covers over her. She worked not to make any noise.

Just as in her previous room, this one had a coffee maker, she'd spotted it the evening before. She tiptoed to the kitchenette and after opening and closing a few cupboards, she found the ground coffee.

Candy got to work making the brew and finding cups and the rest of the things she needed. She glanced at Torrent and sucked in a breath. He was back on the couch, on his back. One of his hands rested on the floor to keep himself from falling off the large three seater. It looked like a tiny love seat with him on it. His other hand was folded behind his head like a make-shift pillow.

The blanket was scrunched in a heap over his lap but his legs and chest were bare. His hair was mussed, his eyes had that clouded barely awake look and his lids hung at half mast. Her heart rate picked up and her breathing did the same. It was like all of the oxygen had fled the room. Like she needed to breathe more deeply to get in the same amount of air.

"Good morning." He gave her a smile. It was beautiful, disarming. If he crooked a finger right now, she might just go. "Did you sleep well?" His voice had that deep, raspy, just-woken-up sound.

"Um . . ." She licked her lips. The smell of freshly brewed coffee permeated across the room. "I slept really well." She pulled a pained face. "You?" She whispered the word, feeling the guilt return with a vengeance.

Torrent's smile grew. "I slept like a baby. I woke up often and longed for a breast to suckle on." He choked out a laugh.

A laugh forced it's way out of her throat as well. She couldn't help it. "You're too much, you know that? A baby huh?"

Torrent nodded. He bobbed his eyebrows.

Candy laughed some more. "Next, you'll be telling me that you are wearing a diaper under there and that you wet your bed."

"No diaper but there is a wet spot"—he narrowed his eyes at her—"it's not pee though." He winked at her.

Heat suffused her cheeks and she looked back down at

what she was doing.

"I'm only joking," he said. Candy could hear him move and when she glanced up, he was in a sitting position.

"Would you like some coffee?"

Torrent nodded. "That would be nice. Two sugars, no milk."

Candy nodded. This was so damned weird. Her hands shook a little and she spilled the milk trying to open it. "Shit!" She set the carton down and went to grab a cloth.

"Are you nervous, Candy?"

She cleaned up the mess and, after taking a deep breath, poured some milk into her cup and then into his. "Shit!" She growled as she poured the milk from his cup down the drain and rinsed the mug. Candy put her hands on her hips. "I guess I am."

"Why?" he leaned against the back of the couch and folded both hands behind his head. His chest was a thing of utter beauty. Sculpted. Wide shoulders, pecs made for biting and abs of the likes she'd never seen before. The blanket was still bunched over his lap. *Thank god!*

"Um . . ." she realized she was staring and got to work finishing making their coffee. "I've never spent the night with a guy before, that's all."

He sat forward and folded his arms across his legs, clasping his hands somewhere in the middle. "You mean you've never spent the night with a male you haven't had sex with before?"

"No." She picked up his mug, and walked over and handed it to Torrent. "I've never spent the night with a guy before . . . ever."

His eyes narrowed. "Never?"

She nodded. "I've had sex with quite a few guys so I'm not a virgin or anything . . . far from it," she added. "But I've only ever had one boyfriend. I was still in school so sleepovers would've been frowned upon. We broke up when Evan went to college. He received a scholarship out of state. Long distance relationships don't work and we were really young." She paused. "It didn't suit my lifestyle to have a boyfriend after that." No sleep-overs were a part of her rules so she'd never stayed over with any of them either.

"Why not? You are a highly desirable female."

"It's a long story," she mumbled.

"We have time. I need to meet with my pinnacle warriors but not until later this morning."

She took a sip of her coffee. "So you have time for breakfast? I saw some eggs in the fridge."

"Breakfast would be great. I will put on some pants and come and help you." He looked up at her since she was standing and he was still sitting, looking even better up close.

She nodded and was just about to turn when he grabbed her hand. His was big, warm and lightly calloused. A real man's hands. His gaze was soft and compelling. "I don't have any experience with relationships."

She nodded.

Using his thumb, he stroked the outside of her hand. "I mean it. I've had plenty of sex with many different females over the years."

Too much info. She didn't want to hear about his sex life just as she didn't exactly want to tell him about hers. It was important though if they were going to be together and if they were going to make a go of it. She'd give it a few days and if she still wanted to stay, she'd tell him everything. "Okay." She didn't know what else to say.

"They were only ever one night stands. It was purely sex. All of it." He squeezed his eyes shut for a moment. "I can hear how your heart rate has increased and not in a good way." He looked back up at her. "I'm messing this up. What I'm trying to say is that I don't have much experience in the relationship department." He seemed to struggle with finding the right words. "We need to talk and to be honest with one another if we are going to make this work. I'll try hard not to mess it up but I might be a bit clueless, so bear with me . . ."

She had to smile at him. "You may have stumbled here or there in the beginning but you're doing a great job now. I guess I don't have much experience either."

He smiled and released her hand. "I'm glad I'm doing a better job and, Candy . . ."

"Yeah."

"You're also doing a great job. I'm glad we spent the night together. That I was your first in that regard. I look forward to spending the night with you in our bed."

Our bed. Crap! *Breathe, Candy.*

"Thanks . . . um . . . I wanted to talk to you abo . . ." There was one thing that had been sitting in the back of her mind. A nagging.

He nodded for her to speak but she chickened out. "It's not important." She tried to walk away but he took back her hand.

"It must be since it is on your mind."

She nodded.

"Sit."

She took a seat next to him. "If we're going to give this a try . . . us a try."

His eyes blazed. "We are."

"If that's the case then you need to be faithful to me," she blurted. "We need to be faithful to each other. It is important to me," she added.

Torrent frowned. "I'm not sure what you mean."

Candy licked her lips. "Sky mentioned that you are within your rights as king to . . ." She paused. "To have sex with another woman if I am unable to . . . help you out." She felt anger rise in her but tried to get a handle on it. "I know that we are different culturally but you need to know that I wouldn't be able to be with you if you . . ."

Torrent pulled her into his lap and she yelped as her thighs connected with his. He smiled at her. No, he was grinning. He was enjoying this. "You think this is funny?" She asked, as the anger bubbled up.

"You're jealous."

"It's not a matter of being jealous." *Hell yeah!* So what if she was? She wasn't admitting it to him though, he was only just getting over his arrogance. "In my culture, if two people decide that they are going to be together, especially if marriage is on the table." She shivered and Torrent banded his arms a little tighter around her. He was so warm and he smelled so good. "If two people are together, they don't have sex with other people. It's considered cheating and I can't have you cheat on me. Not ever. After my dad and—"

"I think it is wonderful that you're jealous."

She felt like kicking him in the shin or slapping that cocky, far too good looking, smile off of his face. "You do, do you? How would you like it if I went out and had sex with the first shifter I came across?"

His whole body tensed. Muscles popped out on either side of his neck. He growled, flashing teeth that looked sharp. "I will kill any male that touches you."

"Now look who's jealous." She squeezed his bicep. It didn't give, not even a millimeter.

The rest of the tension drained from him and he nodded. "Point taken. I don't plan on taking any of the others to my bed. There is only one female for me, Candy. Only one."

She gave a nervous giggle. "Oh, who might the lucky lady be?" She teased trying to break some of the tension that crackled between them. It was nuts how quickly it had morphed into sexual energy.

Instead of answering, Torrent wrapped a hand around her neck and kissed her. He kissed her until her toes curled. Until she pressed herself up against him. He kissed her until she moaned into his mouth. All too soon though, he broke the kiss. Her only conciliation was that he seemed just as affected as her. His eyes were glazed over, his breathing ragged. Then he growled and set her back on her feet. She felt a bit wobbly.

Get it together.

Torrent gave her a panty wetting smile. "Whenever you're ready, sweetheart." He gave a loud sigh. "I need to take a long shower now. There might be a loud roar towards the end. Ignore it. Know that I will be thinking of you." He chuckled as he rose to his feet.

Candy swallowed hard. After that statement and the kiss, she needed a shower too . . . desperately. Only hers would be cold.

CHAPTER 11

The next day . . .

H er gaze was fixed firmly on his cock. Her tongue slid over her lips and her throat worked. He stretched up and flexed his muscles. His dick twitched and her breathing hitched.

"It's all yours, Candy, all you have to do is say the word." He couldn't help but goad her. It was so easy to do. He loved watching her cheeks become red.

Another hitch, sharper this time. She quickly averted her stare. Torrent suppressed a smile since he knew it would piss her off. He didn't want her pissed, he wanted her happy. He just wanted her, full fucking stop.

Candy quickly recovered her composure. It was one of the things he liked about her. She wasn't always readable and she liked to be in control. He couldn't wait to see her unravel and let loose. *Shit!* He was getting hard just thinking about it.

Candy spread out her towel on the white sand. "It's so beautiful out here."

"Yeah it is." His gaze was on her. How the wind caught her hair. How the summer dress clung to her curves. She was tiny but her legs seemed to go on for miles below the mid-thigh hem.

"Thank you for bringing me here, it's so good to be out."

Torrent stepped into the pants Candy had handed to him a minute ago. It was stupid. She'd already seen him naked, since he had to shift to get them here, but hey, he knew it would make her feel more comfortable, so he put them on. "I'll try and sneak you out as often as I can. My brother helped me divert attention."

"Lake?"

Torrent shook his head. "No, Tide."

"Oh." She raised her brows. "You have more than one brother?"

"I have three. What about you?"

"I'm an only child." She shook her head. Candy reached down and pulled her dress over her head.

By all that was clawed and scaly. His dick sprang to life and with a vengeance. There was nothing he could do to stop it. No amount of thinking about other things, about mundane things, about stupid things. Nothing would make this thing go down. He may or may not have cursed out loud.

She laughed, so he suspected he had blurted a couple of choice expletives. She was tiny. Narrow hips, a flat belly and really full breasts. They were barely contained in two tiny triangles. Her nipples pushed up against the fabric.

Green. The bathing suit was a turquoise green. Her favorite color. The males had managed to find one like he had asked, only they'd picked up the sexiest one they could find. There was another tiny triangle that covered her sex. He could make out her mound. *Fuck me!* His cock throbbed.

Candy moved her dress in front of her, covering herself. "It's too much isn't it? Maybe too little is a better description."

"It's perfect." His voice was so guttural he could barely even recognize it as his own. "I don't think I want you wearing it in front of anyone else, but here and now . . . fuck . . . you look so damned sexy."

She smiled, relaxing a little. "It leaves so little to the imagination. You should see the back. Actually, you shouldn't. I'm going to put this back on." She gave her dress a little shake and blushed so hard.

"Don't." He couldn't believe what he was about to say. "You wanted to swim. Go on in." He looked at the ocean. "I won't look." Then he looked down at his hard as rock dick. "I can't help my reaction though. I'm sorry if it makes you feel uncomfortable, but . . ." For just a second, he had the unnatural urge to cover himself with his towel but he fought it. Shifters didn't do such things. His reaction was normal and something his female needed to get used to. If luck was on his side, she'd see a lot more of his engorged member in the not too distant future. And up close and personal at that.

She shook her head and smiled. "It's fine. Thank you.

I'm being silly." She tossed her dress on her towel and turned around.

Torrent grit his teeth to stop from making a choking sound. The bikini bottom didn't cover her ass much. It was cut high up on her ass cheeks. Tight. Her ass was so damned tight. His balls ached.

"Are you checking out my ass?" He could hear that she was smiling.

"Maybe." His voice cracked and he tried to clear it.

She laughed as she looked back over her shoulder at him. Then she looked a little shocked but seemed to shake it off. It was something he had noticed about her. It was like she didn't laugh often. He planned on rectifying that as a matter of extreme urgency.

She dipped her toes in the incoming surf. "Cold."

Torrent jogged towards her. "That's perfect and exactly what we both need." She squealed when he caught her around the waist and pulled her into the surf with him.

She sucked in a breath as he pulled her into the water and then screamed and kicked. "You asshole." He could hear that she was smiling. "It's freezing." She laughed. It was a deep sound that resonated from her belly. He loved hearing it.

Torrent laughed as well. "It's not so bad." He tugged her in a little deeper. They bobbed up over the incoming waves.

"No, it's worse." She laughed some more, her lips were turning blue and her teeth chattered.

"One day . . ." He pulled her into his arms and she

snuggled into him, looking for warmth. She felt so damned good against him. He kept his hips back so as not to scare her. His erection hadn't diminished in the least. "In the not too distant future, you're going to be mated to me. Your core temperature will go up and you'll love swimming in our ocean. I want to show you something." He moved her closer to the shore and dove into the water.

He stayed under for a good five or six minutes before breaking the surface in the vicinity of where he had gone under.

Candy was closer to the beach, about knee deep. She had both her hands cupped over her mouth and her eyes were wide. What the fuck! She was crying. Then she screamed his name, her whole body sagged in what looked like relief.

Shit!

He swam to the shore using hard strokes and ran from the water.

"Oh my god." She was still crying even though she still looked relieved. Candy smacked his arm as soon as she reached him. "Don't ever scare me like that again." She hiccupped and tears continued to stream down her cheeks. "I thought you had drowned or something. Oh my god!"

Torrent felt something clench inside of him. "You were worried." He put his arms around her and she tried to push him away.

"Of course I was worried." She sniffed. "You disappeared beneath the waves. After a minute or two I started to panic. What the hell, Torrent? Don't you ever do that to me again . . ." She pushed at his chest and grit her teeth.

"Oh, sweetheart." He cupped her cheeks. "I'm a water dragon. We can't drown."

"Bullshit! Enough of that cocky bullshit. You're the king. Your people need you and care about you . . . I'm sure. Sky does. She thinks highly of you." Her cheeks were tear soaked, her eyes still held remnants of the panic she must have felt.

He wiped the hair from her face and kissed her eyes. "There was no risk. I can't drown. Water dragons can breathe underwater."

"Really? Seriously? Why didn't you tell me? I was worried sick about you."

He kissed the tip of her nose. "I'm so glad you care so much about me."

She cleared her throat. "I was worried for your kingdom, that's all, I hardly know you."

Torrent couldn't help but to chuckle, he nuzzled into her neck. "If you say so."

She melted into him, her breasts mashed up against his chest. He could feel her hard little nipples. His erection came back with a vengeance and he pulled his hips back. "For the record . . ."

She made a noise of agreement.

"The whole breathing under water thing." He pulled away so that he could look into her beautiful eyes. "I didn't tell you because I planned on showing you. There's a really big tub in my chamber and breathing under water comes in handy."

Her pupils dilated. Candy licked her lips and squirmed. The scent of her arousal surrounded them like an invisible cloak. He buried his face in her hair and inhaled deeply. *Just say the word. Do it! Tell me what you want. Please!*

Candy pulled away. "I think I'm going to catch some sun."

Torrent nodded. Disappointment coursed through him. Candy wanted him, he wasn't sure why she was holding back.

Two days later . . .

There was a loud crashing noise. Candy sat up. She sucked in a breath and put her hand to her chest and tried to get her bearings. It was dark. Not quite pitch black. The moon hung low in the sky, surrounded by a billion stars.

She was on a bed. A really big, four-poster bed. Silk sheets pooled around her waist.

"Sorry." A deep, masculine voice cut through the night. "Did I wake you?" There was a rustling noise of a blanket moving. It came from the floor instead of the couch. It was Torrent.

She sighed softly. "Did you fall off the couch?"

Torrent chuckled. "Yup."

Her eyes slowly adjusted to the light, or lack thereof. The moon was about three-quarters full, so it gave off a ton of light.

"Are you okay?" she asked.

"Of course, yes." She could hear that he was smiling. "I'm a king, the strongest of all my people. Do you think that such a little fall would harm me?"

Before she could say anything, he continued. "I land on my ass at least five times a night. I'm starting to get used to it. That, and sleeping on the floor. The only shocking thing is how you managed to sleep through it. This is the first time you've woken up."

Five times a night! Poor guy. "Oh! I'm sorry. I'm a deep sleeper." Candy chewed on her bottom lip. She could hear that he wasn't trying to make her feel guilty or trying to change her mind about sharing the bed with him. In fact, Torrent had been nothing but sweet and kind over the last few days. Her defenses were weakening. It was time to come clean, to tell him all about her past. She hoped that he wasn't the kind of guy that would be put off by her previous profession. There was only one way to find out.

Torrent rose to his feet, he used the blanket to cover his manly bits but his ass was on full display. Her eyes had completely adjusted to the dark and she could make out his spectacular glutes. She tried not to stare as she settled back under the covers. Tried and failed. *Holy macaroni! Sweet baby Jesus.* What a spectacular sight he made. For a moment she was tempted to turn on the side lamp so that she could ogle him good and proper.

Then he lay back down on the couch, laying on his side, he scooted as far back as he could. There was no room for movement. His big body took up the entire sofa. If he so much as breathed too hard he was going to fall again.

Shit!

What difference did it make if they shared a bed? They were both adults and besides, the bed was huge. They could both lie sprawled out on this thing and not make contact with one another. "Torrent."

"Yeah?"

"You can get in bed . . . with me . . . but only if you promise to stay on your side."

There was a long, heavy pause. "Are you sure? Because I'm okay here. I'm also a really good sleeper. That's probably why I keep falling off this damn thing."

She sucked in a deep breath. "I'm sure. You stay on your side, I'll stay on mine and we'll be golden."

"I can live with that." He got up off the couch and took two steps towards the bed, then he stopped. Torrent ran a hand through his hair, before clasping the back of his neck. "Um . . . should I put on some pants?"

Yes!

Shit!

Candy swallowed hard, trying not to panic. This wasn't a big deal. "You said you can't sleep unless you're naked."

"I'll be fine." His voice was gruff. Torrent turned towards the closet.

"Wait. If you're on your side and I'm on mine, your being naked shouldn't make any difference." *No difference whatsoever.* "Right?" There was a slight shake to her voice.

"Are you sure about this?" He pulled the blanket tighter around his middle.

"Definitely." Maybe she should go and put on some underwear. No! She was in an oversized shirt, which she pulled down. The thing came to just above her knees. They were fine, more than fine. One hundred and fifty percent. No, two hundred percent. Surely!

"Okay then." He walked to the other side of the bed and pulled down the covers.

Candy scooted further onto her side, she turned to face the opposite direction. The bed dipped and the sheets rustled. He really was way over there on that side. Although she could feel his presence, although she could hear him breathing and smell that wonderful manly scent of his, she couldn't feel his heat. They were fine. This was okay. "Good night," she whispered.

"Good night." His voice was low, with a raspy edge. "And, Candy?"

"Yeah?"

"Thank you for this."

"You're welcome."

She lay there in the dark for what felt like ages before finally falling asleep.

"Candy." Torrent whispered her name ever so softly into her ear. He did it in a way that was sexy and seductive. She was wet and needy. Dripping wet. Then she called his name on a sob.

He was there, between her thighs. His manhood thick and ready, a drop of pre-cum on his tip. "Are you ready for me?" He growled, his eyes the most beautiful pale blue.

"Yes," a moan this time. There was a reason she shouldn't be doing this but she couldn't remember exactly what it was. She wanted

him and he wanted her. They were about to take what they needed from one another. It was as simple as that.

He called her name again as he pushed himself inside of her. "*Take what you need.*" *She grit her teeth.* "*Just take me,*" *she ground out.*

"Candy." More urgent this time. "Wake up, Candy."

She opened her eyes on a soft moan and immediately tensed up. What the hell? She swallowed hard and tried to keep herself from panicking. The room was filled with morning sunshine and she squinted her eyes. She began to find her bearings. Please don't let this be real. Please.

Torrent touched a hand to her back. "Easy. It's okay. You're okay."

Her nightshirt rode somewhere up around her hips. Torrent was on his back, still on his side of the bed.

"Oh god!" There was a definite edge of panic to her voice.

Her one leg was thrown over him. She could feel his hard . . . member under her thigh. Her . . . oh good lord . . . *you-know-what* was plastered up against his thigh. She may or may not have been rubbing herself against him. Please no!

It was a dream. A filthy dream. She buried her face into his chest. "Please tell me I'm having a nightmare." Her voice sounded muffled.

He laughed and since her chest was plastered across his, she felt it acutely.

Torrent trailed his hand up and down the top of her back. One of his hands clasped her waist, holding her in place. "I don't know, I was enjoying it, only, I would prefer it if you were awake. More fun that way."

"I'm glad you woke me up." She tried to pull away but he held onto her. "This is so embarrassing. I'm so sorry!" She was plastered up against him. Did she say any of those things out loud? Please no.

"I'm not sorry. Your body knows what it wants and so do you. Stop fighting this, Candy."

"It's too soon for us to be tied together. I would love to have sex with you . . . there I said it." She huffed out a breath. "We can't though, not yet. I need to talk to you about a few things and it's too soon. Too big of a commitment."

"I'm glad you'll at least admit that you want me." His voice was gruff. "That's a start."

"Um, can I move back now? Give you a bit of space? I'm so embarrassed." She wanted the floor to open up and suck her in.

"I love the way you feel against me. I fucking love it."

She covered her face with her hand. He was so hard beneath her thigh. Her pussy was pushed up against him. The dream had made her achy and needy. It was so vivid. Her clit was throbbing. She could feel how slick she felt.

"We don't have to have sex, Candy. There are other things we could do."

"Like what?" *Stupid question.* "Don't answer that."

He chuckled but the laughter soon died and his chest rose higher as he pulled in a big breath. "Let me ease you. Let me taste you, Candy. I want to make you come more than I want my next breath."

She sucked in a ragged breath of her own. She wanted to say yes but oral sex often led to full blown sex and they needed to talk. She needed to come clean. What if he was disgusted with her? What if he couldn't be with someone that had sold their body for financial gain? This was moving so fast. If she was honest with herself, she already had feelings for him. If their relationship became sexual, even if it wasn't full blown sex, she might just fall for him and then what?

He squeezed her hip and eased her nightshirt down, pulling her away from him in the process. "I'm sorry." He put his forehead to hers and closed his eyes. "I messed up. I was supposed to wait until you initiated intimacy. I'm rushing things." He kissed her softly on the top of her head.

She wanted him. She really wanted him. She could feel how much he wanted her right back, yet he was respecting her wishes. Or at least, what he thought were her wishes. "Wait." She huffed out a breath. "No sex, but we can fool around."

"Are you sure?"

"Definitely. I don't think I've ever been hornier in my whole life."

"Me neither." He kissed her softy, his lips soft against hers. "What do you want? How do you want it?" He pulled her onto his lap, so that she was straddling him. His massive cock was flush against his well defined abs. She was sufficiently covered by the shirt.

A shiver ran down her spine. No one had ever asked her before what she wanted. "Um." She took her bottom lip between her teeth.

"Tell me," a deep growl. "What do you like?"

If this was happening, it was happening right. Candy grabbed her hem and pulled her shirt over her head.

Torrent snarled. "Fuck!" He stared at her chest. All out gaped. "I need to touch you."

He was asking for permission? How refreshing. Normally guys just groped her. They had paid after all. It was like she belonged to them and not in a good way. She was more like a possession than a person. Oh shit! He was waiting for her answer. "Yes. You can touch me."

He cupped her breasts, squeezing and kneading them. Then he grabbed her mound. "You have a thin strip of hair."

"Don't dragon females have hair down there?"

He shook his head. "I like pussy hair." He cleared his throat. "I like your pussy hair."

"Thanks, I think." She moaned when he touched her opening.

"Mmmm." A deep rumble. "You're soaking wet. Were you dreaming about me . . . us?"

She nodded. "I'm surprised I didn't call out your name."

"Were we fucking?" His nostrils flared.

She nodded.

"Was it good?" His eyes glinted. "It had better have been good."

"Yes, it was amazing."

"Did you like me inside you?"

"Yes." Her voice was breathy. "A little too much."

"Good." He pressed her opening a bit firmer but without actually breaching her.

The need to ride his hand hit her hard. She managed to stay still after one small thrust of her hips.

"So damned receptive. Such a turn on. Now . . ." His eyes darkened as they narrowed them on her. "Tell me what you want. My mouth? My hand? All of the above?"

She felt her cheeks heat and rolled her head back for a beat.

"Tell me. I can see that it's on the tip of your tongue."

"Okay." Could she really tell him? *Yes.* "I like to be fingered. I want your mouth on my clit and when I'm about to come . . ." She paused and pressed her lips together before pulling them into her mouth.

"Tell me." His voice was as rough as sandpaper. The extra gritty kind.

She pulled in a breath. "When I'm about to come I'd like you to stick your finger in my . . . you know . . . my . . ." She couldn't say it. Couldn't believe she had said this much.

His eyes flared as they widened. His jaw tightened. "Your ass?"

She nodded once.

He grinned for a moment. "Have you ever been taken there?" The hand that was cupping her mound, moved backwards so that his palm was over her pussy and the tips of his fingers were brushing her opening.

She sucked in a sharp breath and shook her head. "I have these rules. I've had . . ." *A client.* "Someone touch me there, but never full blown . . ." She shook her head. "Like I said, I have these rules."

"Not with me. Not by the time we are mated."

"No, well, maybe . . ."

"Not with me." A little firmer this time.

"Not with you, not when we reach that point," a whisper. "I need to tell you—"

He covered her mouth with his and rubbed his thumb over her clit. Candy moaned into his mouth. Torrent broke the kiss. "We can talk later. Lie down, sweetheart. I'm going to make you come now."

She swallowed. "Okay." She did as he said.

Torrent straddled her. He kissed her lips and then her neck. Then he suckled on her nipples until she was mewling like a day old kitten. She dug her fingers into his hair.

"You have amazing breasts. Fuck, Candy."

"They're not real." Why the hell did she say that? What was wrong with her? It was like she was trying to sabotage this.

"Yes, they are." He frowned.

"No, I mean they're fake, silicone." Was she trying to completely destroy the mood? Her pussy sure as hell hoped not. No more talking about bullshit!

"Oh." Understanding flared in his eyes. "It doesn't matter. They are a part of you now." He cupped them in his hands and pinched her nipples between his fingers. A zing of need raced through her. It was also strangely liberating to have told him. She'd never told any of her clients. Torrent wasn't a client. Not even close. She was thankful he was okay with it. Hopefully he would take the rest of the news just as well. She tried not to think about it.

Torrent kissed his way down her stomach. He positioned himself between her legs, taking ahold of each of her thighs in his big hands. His eyes were focused between her legs.

"Even your pussy is a thing of beauty. You have a big, beautiful clit."

"Excuse me?"

"You have a big clit. It is normally a sign of a big g-spot as well. You must come easily and multiple times." He moved a little closer, then she could feel his breath on her slit.

Oh god! He didn't just say that. "Um . . . not really." Her mind raced. He thought her pussy was beautiful. She could see that he meant it.

Torrent frowned. "Surely you . . ." Then he shrugged. "It doesn't matter. Your past is of no concern, only your future. I'm pretty sure that you will come with very little effort. Let's find out." He closed his mouth over her nub and suckled her.

Candy moaned, her back came off the bed. Then he pulled back and licked her clit a few times using soft strokes.

When his mouth suckled her a second time, he pushed a finger inside her. He thrust the finger a couple of times before zoning in on a spot about half way in. "Oh god!" She yelled. Her voice shook, as did her whole body.

Torrent chuckled against her clit. "So plump." Her hips began to rock in time with his finger. *Shit! Shit!* It felt so damned good. Her breath came in sharp pants. This wasn't going to last long. He was right on the money on that count. "Harder," she groaned. Torrent added a second finger and her back bowed.

Oooohhhh! She may have groaned it out loud.

"So sensitive. Your g-spot is a beaut." Torrent spoke against her clit. "I can't wait to have at it with my cock." Then he closed his hot mouth over the bud of nerves and she had to squeeze her eyes shut. None of her clients had ever gone down on her. Her boyfriend had tried a couple of times, way back when, but he was really young. It hadn't been like this. Not even close. Sure, she owned a vibrator but it still didn't feel like this. Doing it yourself was so not the same.

Mind blowing.

Her hands were buried into his hair and her hips rocked. She was whimpering and moaning and panting and growling. Yes, growling. She sucked in air between her teeth and thrust her hips. More!

"Yes," she groaned. "Yes." Everything was beginning to tighten. She could feel the rush, the pull. When he inserted just the very tip of his finger into her ass, it was game over.

Candy yelled his name as pleasure coursed through her. It was like the feelings were emanating from everywhere and all at once. She flung her head back and grit her teeth. Her hips pistoned back and forth until she finally fell into a boneless heap. Torrent still had his fingers in her pussy and one in her ass. He carefully licked the last of the pleasure out of her before removing the finger from her ass. Instead of pulling away like she expected, he began to carefully pump the fingers still deep inside her pussy.

She sucked in a ragged breath. He suckled her clit and his fingers became more insistent inside of her, rubbing her more firmly. She moaned, feeling her hips shoot forward.

Hell no!

The coiling sensation took ahold of her all over again. Candy groaned loudly.

"That's it, Candy," Torrent rumbled against her clit. As soon as his finger found her ass again she screamed, her pussy spasmed around his fingers. It felt like there were three of them. She dug her fingers into his scalp, needing him closer. Her back lifted off the bed. This orgasm was over quicker but was infinitely more powerful.

It was the same again, he slowed his roll, removed the finger from her ass but the thrusting became slower and softer. Suckling turned to licking. She couldn't quite catch her breath. Then he began to pump harder.

Again!

No!

"Stop." Se grabbed his hand.

"You can come again . . . easily." She looked down. His hair was a mess thanks to her grabby hands.

"Just because I can doesn't mean I should. I don't think I'll survive it."

Torrent slipped his fingers from her and kissed her belly. "At least I know where your hot buttons are. I'm sure you have more."

"My what? More?" Her voice sounded thick.

"That thing that makes you come in an instant."

She felt herself blush.

"I didn't take you for an ass female."

She choked out a laugh. "I'm not an ass anything." That one time her client had touched her, it felt good, yet it didn't get her off. She'd always wondered how it would feel with the right guy in the driver's seat. Someone she was actually attracted to. Candy had never expected to be so bold so soon. Torrent made her feel a little wild.

"One of these days I'm going to take you here." He gripped her ass. "And you're going to love it."

She could hardly breathe just thinking about it. She was appalled at how turned on she was despite having just come twice.

Candy sat up and pushed him to the bed.

"What?" His eyes widened.

"It's my turn to make you come." Ellis wasn't wrong. She was the blowjob queen. Not that she gave head very often these days but still.

Her hands pressed against his chest for a second time. "Lie down."

"As much as I love the thought of those lips wrapped around my cock." He looked pained. "You don't have to do this. When I eased you it wasn't because I was looking for something in return."

"Lie down." She gave him another shove and this time he allowed himself to be pushed. "I'm not even sure my mouth will fit around that thing but there's only one way to find out."

His eyes narrowed and darkened. His chest heaved. His cock jutted from his body. Her mouth watered for a taste. She couldn't wait to give him the ride of his life.

CHAPTER 12

Torrent watched as Candy licked her lips, her eyes were focused on his cock. Her cheeks were flushed, her hair tussled. She was a stunner. An absolute stunner.

She was also so tiny and fragile. Even through his haze of need, something in him shifted. She was beginning to trust him. Beginning to accept their bond. He couldn't wait to make her his.

She glanced up at him from under her lashes and his heart skipped a beat. Her skin was the color of milk. Her breasts swayed as she leaned forward, putting her hands on either side of his body. Her nipples were a dark pink. They were hard little nubs. His legs were open, with her between them.

Candy stayed that way for several long seconds. Then she went onto her haunches, taking his length in one of her tiny hands. He hissed out a breath as she squeezed him softly. Then her other hand went to his balls. She took ahold of him there, giving them a fondle.

Torrent groaned.

Infinitely slowly, she leaned down, her mouth just an

inch from his cock. He could feel her breath on him. Torrent let his head fall back on the pillow. He swallowed thickly, anticipation buzzed through him.

Her mouth closed over his tip.

Fuck yes!

Finally!

Torrent groaned deeply. Her mouth was warm and so fucking wet. She released him and another groan was torn from him. This one born of frustration.

"Female." He gripped the sheets to keep from grabbing the back of her head.

She gave a husky chuckle and blew a breath onto his head. He felt goosebumps rise on him. When he looked down, she was smiling. Using just the tip of her tongue, she licked the rim of his cock in a seductive sweep that had his blood running hot and his breath coming in pants. "So you like to tease?" His voice was a rough rasp.

Instead of answering, she wrapped her lips around his cock again. The sight of her mouth on him almost made him come right there and then.

He sucked in another breath, his teeth clenched. His hands fisted. This time, instead of taking just his tip in her mouth, she deep throated him.

"Fuck," he growled softly.

Candy deep throated him a good couple of times. He felt his brow sweat up. He felt his breath turn ragged. He felt his heart just about beat out of his chest. Much more of this and he was going to embarrass himself.

Then she released him and his lip curled back on a soft

growl.

His frustration didn't last long because she wrapped her hot little mouth around one of his balls. She made a low humming noise and it vibrated right through him. Right through. A zing of pleasure raced through him. Every muscle tensed. His belly tightened. Candy hummed some more, moving from one ball to the other.

He swore. It was loud and rude but didn't deter his little minx. She took in more of him, now fondling one ball while she hummed on the other.

When she took back his cock, Torrent felt everything in him tighten, his balls pulled up. It felt so damned good that it almost hurt.

Candy must have sensed that he was about to come because she licked his rim again. Trailing her tongue slowly around the edge before sucking softly on his tip. It was enough of a reprieve to allow him to catch his breath.

Then she was deep throating him again. Her lips thin as they stretched around his girth. Her head bobbed up and down. Her little hand pumped on his shaft base.

"Fuck." He was about to come harder than he ever had in his long life. "Candy." He forced her name out. His blood rushed through him. His heart went nuts. Just as he was about to explode, she moved back to his balls.

She stopped just a second short and he growled loudly. His chest vibrated with the force of it.

Her mouth felt so good on his balls. Her hands knew where to touch and with just the right pressure.

Torrent was so wound up. He'd been so close to this

female for days and hadn't been able to touch even a hair on her lovely head. Making himself come wasn't the same. The need for release rode him harder than he'd ever experienced before. "Please." He couldn't help but thread his fingers into her hair. "You're killing me," he groaned.

"Poor baby." She sighed as she moved back to his cock.

"Please, Candy." He'd never begged anyone for anything before in his life. Torrent found that he didn't care. He would get on his knees if he had to.

This time when she took ahold of his base and took his dick deep in her mouth, she didn't stop.

His entire body tensed. His hand fisted her hair and he forced himself to let go. Her head bobbed quickly. Her breasts swayed and bounced with each jerk of her head. His balls were somewhere in his throat.

"Stop," he ground out. "Fuck . . ." It was all the warning he could give her. Candy moved quicker, her hand clutched him firmer. He snarled as his seed erupted from him. It burst from his body in a solid stream. Ecstasy coursed through him. His body went nuts after being held on the brink for so long. She swallowed him down, her porcelain throat worked. She slowed, her hands, going back to his balls and another spurt was forced from him. She made slurping, swallowing noises that made him want her more. As in, inside her, deep inside.

He thread his fingers through her hair, feeling how soft and silky it was. He forced out a breath before pulling in another one. Candy trailed her tongue down his shaft.

Torrent chuckled. It came out sounding pained. "That

was . . ." he laughed some more. "My god, female . . ." He cupped her chin and lifted her face. Her lips were swollen and wet. She looked up at him from under her lashes. "If you're waiting for me to get soft, you're going to wait a long time."

"I thought that since you gave me more than one that . . ." She pulled her bottom lip in-between her teeth.

Torrent shook his head. "I'll die if you do that again. I couldn't take it."

"I thought you were a king, the strongest of your people." She smiled.

"I am, wiseass." He pulled her up and held her to his chest. "Coming in your mouth made me want you more. All I could think about was being inside you." He felt her tense. "No pressure. I understand your need to wait. I need a little bit of time to recover. Where the hell did you learn to do that?"

She tensed up all over again.

He hugged her tighter. "No! On second thought, don't tell me. I know you've been with other males but I don't want to hear about it . . . ever."

"Um . . ." She sighed. "Okay. We should talk about some of that stuff though."

"It's not important, Candy. You had other males. I had other females. You are my first relationship. We are highly compatible and that is all that counts. Now . . ." He smiled at her. Candy was frowning. "Tell me more about you. What is important to you?"

The frown disappeared and her eyes lifted in thought.

"Animals. I'm an animal lover."

"I remember you telling me that the other day. Good to know considering I'm part dragon." He smiled at her.

She smiled. "Who's being the wiseass now?"

He ran a hand down her back. She felt so good against him. In his space.

"I do a lot for our local shelter. I walk the dogs. I donate money. I had planned on becoming a vet but I can't stand the idea of putting an animal to sleep so I've decided that maybe the medical field would be better. We try and save people, we don't put them to sleep. I recently quit my job and have enrolled in medical school."

He didn't know what to say. Candy was supposed to be desperate and in need of help. She sounded anything but. He realized he needed to say something. "A doctor . . . wow . . . that would take years of hard studying. Before you ask me how I know that, I've bedded a doctor or two and a nurse, oh, and a paramedic."

Candy smacked his chest. "We weren't supposed to talk about previous conquests, you manwhore."

Then her whole demeanor changed. She looked away and buried into his chest. "Sorry, I didn't mean that," she mumbled.

He squeezed her to him. "I have been going into Sweetwater, Walton Springs and other surrounding towns for many years. It was a necessity. You need to know that. As a male, I have needs and—"

"You don't need to explain. I understand."

"I hope you do." He kissed the top of her head.

"Shifters have a high sex drive. We are wired to procreate. There is the stag run and then there are female dragon shifters, I have taken every opportunity that was presented to me but it meant nothing. I can safely say that I have never come so hard as I did just now. I've never wanted a female more and I've never enjoyed being with someone as much. I'm not just saying that."

"I know." She lifted her head and gave him a shy smile. "I feel the same."

He had to grin. He could feel it wide on his face. They were going to be okay. For the first time he felt it. Really felt it. If she wanted to study he would find a way to make that happen for her. Whatever this female wanted, she would get. Candy was his queen after all.

Her legs were spread. As wide as they would go. Steam wafted from the surface of the water. Clusters of bubbles drifted aimlessly. Candy choked out a sob. She tried to thrust, causing both of her knees to come up, both legs hung over the sides of the large tub.

Torrent's tongue was buried deep inside her. Her hands clutched the porcelain edges.

Oh god!

She moaned as the tip of his tongue stabbed into her repeatedly. Her hips rocked and soapy water sloshed over the edge. Candy didn't give a shit. She was trying not to come. Torrent replaced his tongue with at least two fingers. His mouth suckled on her clit. More water sloshed over the edge.

Oh! Oh!

His broad back was just above the water; his face was buried firmly between her legs. Soapy suds clung to the skin that was exposed. His blond hair swirled in the water. His hands held her ass. His big shoulders kept her legs open. Who knew that breathing under water could come in so handy?

Who freaking knew. Water sloshed over the edge repeatedly. She was moaning like mad. It was weird considering that her wild moans and groans and the water spilling onto the floor were the only noises in the large chamber.

She was trying so hard not to come. This felt too damned good. Torrent had other ideas. When the tip of one of his fingers entered her back end, she went off like a firecracker. Her orgasm was big and explosive. Her legs clamped closed, or tried to, and she made a drawn out guttural wail. Her whole body vibrated. Torrent licked at her clit. His pumping fingers slowed as she came down.

She slumped back against the tub, her breath coming in sharp gasps. Torrent came up. Water trailed down his chest. It covered every inch of him. He wiped sopping hair from his brow and grinned at her, looking both gorgeous and wicked.

"I told you you'd like it." He wiped a hand over his face.

"Understatement of the year." She still struggled to catch her breath. "You can bathe with me anytime."

Torrent chuckled. He leaned in and kissed her softly on the corner of her mouth. "I need to show my face. I've been buried between these thighs since yesterday morning."

"That's a bad thing?"

He made a pained face. "Not at all. I also have a meeting with my brother." He stood in one graceful move. Water cascaded down his body and her mouth went dry.

He was too darned good looking. So strong. He embodied exactly what a man should look like. Tall, built, bronzed skin. His . . . member was big and hard. It jutted from his body. "Don't you want me to take care of that?" She narrowed her eyes on his dick.

Torrent groaned and his dick gave a twitch. "No time. I'll pack a picnic and we can go out later. You can make good on that offer then." He fisted the base of his cock and gave his entire length a tug, his eyes glazed over. "I'll look forward to it."

It suddenly became hard to breathe. Hard to even think. Despite having just had an incredible orgasm, her channel clenched with longing. It was becoming harder to resist him. It was crazy because she hardly knew Torrent but she was beginning to imagine a future with him. She was definitely falling for him in a big way. There was no doubt about it.

Torrent stepped out of the bath and grabbed a towel. He wrapped the piece of wool around his waist. Then he disappeared into the bedroom for a few minutes before reappearing. He grabbed something from the closet and tugged on a pair of pants.

Within a few strides he was next to the tub. Torrent

crouched next to her. "Sky will be by in a bit." He looked at her with concern. "Do you need a few more of those books you like to read?" He smiled at her.

"I'm still good." She nodded once. "I'm still reading the first one."

He made a humming noise. "The one about the demon king and his concubine."

"Yup." She nodded.

"Surely if it were any good you'd be finished by now."

"A certain dragon king has been keeping me very busy." She leaned forward and kissed him.

He didn't allow her to deepen the kiss. "I've enjoyed every second." He paused. "I'll miss you."

Her heart paused for a second. "Well then come back soon."

He nodded. "I'll see you a bit later." Then he kissed her, this time sweeping his tongue into her mouth in a panty wetting kiss. He tasted of mint and smelled so good.

After a couple more kisses, he pulled away and stood. "I'd better go before I change my mind and we get stuck in bed all morning."

"You make it sound like a bad thing."

"Not at all." He nibbled at her lower lip. "But duty calls." He made a growling noise that clearly showed pent up frustration. "I'll see you later." He kissed the side of her mouth and left. The door clicked behind him. She waited for the sound of the key turning in the lock but it never came.

Okay. So he trusted her to stay put. The funny thing

was that she didn't feel like going anywhere. Yeah sure, she wanted out of the room but she didn't want his people to find out that they hadn't been intimate. She didn't want them to think badly of their king. Of Torrent, of the man she was steadily growing feelings for. She made a groaning noise and dunked her head under the water. She realized that she was smiling. The thought wasn't as daunting as it had been. Could she do it? Could she take that next step, become his queen?

Candy lazed in the bath for another ten minutes before getting ready for the day. She'd just read two or three pages of her book when there was a knock at the door.

"Come in."

Sky put her head around the jamb first before entering. She closed the door behind her. It was the first time Candy had seen the other woman in a couple of days. She was smiling from ear to ear and her cheeks looked rosy. She looked different somehow. More relaxed, happier. "What's going on?"

Sky shrugged, she put down a tray. "I brought croissants. I'll put the kettle on."

Candy put her bookmark into the book and closed it, placing it on the coffee table. "Sounds good."

"I went into heat." Sky blurted. She covered her mouth for a second. She was smiling hard. "I can't really believe it."

"You went into heat as in . . ."

"A female can become pregnant when in heat."

"Oh." Candy nodded. "You ovulated. How do you

even know?"

"Dragon females know. Firstly, we begin to scent differently. It drives males crazy. Then we start to need sex. Our bodies crave our mates. Lake took me to one of the caves and . . . yeah, I'm sure you can guess the rest. We were holed up for a few days, that's why you haven't seen me."

"A cave?" Candy raised her brows. "As in, a dusty hole in the mountain?"

She nodded. "Yeah, something like that. They are rustic but we need very little during the heat, save our partner and plenty of sex. The caves are kitted out with the basics."

"Oh, okay. Wow! Does that mean?" Her eyes tracked to Sky's belly.

The she-dragon covered her stomach with an open hand. She was smiling broadly and looked so happy that Candy couldn't help smiling along with her.

Sky nodded. "I hope so. It is rare for a she-dragon not to become pregnant if a male is with her during her heat."

Candy squealed. "That's so exciting. I'm thrilled for you. You must be—"

"No!" Sky held up a hand. "Don't congratulate me yet, it is considered bad luck."

Candy held up her hands. "I won't, but it is exciting. How long before you find out?"

"It shouldn't take more than a week." She narrowed her eyes on Candy. "What's been happening with you? I ran into Torrent on my way here and he looked relaxed." She sniffed the air.

"You haven't rutted, but . . ." She sniffed again.

Candy felt heat flood her cheeks. She busied herself with grabbing some mugs and plates. "Stop it. It's none of your business." She couldn't help but smile though.

"No sex . . . yet . . . but you've moved things forward." She clapped her hands together. "I'm so glad. How are things between you? Is he still being an arrogant ass or is he showing his . . . sweet side?"

Candy shook her head. "He's really been amazing. He's trying really hard and . . ." She chewed on her lip for a moment. "It's working." Then she felt herself frown.

"What's wrong?" The kettle clicked off.

"It's nothing."

Sky snorted. "It's not nothing. Out with it."

Candy leaned back against the counter and folded her arms. "I just feel like this is moving so quickly."

"You are with a shifter. Quick is normal. In fact, for Torrent, this is moving really slowly. Try and see it from both sides. It is important that you try and trust your gut. Not just your gut but your heart too. Forget about what your head is telling you." Sky paused. "Sometimes overthinking things can make them more difficult."

She sighed. "Yeah, you're right." Worry churned in her gut anyway despite Sky's wise words of wisdom.

"There's more." Sky scrutinized her, raising her brows. "What's eating at you?"

Candy nodded her head. "There are some things about my past that Torrent needs to know." She knew this day would come. The day she met someone that she could see herself with. The day she would have to come clean. She may have been a high priced call girl, she may have only had a handful of clients over the years, but the fact of the matter was that she had sold her body for money. It didn't matter that she had strict criteria. That she didn't always sleep with the highest bidder. That it wasn't always just about the money. She was probably worrying for nothing. Torrent might be totally fine with it.

"Hey." Sky touched the side of her arm. "I can see that this is really worrying you. I'm sure that your past will be of no concern to Torrent. You are who you are. Your future together is what counts."

"Maybe you are right." Some of the weight lifted. *Please let that be true.*

"I know I'm right. I wouldn't worry so much about it." Her eyes widened. "Unless you are mated to another male."

Candy laughed. "No, nothing like that."

Sky huffed out a breath and put a hand to her chest. "Thank claw! Okay then. If you need to speak about your past in order to move forward with Torrent, then do it. You will see that it will be fine."

Candy smiled. She took Sky's hand and squeezed it. "Thank you for the advice. I'm going to take it. I'm feeling a lot better."

"I'm glad I could help out." Sky put a teabag into each of their cups.

Candy gave a shake of the head. She removed one of

the bags and replaced it with a herbal teabag. "Just in case."

Sky gave a nervous giggle. "I hope you're right." Her hand moved back to rub her belly. "You will be next." Her smile widened.

Candy felt both excited and apprehensive at the idea of being a mom. She sucked in a deep breath. "Hold up, one thing at a time. It's far too early to even think about kids."

"Mmmmm, we'll see. Torrent will be able to think of nothing else, especially when you enter your first heat as a mated couple."

Candy put her finger tips to her temples and squeezed her eyes shut. "You're giving me a headache. Too much too soon."

Sky laughed. "We'll see."

Candy dropped her hands back down to her sides and locked eyes with the other woman. "He can hold his niece or nephew if he gets broody."

Sky shook her head. "I'm sure he'll be a proud uncle but that won't work."

"I'll have that talk with him today. We can't take the next step until the first happens. It is no use even thinking about starting a family before we're married." She huffed out a breath. "It's too soon for that. Way too soon."

Sky's eyes widened. "If I'm reading between the lines, you're ready to allow him to claim you fully."

Candy blew out a breath, her heart pounded in her chest. "I think so." Her heart beat faster at the prospect. A lot depended on the conversation they were about to have but it looked like it might just happen and soon.

It was Sky's turn to squeal. The other woman pulled her into a hug. "I'm so happy for you. For both of you."

Candy broke the hug. "Don't congratulate me prematurely. What was that you mentioned about bad luck?"

Sky laughed. "You're worried for no reason."

Candy hoped that the she-dragon was right.

CHAPTER 13

The ground seemed to rush up to meet her. The grass was long, green and soft looking, it leaned with the wind. The fields were vast and hilly, reminding her of something from the *Sound of Music* or *Heidi*.

Their descent suddenly slowed dramatically. The last few feet took a few seconds. Her feet touched the ground and Torrent's claws opened.

Candy almost fell but managed to find her balance by spreading her arms. She watched as the majestic dragon lifted, huge wings beating slowly. Torrent moved slightly to her right before coming back down. An enormous beast, he touched down slowly and carefully. There was such grace and power beneath the shining scales and arched neck. His eyes were the same pale blue but slitted. His tongue was forked, his tail sweeping. Torrent's chest was golden with flecks of green. Easily recognizable in his dragon form. He was beautiful and took her breath away. Within seconds, he folded into himself. There were tearing and cracking sounds that made her think that the change must hurt, surely. Then a man stood before her. A magnificent specimen of a man. She would never tire of looking at him. *Easy, Candy.* Next thing she knew, she'd have to wipe drool from her chin.

Torrent smiled. "How are you feeling?" His eyes were filled with concern and he touched the side of her arm.

"Good, thanks." She put a hand to her stomach. It reminded her of Sky so she quickly removed it. "I seem to be getting used to being carried above the earth." The first couple of times he'd carried her, she'd felt quite nauseous during the flight and for a few minutes after.

He moved to her and helped remove the backpack from her back.

Torrent opened the pack and removed the blanket. He spread the blue and white checkered fabric across a thin patch of lawn. Next, he removed a pair of pants and put them on. He gestured towards the blanket. "Take a seat."

Her hands were shaking. Her heart was pretty much in her throat. Maybe she should wait until tomorrow. This conversation could wait. The setting was just too picturesque. This moment too beautiful to ruin with the sordid details of her past.

She did as he said and sat down, folding her legs underneath her.

Torrent did the same, sitting across from her. He began to unpack various items. A wooden board and some knives, two plates and a couple of napkins. The material kind. Next was a crisp looking baguette that had been wrapped in cloth. There was also cheese, olives, a hunk of ham and what looked like smoked salmon.

He smiled and handed her a plate. "Thank you."

"So formal." He smiled back. "Is everything okay? You don't seem quite yourself. Are you sure you're feeling okay?"

She nodded. "I'm fine. I promise."

"Maybe this will help relax you." He pulled a bottle of wine out of the bag and held it up. "Can I offer you a glass?"

Candy nodded. "Why not?"

It took Torrent a minute or two to uncork the wine. It was clearly something he didn't do often. He poured them each a glass and he handed her one. "To us." He kept his eyes locked with hers. "To our future . . . together."

Candy nodded. "To us." They clinked glasses. She took a small sip but her stomach lurched. She wasn't sure if it was because of the flight, after all, or whether it had to do with their relationship and how fast it was moving. It was probably a little of both.

He must have noticed her grimace because he leaned forward. "You don't look well." Concern was evident on his face.

She forced a smile. "I'm okay, I think I just really need to eat something before drinking any of this." She held up her glass. "It would be terrible if I got tipsy and took advantage of you."

He laughed. "I could honestly think of nothing better, but when you finally do take proper advantage of me . . ." He winked at her. "I don't want it to happen because you're tipsy."

"I'm sure that cold shower would sober me right up."

"I'm sure it would." He balanced the glass on the edge of the wooden board and tore off a piece of the baguette before placing it on her plate. "Can I cut you some ham or would you prefer the salmon? Or both?"

The thought of fish didn't appeal which was strange because she loved salmon. Maybe she wasn't quite as used to flying yet as what she thought. "I'll have the ham please."

Torrent rummaged in the bag and removed a knife and a jar of mustard. "Nearly forgot this." He opened the jar and placed it in front of her. Then he got to work carving some slices of ham, stopping abruptly. "Ahh!" He put the knife down and reached for his napkin but not before she saw blood blossomed from a slice on his index finger. It was about a half an inch long.

Nausea tugged at her stomach. It rushed through her, causing bile to rise in her throat and sweat to form on her brow. She put a hand over her mouth and made a gagging noise. Okay, so the flight really had affected her.

Torrent frowned. "Are you okay?" He quickly wrapped the finger in his napkin.

As soon as she couldn't see the wound anymore, some of the queasiness subsided. She took in big gulps of air. *Don't puke, Candy.* Whatever you do don't puke.

She could still taste bile and swallowed thickly, licking her lips.

Torrent touched her knee. "Are you are alright?" The creases in his forehead were all the more pronounced, his voice thick with concern.

"I'm sorry." She managed to get out between breaths. "I've never been able to stand the sight of blood. It makes me feel ill."

Torrent burst out laughing. He laughed so loud that his eyes filled up with tears.

"This is funny to you? Seriously? My feeling sick to my stomach is funny to you?" She leaned forward and punched him once on the side of the arm.

He grabbed ahold of her fist and brushed his lips across her knuckles. Torrent shook his head. "No, that's not what I find amusing. You want to study to be a doctor yet you can't stand the sight of blood. There is no logic there."

"I'm sure I could work through it . . . around it."

He leaned back, taking a look under the napkin. "All healed." He announced. "You might want to turn away while I wash off the remaining blood."

Against her will, she pulled a face at the thought of blood.

Torrent chuckled. "Work through it, huh? Whatever you say." He put his hand in that bag of tricks and pulled out a bottle of water, turning his back to her. She could hear the water trickle onto the grass. "There we go." He turned back to her, and flexed the hand in question. There wasn't even a scar or a pink line or anything. It was like the injury had never happened.

"That's amazing. Truly amazing."

He pulled out another bottle of water and handed it to her. "Are you feeling better now?"

She nodded, taking the water from him. "Maybe you're right. I guess I never really thought things through. Maybe being a doctor isn't the right career choice for me. I want to do something meaningful with my life though, you know. I want to prove that I'm intelligent. That means becoming a doctor or a lawyer or—"

"No it doesn't. There are many things you can do. It might mean studying and it might not. It sounds like the work you did with your animals was beneficial. It certainly was to them."

She shrugged. "I guess." She knew he was right. "I love volunteering at the shelter. It's extremely fulfilling."

"What else did you do besides take care of the animals? I know that humans have jobs . . ." He lifted his eyes in thought. "Just like dragons do. We are also assigned to different tasks. I know you said that you just recently left whatever your job was and I know that you are reluctant to speak of it. I feel that we have grown closer and I'm hoping you will confide in me."

Oh shit! What now? She needed to come clean. She planned on coming here this afternoon and on telling him everything. Then she chickened out. She couldn't keep running away though, falling more for this guy every day. Candy needed to tell him right now while she could still walk away. She only prayed that Sky was right and that she wouldn't have to.

She took a sip of her water but her mouth still felt dry. "Okay." She nodded once. "I'll tell you but only if you promise to hear me out before you judge me."

"Judge you?" His face scrunched up in disbelief. "Of course I will listen to you. Why would you even think such a thing?" Torrent leaned forward and cupped her cheek in his hand. She couldn't help but to lean into him. "You can tell me anything. I may not have fully claimed you . . . yet . . ." The word came out sounding rasping. "But, actually, there are no buts—I feel deeply bonded to you. My feelings are growing by the day." He traced the tip of his thumb along her lower lip. "You need to know that."

She did. She'd felt them grow closer. She enjoyed holding him at night. Talking to him. Spending time with him. She loved watching his eyes glaze over with pleasure when she pushed him over the edge with her mouth, how they heated when he looked at her. She wanted more, she just had to get through this first.

"Okay then." Candy clasped her hands tightly in her lap. "I told you my dad left when I was young and that my mom went through men like she did handbags. She wasn't a bad mom, not really. She was just too caught up in herself to ever be a really good mom."

His jaw tightened and he nodded once.

"When I turned sixteen, one of her boyfriends started . . . I don't know . . . I guess, flirting with me. He would do it when she wasn't in the room. He hugged me just that little bit too tightly, that little bit too long. I would catch him staring at my ass. One night, he let himself into my room and tried to . . . touch me inappropriately. Even though he told me to be quiet, he even threatened me, I managed to yell before anything could happen." She gave a humorless laugh. "My mom came running in and the SOB tried to pretend that I had a nightmare and that he was there to check on me. In my mom's favor, she kicked him out the moment I told her." She shook her head. "Unfortunately within a week she'd replaced him with another bozo. Some of the guys were okay, but others . . ." She paused. "I guess I'd reached an age where men had begun to notice me. That asshole that tried his luck wasn't the last. I put locks on my door and tried to keep to myself as much as possible."

"You're right." Torrents rough growl was unexpected. "This is difficult for me to hear. Go on. I'm sorry I interrupted."

"It's just the beginning. I'm not trying to make you feel sorry for me but I need you to understand what my life was like. I was seventeen when I graduated high school. It couldn't have been two weeks after my graduation. I was still trying to figure out what I was going to do with my life. I'd managed to secure a partial scholarship at one of the local colleges but there still wasn't enough money for me to attend. I was trying to figure something out. Maybe I could work part-time. Stay living at home. My mom had been with the same guy for about six months and things were fairly stable. Life was pretty okay. The only problem was that he drank quite a lot. My mom started drinking too."

She paused.

"One night, they'd both been drinking heavily. My mom was passed out. I had become complacent. Rick didn't seem the least bit interested in me. He was a truck driver, on the road regularly. He would be gone for a couple of days and then home for a couple days and they would go on their benders. I left my door unlocked . . . mistake. I guess I was unlucky and that he was sober enough to get up and come after me. Luckily for me though, he didn't have great reflexes and was a bit wobbly on his feet. When he came at me, I was able to grab my bedside lamp and hit him with it. He went down and I hit him again."

"Did he . . . ?" A soft, menacing growl. "You know?" His voice cracked.

She lifted her eyes. Torrent looked angry. Actually angry wasn't strong enough of a word. His face was red and his muscles bulged.

She shook her head. "No, but it was close. Too close. I packed my bag and left. Ellis found me the next day, I'd been on the street for all of twenty-four hours. I was hungry and cold and more afraid than I ever thought possible. I didn't trust Ellis at all but what choice did I have? I couldn't go back home. I went to his place and crashed in his spare bedroom. He drove a fancy car, wore fancy clothes. He told me he was going to help me, that we were going to help each other. It took a while before I started to trust him. It was one hell of a mistake."

You can do this, Candy. You can do this.

"Ellis owned his own business. It was a dating agency. An escort agency is the right term. He offered me a job and I leapt at the opportunity. He bought me beautiful clothes and dresses and all I had to do in return was go out on dates with, mostly, wealthy men."

Torrent frowned. "I don't understand."

"It might be a human thing." She huffed out a breath, struggling to find the right words. "I mostly dated elderly gentleman or young rich guys who needed a date. Guys who needed a partner for functions and didn't want to go through the hassle of finding someone to attend with them. Guys that had lost their wives and weren't interested in going through the motions again. Or men that were tired of money grabbing women." She pictured Charles. "They didn't want the hassle, so they'd call Kitty's and organize themselves a date."

"Let me see if I understand this correctly, human males would pay money to go out with you. To spend the evening in your company? Am I correct?"

Candy nodded. "Yes, I'd dress up for the occasion and would essentially be shown off on their arm. Fathers sometimes hired escorts for their sons. A slightly older, good looking woman. It is often for show but some of the guys were genuinely lonely. I sometimes spent evenings playing chess or just talking or sharing a meal."

Torrent smiled. "You are good company, Candy, I can understand that these men would pay good money to have you spend time with them."

She tried to smile back but there was a huge lump inside her throat. "That's what I did for the first year or so that I worked at Kitty's. I went out on a couple of dates a week, got myself my own small apartment and managed to start a savings account. Even back then, I had this dream of proving myself, of doing something with my life. I could see that it was going to take too long though. I didn't want to be an escort for years and years. Some of the girls at Kitty's were making bags of money."

Torrent frowned. "They were doing the same thing as you and yet making more, that is not fair I hope that you spoke to this male . . . What is his name again?"

"Ellis." She grit her teeth, just saying his name made her angry. "It was around that time that Ellis approached me. Those women that were making more money than me, they weren't just simply going on dates. They were offering more to their clients."

Torrent's frown deepened. He picked up his glass of wine and took a big glug.

"They often granted their dates sexual favors in return for more money. Lots of money."

"Did your boss know about this?" Torrent's eyes were so pale that they practically glowed. His voice was low and evenly delivered but his body radiated tension.

She nodded and swallowed hard. "Oh yeah, he knew all about it. He encouraged it. Ellis took a big cut of all of the income. I had become accustomed to being independent. I had big dreams. I realized that I was never going to get out of the hole I found myself in, that I was never going to be able to study or further myself unless I did something drastic. Something short term that would bring in good money. When Ellis approached me . . ."

"You had sex with males for money?" His voice was hard as flint. "Is that what you're going to tell me?"

"You promised to hear me out," she whispered.

Torrents eyes were definitely lighter, they even seemed to be glowing a little. He reached out and picked up his wineglass, and then drained the contents. "Go on. I will listen to all you have to say." His eyes stayed on the glass in his hand.

She pulled in a deep breath. "Ellis approached me, and I agreed but on my terms. I agreed to try it out. Some of the men that I spent time with thought that they were God's gift to women. Some of them were downright assholes. I knew that a ton of the guys were married."

Torrent growled but caught himself doing it and snapped his mouth shut, pursing his lips together. His hands were fisted in his lap.

"The agreement between Ellis and I was that I got to choose who I dated, who I had sex with. There was no way I was going to disrespect other women and have sex with a married man. I saw what it did to my mom and . . ." She paused. "I had rules regarding the sex. What I was comfortable with and what I wasn't."

Torrent jumped up to his feet. "I'm sorry." His voice was gruff. He looked distraught. Candy felt tears prick in her eyes. This was not going well. It was a disaster.

He grabbed the back of his neck and squeezed. "I wasn't expecting this. I need a minute." He strode away, walking for about a hundred yards and just stood there. After a couple of minutes, he made his way back and took a seat in front of her. His chest heaved. He still refused to look her in the eyes. Torrent nodded. "Go on." He clenched his teeth.

If he couldn't accept her past, this wasn't going to work. Her eyes burned. Her throat felt tight.

You can finish this. *Suck it up.*

"There were two guys that I initially agreed to have sex with. Two quickly became four. I refused to allow Ellis to increase the number. A lot of Kitty's is based on referrals, the guys talk. It quickly became known there was a woman, an escort that was exclusive. That turned away huge amounts of business. As a result, more men wanted to date me and my price increased. I refused to take on any more clients. If someone dropped out, only then, would I agree to date a new person."

"Only you weren't dating them, were you?" His eyes lifted to hers, they were full with . . . hurt. Just as quickly they seemed devoid of emotion. "Were you fucking them all?"

Candy cringed at how horrible it sounded. "Not always." There was a definite edge to her voice. "They still enjoyed spending time with me, going out with me, doing mundane things with me. Most of these men were lonely. It wasn't just about the sex."

"Maybe not to them." He interjected.

"It wasn't about the sex for me either. It was about the money . . . period. I went into this with my eyes open. I needed to make money quickly in order to move on with the rest of my life, except . . ." She paused. Her lip quivered. She took in a breath to soothe her nerves. "I was wrong. Selling myself like that, it wasn't for me. Some women love it, they thrive off of it. It makes them feel powerful. Being desired by so many different men and to such a degree. These guys throw enormous amounts of money at you. Some of the women loved the sex. They loved climbing from one bed into the next. They got off on it."

Torrent poured himself another glass of wine and downed half of it.

Candy reached for her own glass and took a tentative sip. It felt like vinegar going down her throat. "It wasn't like that for me. It was soul destroying. I needed the money but I wasn't willing to just do anything or anyone to get it." She needed to tell him everything but it was a struggle for her. She squeezed her eyes shut for a moment. "The sex did nothing for me. It was all fake. I never had one orgasm, not ever."

He didn't say anything. Didn't even look at her.

"Then one day, one of my clients left, I refused to have him replaced. You won't believe it, but that started an even bigger frenzy. There was a waiting list. Ellis went to my three remaining clients and they agreed to pay more. One of the three guys I saw started dating a woman and then there were two."

Torrent nodded. "How long were you"—he cleared his throat—"an escort?"

"I was seventeen when Ellis put a roof over my head. A few months later I started dating and by the age of nineteen I was having sex with my dates for money. I'm twenty-four now, so that's almost five years."

"How many men have you had sex with?" His jaw was tight. His brow furrowed.

"How is that even relevant? How many women have you had sex with? I'm sure your list is a hell of a lot longer than mine. All of my sexual experiences barring two were business transactions."

"Two." He said, finally looking at her.

"My first boyfriend and you."

He made an irritated snorting noise. "I didn't pay anyone or expect anyone to pay me."

His words stung. "At nineteen, it seemed like a good idea. By the time I was twenty-four, not so much. Like I said, I was down to two clients. I only had sex with the one. Harold is impotent."

Torrent finished the rest of his wine. "What do you mean? Impotent . . . I'm not sure . . ."

"He couldn't get it up." Candy huffed. "If I'm honest with myself I wanted to get out much sooner. I spoke to Ellis about it. He kept on talking me into staying. My rate kept on going up and up. *It's money for jam, Candy. Don't do something stupid, Candy. You'll regret it if you leave, Candy.* He knew exactly what to say. My list of rules grew longer and my clients fewer."

"So that impotent male didn't have sex with you?"

"No." She shook her head. "He had been married three times and was so afraid of women being after him for his money that he stopped dating altogether. He said that he preferred to take care of the money side of things upfront. At least with him and I, there were no lies. I went with him to functions and just spent time with him. He's a lonely old guy. It still felt wrong though."

"Maybe because it was." Torrent's throat worked. "Tell me about the other male."

She shrugged. "Why is it important? I'm not asking you about all the women you had sex with . . . am I?"

"I want to know." He looked deadpan and emotionless.

"Charles is a really sweet guy. He's also pretty old, must be in his late 70s. His wife died a couple of years back and he can't bring himself to date 'real' women."

"Real women." Torrent made a snorting noise

"Well, although Charles and I spent plenty of time together, we never had a real relationship and therefore he never felt like he was cheating on his dead wife. It was a business transaction. Probably a tax write off." She laughed, it came out sounding a little high pitched.

"Did you rut with this male?" There it was again, that look of hurt. It lasted just a split second, if she blinked she would've missed it. His jaw tightened up some more.

Candy nodded. "On occasion."

"When did you last have paid sex with a male?"

"Why do you want to know all of this? It's not important. I didn't enjoy having sex with these men. At first it was just a duty I was expected to perform and then it slowly became something I hated. I would never put down the women I worked alongside, but it wasn't for me."

He blinked a few times. "When did you last have sex with this male?" he repeated the question like he hadn't heard her response.

It irritated her. "It's not relevant. When did you last go on one of your stag run thingies? When did you last have sex with one of your she-dragons? Was it good for you, if so how many times did you come?" A tear escaped and she wiped it away. "Well?"

"When did you last rut the male?"

Another tear fell. She ignored it. "I don't know." She was struggling to think. "A while ago."

"Was it days before you came here? Weeks? Months?" His eyes were hard and so light. They reminded her of when she'd first seen him. When he was in full hunt and attack mode. Two cold, hard glaciers.

She shivered. "Months. It was months okay? I've been trying to leave the business but Ellis wouldn't let me. I finally stood up to him the day I was taken by one of your dragons. Ellis wanted me to take on another client. He wouldn't listen to me." She was breathing hard. Tears coursing down her cheeks. "I could tell that he was never going to let me go. He'd lined up another client for me and was taking me to see the guy that afternoon. He didn't give a shit about what I wanted. I was an asset to him and nothing more. We argued. He hit me."

Torrent snarled. The sound was loud and terrifying. His entire face morphed into the picture of violence. He sprang back up to his feet and walked away, cursing loudly.

He paced and stomped and paced some more. His hands rather than fisted at his sides, were clenched onto his neck. After what felt like forever, he strode back to her. "Come. We are leaving." He began tossing things into the bag.

"We need to talk about this."

"There's nothing to talk about. Thank you for telling me about your past. We won't speak of it again."

Candy narrowed her eyes at him. "We have to talk about it. I should have told you about it sooner."

Torrent shrugged. "It makes no difference."

"I can see that you're upset. Speak to me."

"I don't like the idea that you had males pay you for sex. I knew you had a past, you mentioned yourself that you weren't a virgin. You said far from it. I knew you had lovers but this is a difficult concept for me. It doesn't matter though. None of it does. We are bonded." He grit his teeth together in a semi snarl. "Soon to be mated."

"Of course it matters. It matters a ton."

"It doesn't. I chose you and you chose me. We are one step away from becoming mates." He shrugged again. "Let's just go." He threw the rest of the items into the bag, haphazardly. Torrent yanked off his pants, tearing them in the process. Within seconds, he was in dragon form. Not before she noticed how hard he was. What the!? She didn't understand it. Torrent was spitting mad and yet his cock was as hard as rock. She'd just told him something that had upset him. It didn't make sense.

Candy didn't have time to think on it, she barely had time to put the backpack on her back and he was lifting her into the air. Her stomach lurched as they acclerated quickly into the sky.

CHAPTER 14

The next morning . . .

C andy reached for the space next to her. The sheets were cold and empty. Within minutes of returning back to the chamber, Torrent had left. He mentioned something about having a meeting. Candy could see that he was talking rubbish. It was written all over his face.

She felt empty and filled with sadness and all at the same time. Candy chewed on her bottom lip to keep it from having a wobblefest. She squeezed her eyes shut to keep from crying. He needed his space, time to think things through. Hopefully he wouldn't leave her waiting too long and hopefully he would open up and talk a little more about his feelings without being an asshole. Maybe they could still work through this. She was still here, so there was hope.

It was strange how a couple of days ago, she would've jumped at any opportunity to go home, yet right now, all she wanted was to make things right with him. To stay and make a future with Torrent. Her chest hurt. Her heart ached.

She forced herself to throw off the covers and get out of bed. If she stayed in this fetal position, she was sure to feel worse.

Candy got up, showered, ate breakfast and went through the motions of a normal day. There was no sign of Sky. She longed for companionship and someone to talk to. She mainly prayed that Torrent would come home.

Home.

It was weird how she'd come to think of this place as home and in such a short time. It didn't matter that she hadn't met anyone or experienced life amongst the dragons. She hoped to get the opportunity.

Candy made lunch and read a bit. Then out of sheer boredom and frustration she put on some workout gear and spent an hour going through her aerobic routine. After a shower and a change, she felt no better. Anger had started to creep in. How dare he judge her like this? No one had the right to judge another person without walking in their shoes. Here was a guy that had been born with a silver spoon in his mouth. He'd never wanted for anything a day in his life. He was a complete manwhore by his own confession and yet he judged her.

Asshole.

In many ways, he was just like those arrogant dickwads she avoided. The ones that were against her rules. The ones she never agreed to date. Men with more money and arrogance than what they knew what to do with.

If he walked through the door right now, she was going

to give him a piece of her mind. It was a half an hour before the door finally did open and if anything, she was even more angry.

Torrent didn't know what to do with himself. He spent the night in his office. Hadn't slept even a wink. All he could think about was Candy.

He knew that she had rutted other males. It was something he tried not to think about. She had a past and previous sexual encounters, just as he did. It was a given. It was something he always thought that he could handle. Something he never questioned.

Hearing her talk of accepting money for sex made him want to go into a blind rage though. She had been young and gullible. That male, Ellis had used her. That much was clear to him. Even if she hadn't gone into this with open eyes and a clear mind, it had been for the right reasons.

To have a future. To better herself in the long run.

Torrent could understand these things. But fuck! It filled him with rage. Moreover, it filled him with the need to claim her. To make her his.

It made him mad with need. His dick was hard and throbbing and had been ever since she'd told him. Call it instinct, driving need. It didn't matter. It was there and it rode him hard. Torrent felt sure that once he finally claimed her, he would be able to move past this. Not a minute sooner. In fact, the rage and frustration was growing by the second. Need was also a fantastic contender in the race of emotions.

All of this turbulance raced through him. His teeth felt sharp, he could feel his scales rasping beneath his skin.

Claim!

Now!

Candy was his. *His.* He moved swiftly down the hallway. It was time to claim her. No, it was way past time. So overdue, it wasn't funny. He would finally have her and they would never speak of it again. Not ever.

Torrent unlocked the door and tried to open it carefully. One of the hinges tore from the frame. Not too bad, considering. He righted the door, pushing it back into its frame.

Candy stood on the other side of the couch. She had a hand to her chest and her face was pale, her eyes were wide in her head.

"Mine," he rasped, his voice barely human. "Mine." He tried again. Still guttural but with better pronunciation.

Her eyes widened even more and she sucked in a breath. "What's going on?" she stammered.

"I'm done waiting." He could only pray that she understood what he was saying. It didn't really matter. This wasn't about words anyway.

"We need to talk." She held up a hand.

Torrent chuckled. It seemed his female had other ideas. Well tough luck. He advanced on her.

Candy backed up one step and then another, and another. "Wait." She held up both hands. "We really do need to talk."

"There's nothing to talk about." He was pleased with

how calm and understandable his words were even though they came out in a deep rasp.

"There's a ton to talk about. I put it all out there and I can see that you are not taking it well."

"I didn't come to talk." He closed the distance between them and clasped an arm around her waist.

"Torrent, wait," Candy pleaded. She pushed against his chest.

"Don't you want me?" He narrowed his eyes. He didn't know what he would do if she denied him. He wasn't sure that he could control his beast for much longer.

Rut.

Take.

Claim.

"You know I do."

"Well then." He lowered his head and buried it into her neck, nipping at her flesh. The scent of her arousal met his nostrils and he growled deeply.

On a hard rip, he shredded her sweater, curling his hand around her lush flesh. Her nipple tightened. Candy gave him another hard shove. "Wait." It came out sounding breathless. "We can't."

"No more waiting. You are mine. Do you hear me?" His free hand cupped her mound and she made a whimpering noise.

"Yes . . . no."

"You. Are. Mine." It ended on a snarl. Shit, if he carried on like this he was going to scare her. "I need you," a rough whisper.

"No!" More forceful this time. She slapped the side of his arm. "Stop!"

"Candy." His voice sounded pleading, so close to begging it scared him. "I need to claim you now. I need to make you mine. Need to have you." He pushed a hand past the elastic of her pants. "Stop denying me."

She shoved at him some more. "We need to talk first." She squirmed.

"Fuck!" He snarled, pulling away from her.

"I do want you." She sniffed, she was crying. "I want for us to be together but not like this. You're angry. You hate the idea that I was a call girl, a high-priced hooker. A whore." She was openly sobbing now but her hands were fisted as well. She pulled her clothes together in a hard tug.

"Don't call yourself those things." Anger rose up in him. A lump formed in his throat.

"I had sex for money. It's who I was. *Was.*" She practically shouted the word. "It's in my past. It is a part of who I am but it doesn't define me."

He could hear what she was saying. Torrent could sympathize and empathize but it didn't make him feel any better. His dragon prowled and growled. Hearing her say those things didn't calm him. "You've told me. I will come to terms with it. I need you . . . now. Don't deny me. Don't deny us."

She shook her head. "We're not ready to take that step. I thought that we were but I was wrong."

"What will it take?" He growled. The sense of urgency rose even higher and along with it a feeling that he was losing her. Candy. She was his.

She shrugged. " I don't know." Candy shook her head. "You need to come to terms with what I used to do. You need to get the hell over it or let me go . . . one or the other."

"I'm never letting you go," he growled. "You are mine."

"Stop saying that." She poked her finger into his chest. "You're acting like a complete jerk. I did what I had to do. Something that *I* have to live with, that *I* have to deal with. You are the one that needs to get over it though." She turned and paced away from him. Candy opened the closet and grabbed a shirt. Then she changed out of the ripped sweater and pulled on the fresh shirt. Her movements were jerky and angry.

Torrent ran a hand through his hair. He was losing her. What was wrong with her? He didn't understand it. He was offering her everything. A whole new life. An opportunity to be a queen, to be his mate and it didn't seem like she wanted it.

Maybe she didn't want him.

A king.

Why didn't she want him? She allowed human males to pay her money to rut with her and yet she refused him at every turn. White hot anger coursed through him. It was unacceptable. Did she not realize that she was lucky to even be here? It was her that should be begging him and not the other way around.

Torrent went to his side of the closet and yanked open

the door. He opened the golden chest in the far corner and and chose a couple of items.

Candy was at the far end of the chamber. She was staring out at the view, deep in thought.

Torrent swallowed thickly. Something gave him pause. A voice maybe. Something that told him not to do it but he ignored it. Candy was his female. She'd had sex with others for far less. Rutting her was his right. She was his dammit. Why was she being so stubborn?

"Here." He held out the jewelry to her. Torrent had tried to speak with her but they had gotten nowhere. Hopefully she would understand this.

Candy looked from him, to the pieces in his hand and back again. She looked at him like he was mad. "What's that?"

"Some pieces that my family has collected over the years. An emerald ring. A diamond and ruby encrusted brooch. This . . . he held up the necklace and pendant, is a two carrot diamond."

She frowned. "Okay." Her frown deepened and she took a step back.

"They're yours." It was too late to back out. By now the voice was screaming to him not to do it.

Fuck it!

"I want to rut you. I will give you the jewels as payment. This"—he rattled the priceless heirlooms in his hand—"is what you understand. Am I correct?"

"Fuck you," a whisper.

"Yes." He raised his brows. "I want you to fuck me.

You did it with all those humans and for less, I am sure."

Her hand lashed out and she slapped him across the face . . . hard. "No." Her voice trembled. She cleared her throat. "You misunderstand. Fuck you!" She yelled. "As in take your money, your diamands, your title . . . you can take it all and shove it." Candy sucked in a deep breath.

Fear gripped him. "I don't understand. You'll fuck all of those—"

"I wouldn't lower myself and have sex with you if you were the last guy on the planet. Guys like you are the reason I had a whole list of rules in the first place. I'm leaving now. I want nothing to do with you. Don't you dare try and stop me." Her eyes shone.

"Fine," he snarled. "Whatever! There are other females out there. In fact, I heard something about another hunt in a week or two." It was a lie. There was a hunt but he wouldn't be bringing a female back.

Candy flinched like he'd physically hurt her. "Just take me home, or better yet, get one of your guys to do it. I don't ever want to see you again."

It hurt so much he could hardly breathe. What the fuck had he done?

No! Wait just a minute.

Torrent had tried everything. It was Candy's fault. Her own damned fault. She didn't want him. He'd tried hard. He would've done anything for her. Right now, he was taking his own advice, there were more females out there. Torrent shrugged. He pretended not to care. He tried to get his heart rate under control and tried to breathe, even though it felt like a mountain was sitting on his chest, squeezing the life out of him. "I renounce you as well. You'll be back in Walton Springs before nightfall." Torrent turned and strode from the room. He tripped and almost fell as the door closed behind him. His eyes stung and his throat felt thick.

It was nothing. She was nothing to him. Less than nothing. A mistake. Once he had another female under him, he'd perk right up. He was weak from lack of sex. That was all. It was a problem that would be easily rectified.

CHAPTER 15

"Hat are you doing here?" Blaze pushed back from his desk and stood up.

"Hello," Torrent said. "It's good to see you too." He could feel that he was frowning.

"Save me the dramatics." Blaze smiled. "Why aren't you with your new bride?"

The male had spent too much time with human females. With one human female in particular. Blaze thought that the others hadn't noticed just because his visits had dried up before they could call him out on it. It was the first time that Torrent wondered what had happened.

Bride.

Fuck!

"The female is not my mate. It was a false rumor. A misunderstanding." He shifted from one foot to the other. A mistake! His chest tightened just thinking it. A stupid damned mistake.

His youngest brother, Storm, would be dropping her in Walton Springs right now. Good riddance.

Blaze raised his brows. "Oh! I had heard that you sealed the deal."

He shook his head. "Nope. I sent the female home. We were not compatible."

"Oh! That's a shame." Blaze looked amused.

"We didn't rut." He felt the need to set the record straight. "We were not compatible as people."

"An even bigger shame."

"I'm here to enquire about the dark haired human. I had my sights set on her from the start. It is probably the reason it didn't work out with Candy." *Liar!* The words almost stuck in his throat. They felt hollow. It felt like he was betraying his female.

No!

Not his.

Candy left him. She left. It wasn't his fault. Not at all. *That wasn't entirely true.* The same voice that had tried to stop him earlier began to shout at him. It called him choice names. He pushed it down and drowned out the pesky droning. "I heard that your brother has not yet mated her."

"No, but he seems to like her." The fire king looked thoughtful.

"I want her," he blurted. Torrent had called Ocean to his chamber as soon as Candy had left but the female did nothing for him. Absolutely nothing. She'd stood before him naked and his body hadn't so much as stirred. He'd apologized to her and had sent her away. He'd felt like the biggest prick. No! It wasn't his fault. It wasn't.

It was simple, he needed a human replacement. The dark haired one. The one he had wanted in the first place. It was simple!

"I don't know." Blaze rubbed at the stubble on his chin, he was deep in thought.

Interesting, the male was considering it. "Surely they would be mated by now if she was the right one for him? All of the other females are mated. I sent mine back . . . after all this time, we should have been mated as well but we were not compatible." He almost stumbled over his words. "It is the same with this human and Coal. They don't belong together. You know I am right."

Blaze nodded. "I must admit that I am concerned. You need to know that she"—the male stopped talking—"you might be right." His whole demeanor changed. "Why the hell not? Do you agree to forfeit the next hunt if I give her to you?"

"Yes." Torrent knew it was rash but he didn't give a fuck. The dark haired one was just what he needed to forget Candy. All human females found him attractive. Candy was the first female to ever resist him. He felt his blood boil all over again just thinking about it. She would accept money from mere humans and wouldn't let him near her. That wasn't entirely true it . . .

Fuck!

Candy didn't want him. She didn't. The human had proven that time and time again.

"Are you sure?" The fire king asked.

He paused for a time. Why was he second guessing

himself? Fuck that! "Yes." His voice rang loud and true. Of course it did! The dark haired one would fall at his feet. She was the one for him. His throat constricted further and his chest felt all the tighter. He needed a female. He would feel better once he was inside of one. Anyone. He would.

Blaze nodded. "It is done." They both touched their markings as a show of faith. Torrent pushed his hand deeper into his chest, trying to still the emotion swirling beneath the surface.

"Coal should be on his way now. I will inform him of my decision."

"I will wait."

"Come back in the morning."

Torrent shook his head. "I will take the female today."

"What is the rush? I will inform Coal and allow him to break the news to the female. You can come b—"

"I will wait." The thought of leaving empty handed was appalling to him.

Blaze narrowed his eyes on Torrent for a long while. Torrent could feel his heart beating out of his chest. The male finally nodded.

Something inside of him released but the weight on his shoulders felt like it increased by ten fold. What was he doing?

Torrent breathed out. Things would be fine once the dark haired female was his.

"I will inform Coal and then you can take her soon after. Stay out of sight until she has been informed." He paused. "She is a difficult female." Blaze shook his head.

"They are all difficult." Torrent forced a smile.

"Indeed they are. Please wait in the great hall until one of my males calls you."

"I will do that." Torrent gripped Blaze's wrist. "Do not back out."

Blaze frowned. "Go and wait in the hall." His voice had a steely edge.

Torrent was going to stay close. He was going to do everything in his power to ensure that the fire king kept his word.

It wasn't long before Coal arrived. The fire prince disappeared into Blaze's work chamber.

Within ten minutes of the male's arrival, the dark haired beauty appeared and rushed into the chamber as well. She looked upset. Good!

The female was just as he remembered. She was to his taste. Taller, more robust. There were more hips and thighs to her. At least as much breast. Her cheeks were flushed and her skin had more of a honey tinge as opposed to pure milky white. She was perfect!

He waited to become aroused by the sight of her. By her scent.

Nothing.

She lacked the exotic edge to her scent like Candy . . . stop! Perhaps she had arrived and disappeared into the chamber too quickly. He needed her up close and personal. Yes, that was it. She was exactly his type. To a fault. Blaze had given the female to him and he would make sure that the male made good on his promise.

This dark haired one would work for him. She would want him. He was sure of it. It wouldn't be long before Candy was a distant memory.

Candy.

The pain that coursed through him as he pictured her sweet smile, her beautiful blue eyes, her . . . no! He needed to forget the human.

Shouting interrupted his chain of thought. It was coming from Blaze's work chamber. The dark haired human was angry.

Good! It would make this easier. One night with this female and Candy would be a distant memory. He swallowed hard. Fuck!

"Save it!" she yelled. The dark haired one walked out the door. Her cheeks were flushed and her jaw was set. She looked pissed.

"Wait. Let me explain. We need to talk!" Coal followed the female. His voice was pleading. His whole demeanor was pitiful. The male looked like he was on the verge of groveling.

"Let her go," Blaze said, as he followed behind his brother.

"No!" Coal shouted. "I've listened to you enough. I need to . . ." The male growled, he was just behind the female. Following in her footsteps like a puppy.

"Let her calm down first." Blaze called after his brother. "Save it for behind closed doors."

"Julie!" Coal shouted.

Torrent felt like laughing. This male was so far fucking gone that it was both amusing and nauseating to watch. "We belong together. Please let me explain."

"There is no *we!*" The human shouted. Julie. Her name was Julie. A bit on the boring side. It wasn't like she was named after sweet treats, named after anything for that matter. The female didn't turn back, she kept on walking. The pitiful prince on her heels.

"Don't say that," Coal said. The male paused and looked around the room locking eyes with Torrent.

The male visibly blanched. He even stumbled over his own feet. Torrent could see that his mind was racing at a mile a minute. Coal roared and his hands fisted.

The female was still oblivious. She turned sharply, Coal almost walked into her. "Let me just tell you something." She pointed a finger at the male.

This was going to be easier than he thought. Coal might be head over heels over her but she felt nothing for him. That stupid voice disagreed with him but he ignored it.

"Not now," Coal ground out, his eyes darted to Torrent.

"Oh, I'm only permitted to talk when it suits you?" She stabbed the poor bastard with her finger. Torrent knew exactly how that felt "Well sorry for you. It doesn't work like that."

"Julie, listen to me—"

"No damned way am I listening to you. I've listened to you enough, don't you think?" The human didn't wait for a reply.

Coal glanced at him again. His eyes were wide and held fear the likes Torrent had never seen. What a complete pussy. For the first time since Candy had left he felt thankful that he was no longer with the female. Truly thankful.

The human, Julie, put her hands on her hips. "You are an asshole. A jerk of the highest order. I'm done listening to you. All you seem to be able to do is talk a bunch of bullshit."

"There were a couple of things I kept from you, but they—"

"No!" The human yelled, cutting him off. Torrent felt bad for the fire prince He would be helping the male by taking this female. "There were more than just a couple of things." The female continued. He didn't know what they were on about and quite frankly, he didn't give a shit.

"I have never lied to you about the things that truly mattered. I swear. Please." He tried to touch her but she pulled away with a sharp jerk. "Let's go back to my chamber, we can discuss it." Once again, Coal's eyes flashed to Torrent. He almost felt sorry for the bastard. Almost!

"There is nothing to discuss. I want to leave. I've already packed, although the stuff isn't mine. Where is my backpack? I'm leaving." Her eyes welled. For just a second he considered walking away. The female had feelings for the fire prince even if she wouldn't admit it.

Fuck it!

He wanted the female. The water fucking king. Blaze

had given her to him. Moreover, the human had just renounced her bond with Coal. She was free for another male to claim. The fire prince could step aside.

"No. Don't say that. Please." Coal visibly paled.

"No, Coal. There is no we or us. There never will be." She snarled. "Do us both a favor and let me leave. We are done."

Hallelujah! Any question as to the renouncing was washed away right then.

"I'm glad to hear it." Torrent pushed off the wall. "I'm glad you're packed. We are leaving right away." He allowed his gaze to roam her abundant curves. He willed his body to react.

Nothing.

Damn.

Torrent needed to get her home.

"Who the hell are you?" The human looked Torrent up and down.

The female was about to get to know him in every way possible. He could scent that Coal had recently rutted her. He pushed that annoying voice from his head once again. "I'm the water king and you are quite lovely."

Coal snarled. "Touch her and I'll . . ."

The idiot had no dignity. None whatsoever. "You'll what?" Torrent took a step towards them to show how serious he was. "You'll do nothing. Your female has renounced you. Your king has already given permission for me to take her . . . not that I need it after that display, but . . ." he shrugged. "It's good to have anyway."

"What is he talking about?" The female moved in behind Coal. Like that would save her.

"You publicly announced that you no longer wish to be with the fire prince, that makes you available. Free for someone else to claim you." His chest hurt. He felt more tired than he'd ever felt in his life.

"I'm not available." The human tried to step from behind Coal but the fire prince gripped her waist and pushed her back. It was touching but useless.

"This female does not understand our ways. She does not wish to go with you." Coal looked like he was about to burst into tears. It was hilarious how a female could bring a male to his knees. Thankfully he had managed to circumvent such a thing form happening to him and just in the nick of time.

"Her wishes are no concern to me." Torrent spat, he shook his head. They needed to know that he meant it.

"Stop this, Torrent." Blaze said as he entered the hallway. "Don't do this." He stepped in between the couple and Torrent. He tried to show how superior he was. He didn't have even half a leg to stand on. "When I said that you could have the female, I didn't realize what she meant to my brother. He just told me that he has feelings for her."

Torrent laughed, there was no humor there. "Feelings. How unimportant. Their feelings do not concern me." He said. "The female renounced Coal and I am stepping up. You"—he pointed at Julie—"are coming with me. Now."

"No, I'm not. I want to go home." There was a slight

quiver to her voice but she also sounded angry. He ignored the emotion. It meant nothing to him. He would convince her by any means necessary.

Like you convinced Candy. *Fuck off!* He pushed down that irritating voice . . . yet again and pushed out another laugh. This one sounded real. Almost. "Not happening." He ground out. "You're coming with me and that is final."

"Be reasonable," Blaze implored him. He took a step towards Torrent. "There will be another hunt next month. Coal and the female are having an argument. They care for one another." He grimaced as he said the word care. "Don't do this." His voice took on a harsh edge. Fuck him. No legs to stand on!

Torrent shook his head. "I tried to be reasonable but look where it got me. I don't have a female to show for it. She left." His heart felt like it was going to burst as he said the words. It hurt so fucking much . . . *no it did not!* "I will take this one in her place. This is the one I wanted from the start." Torrent reached past Coal. Once he rutted this dark haired one . . . Julie . . . all would be well again. Equilibrium would be restored.

The idiot, Coal lunged at him but Blaze pulled him back, taking him in a headlock. "Don't do this, Torrent!" The king shouted.

Coal didn't know it yet, but Torrent was doing him a favor. It complicated things to feel too much for your partner. "It's already done." Torrent wrapped his arms around the human who struggled against him. Not for long. She would soon give in.

Coal roared. Flames erupted. Torrent ignored the male. Coal roared again as Torrent gripped the human to his chest. She kicked at him and even punched him in the face. The screaming hurt more than the blows. Torrent only gripped her tighter. It wouldn't do if she fell.

If she wasn't careful he *would* accidentally drop her. Idiot human! "Stop," he choked out. "Behave," he said on a growl.

Julie sank her teeth into his neck. Torrent roared in pain and rage but kept moving. He could hear Coal screaming and shouting behind him. The male would get over it.

Torrent's clothes ripped as he shifted. He clutched the female to his scaly body. She continued to fight him even though she would fall to her death if he released her. Human females were strange creatures.

"I'll come for you!" Coal yelled at the top of his lungs. Torrent could still hear him, even though the human wouldn't be able to.

Coal wouldn't come. It was against the lores. He beat his wings as hard as he could. The sooner he returned to his lair, the better. The sooner he made this female his, the better.

CHAPTER 16

Torrent hovered over the balcony that led to his chamber, he slowly descended and deposited the female carefully on the floor. The female was weaker than she looked because she fell into a heap. Quick as a flash, she was up and running.

He wasn't sure where the hell she planned on running to. She was liable to hurt herself. What would Coal say then? Fuck the fire prince. The female was his now. He didn't understand why he'd even thought of the male. Torrent hooked an arm around her waist.

"Let go of me!" She yelled. The human twisted and the palm of her hand managed to connect with his face.

Two slaps in one day. It was a record.

The female grimaced and looked at her hand. Silly human was definitely going to hurt herself if she wasn't careful.

"Feel better?" He kept his gaze on her.

"No. I wish I was stronger." She cradled the hand against her chest. "I would punch the snot out of you. What the hell is wrong with you?"

He didn't have the time or the inclination to have a discussion with her.

She scented delectable. He willed his body to react but it didn't. Torrent wanted to growl in frustration. He needed to touch her. He needed . . ."I'm going to kiss you now, female." He clenched his jaw, trying hard not to allow that pesky voice to start in on him.

Her eyes narrowed. "Touch me and I swear to god I will hurt you!" She yelled. The human pulled away from him and he let her go. Once she was far enough away, she turned to face him.

"We just established that you are not capable of hurting me." He couldn't have her hurting herself. He needed her in perfect condition. He just needed her. His body would come to the party soon.

The human swallowed thickly. "I'll just have to find a way." She glanced down at his cock. There was nothing but anger and contempt written all over her face. Julie locked eyes with him again, trying to act normal.

It was the oldest trick in the book. "Don't even think about it." He shook his head. Did she really think she could hit or kick him in the junk?

"Let me go, you big . . . horrible . . . disgusting ape." Her fists were clenched at her sides.

Torrent frowned. "I'm not a primate, I'm a dragon." He sounded bored. He felt . . . no . . . it didn't matter how he felt.

"You're an asshole of epic proportions."

That was the second time he had been called an asshole

today as well. Another record. He didn't give a fuck. He sure as hell needed one though. Her scent was spiced with anger but there was something else there. His nostrils flared as he took it in.

"Stop that!" she shouted, her face was flushed. Her eyes blazing.

He ignored her and sniffed harder.

Julie kicked him in the shin and her face registered pain.

Idiot human. "Stop that. You do know that dragons heal at an alarming rate, so even if you were to harm me . . ." Maybe he should just take her back. "I would heal too quickly for it to mean anything?"

No! He would see this through. It was only a matter of time before interest flared between them.

He sniffed at her again. "You're nearly in heat." Her current situation helped things. Surely . . . surely . . . come on! His dick didn't stir at all. What the . . .

"Don't even think about it. You barbaric piece of shit."

Enough with the name calling. He needed to put his cards on the table, as the human saying went. "We should rut. I am a skilled lover. I have made humans weep from the sheer pleasure."

The human feigned a yawn. "Tell someone who cares. I wouldn't have sex with you if you were the last person left on the planet."

Again, another record for him. Candy had told him the exact same thing a couple of hours ago.

It was time to spell it out. This female may not want him but it didn't mean that she wasn't perfect for him. In fact, he would prefer to keep his feelings separate from his relationships going forward. "I am not looking for love." His chest ached. Damn . . . it hurt! "I"—he swallowed thickly, pausing for a moment—"we . . . could work. No love or any of the other emotions. Let's test compatibility. We could mate and procreate. I would look after you. It could be a win win." How could she possibly say no?

"More of the same bullshit!" She yelled, making him want to cover his ears. Then she choked out a hysterical sounding laugh. "You assholes are all the same. What's so wrong with love? Why don't you want it? Love is amazing. It's wonderful. To feel like that about another person is—" Her eyes filled with tears and his own eyes pricked, although he couldn't say why.

He hated the emotions coursing through him. He especially hated the voice that told him to go after Candy. To get on his knees and beg for forgiveness if that's what it took.

No!

Fuck that!

His resolve hardened. "Heartbreaking," His chest vibrated as he growled out the word. "To let someone else in enough to break you. No. It is a mistake. One I will not make again. Get on the bed. We are rutting now." He choked the words out.

"Heartbreaking." She looked up in thought. "Yeah, I suppose there's that too." She frowned and then her eyes widened and she seemed to realize something. "You don't want to have sex with me." Her eyes locked back with his.

She definitely had this bewildered look.

"I do," he rasped. There was only one way to get over Candy. Only one way to stop this pain. Surely? "You are almost in heat. You have a delectable scent." Pity his dick wasn't in the least bit interested. Torrent glanced out the window and then ran a hand through his hair. What the fuck was wrong with him? He sucked in a deep breath.

"You really don't." She spoke softly, carefully, like she was addressing a wounded animal.

Everything in him screamed to go after Candy. He clenched his teeth. His female didn't want him and after the way he had behaved, he couldn't blame her.

"What happened with Candy?"

He growled, it came out sounding wounded and anguished. It was over between them. He needed to face it. Move on! "I don't wish to discuss it. She is gone and you are here."

"Oh my god." She covered her hand with her mouth for a second. "You're in love with her."

Bullshit! His ego was bruised. Yeah, that was it. It was nothing more. "No. I feel nothing for her."

"Rubbish. What happened between the two of you? Maybe I can help." She folded her arms.

"It doesn't matter. She is gone. She's not coming back." He moved to the nearest sofa and sat down heavily. His shoulders were slumped. He probably looked like a complete loser but right now, he didn't give a fuck. Not even the tiniest of fucks.

"It wouldn't help, you know? Sex with me."

The human was right. She was completely, one hundred percent correct. There was no way he was having sex with anyone. Even if he wanted to, he couldn't. His body craved one female. One tiny human female. He swallowed hard. "I feel empty inside." Like someone had carved out his insides and replaced them with shards of glass. Sharp and cutting.

The human, Julie, took a step towards him. "Sex with me will only make you feel worse. When you finally stop moping and go after her, she might actually forgive you if you don't screw anyone else. You have no hope if you fool around with other people."

He lifted his gaze to her. "I don't wish to rut anyone but her. I am a fool. I won't go after her though. She made her decision when she left me."

It was your own fault.

You did this to yourself.

He clasped a hand to the back of his neck and squeezed his eyes shut, trying to get the voices to shut the hell up. Only because the voices were right.

"You really should put your pride aside and go after her. You have it really bad."

When he glanced at the female, she was smiling.

Put his pride aside? Go after Candy? To what end? She would just shoot him down again? "No." He shook his head. *It was your own fucking fault she left!* "I did something I should never have done. She won't forgive me for it." That heavy sensation became stifling. That cutting feeling worsened. It felt like he was being torn up inside.

"She will if she loves you," Julie whispered. He watched as several emotions crossed her face. This female had it bad for the fire prince. He was an idiot to ever think he could take her from the male. He was an idiot full stop.

Torrent shrugged, it was an effort to lift his shoulders. "Maybe." He sounded pathetic but it couldn't be helped. "I will think on it." He paused. "Would you like me to take you back now?" Coal would be happy to see his female. It gave him a small amount of solace and made him feel like a colossal dick for taking her in the first place. He vowed that if the male felt the need to hit him, he would take it. He deserved it.

Julie seemed to think on it for a few beats. "You can take me to Walton Springs. Do you know it?"

The pain intensified. "It is where Candy lives." His voice cracked as he said her name.

Her face became animated even though her eyes were sad. "I'll tell you what, drop me off and go after her. Two birds with one stone." She held up her fingers.

What was she saying? Crazy female. "You have given me advice and I feel that I need to do the same in return. Coal loves you."

She shook her head so that her long dark tresses flew about her face. "No. You're wrong. Do you know that he asked someone else to mate with him just the other day? He goes through women like I go through shoes. Not that he wears shoes but . . . you know what I mean." She mumbled the last part.

"I know that people make mistakes." He had made one.

A huge one. Fuck!

"He lied, a lot." She looked down at her lap and chewed on her lip. It was something Candy did too. *Stop thinking about her!*

He needed to fix things between Coal and the human. He'd taken Julie and he shouldn't have. "I don't know what happened between you two, but I do know what I saw. That male was a like a puppy dog on your heels—did I say that human saying correctly?" He raised his brows.

"Yes, it's only because his brother commanded him to mate me though and—"

"Nope." It was funny how people didn't see what was right in front of them. He shook his head. "He was desperate and needy. He is in love with you. It doesn't matter about previous females in his life or things he didn't tell you, probably to protect you. The male is desperately in love with you. He looked completely pathetic. Maybe it is better that Candy is gone." *It is better.* "I don't ever want to be that pathetic." *Too fucking late.* No!

She sort of smiled and then turned serious. "It's not better that she is gone and you know it."

It is better! Good riddance. She didn't want him. The human hadn't welcomed him to her bed but she had accepted money from human males. Why them and not him? Why? His chest hurt and he struggled to draw breath.

You know why! You deserved everything you got.

Fuck it!

"Are you ready to go?" His voice came out sounding gruffer than he intended.

She nodded once. He could see her shoulders relax. The female was deep in thought. Then she smiled and gave a small nod of the head. Coal was one lucky SOB.

"I take it I'm taking you back to the fire prince?" Torrent smiled, something lightened in him. At least things would work out for Julie. She was a sweet female. Clueless but sweet.

"How did you know I'd changed my mind?"

"You gave a little smile just now and your cheeks are flushed. I can tell that you were thinking about the male. It seems that you have it just as bad as he does."

She shook her head, preparing to deny it but sighed instead. Maybe not so clueless after all.

Torrent laughed and although she first rolled her eyes, she couldn't seem to help but to smile along with him. "Let us go." He put his hand on her shoulder as they walked towards the balcony.

The double doors leading to the balcony flew open. Glass exploded out as both panes of glass were obliterated. Coal stepped into the wide opening, taking up the whole space. He was a bundle of tension. Every muscle was corded. Smoke curled around him. Small flames erupted from his nose and mouth. His eyes were slitted. His frame enormous, his beast, barely contained within his human skin.

What was that he had promised himself earlier? Something about taking a punch or two if need be.

Fuck! He needed to explain and it needed to happen quickly.

Julie had the same idea because she sucked in a ragged breath.

The fire prince cut her off. He cut them both off. "Get your filthy hands off of my female!" His voice boomed. Shit, the male was pissed. There was more smoke and Torrent could see scales beneath the prince's skin. A whole bunch of them.

Torrent took his hand from the human's shoulder. All he needed to do was explain, Take a punch or two and Coal and Julie could be on their way. "I'm glad you are— "

Coal wouldn't allow him to speak. Torrent could see that he was barely holding it together. "Step away from him, Julie. Do it now." His words were barely understandable. More of a guttural bark than human speech. Shit! Coal was physically vibrating. His eyes slitted further

"No . . . you don't . . ." Julie pleaded, but Torrent could see that Coal wasn't listening. He was on the verge of attacking Torrent or erupting into dragon form. Or both. If either of those things happened, the human would be injured. Torrent had caused enough trouble for one day. He needed to let the male hit him a few times. Hopefully reason would return enough to stop him. If not, he would take it. He deserved it.

Torrent gave the human a light shove. He wanted her out of the way so that neither of them could harm her accidentally. From the corner of his eye, he saw her land in a heap to the right of them. She would hopefully be far enough away.

"You bastard!" Coal snarled as he leapt at him. The male wasn't thinking clearly. Torrent could have lifted a knee, or punched the male in the face using his own momentum against him but he refrained. Hopefully he wouldn't regret it. The force of the blow knocked him back.

"Wait!" Torrent shouted as regained his footing. Coal wasn't listening. *Shit!* "Let me—"

Flames erupted from Coal's throat. White hot. He felt his flesh char. He felt his hair singe. He felt so much pain that all he could do was roar and maybe pray. He could scent his own flesh burning. At long last Coal took a breath and the heat subsided. Torrent almost fell to his knees with relief. He could already feel his flesh begin to knit. It hurt like a bitch and he grimaced. His lips pulled tight and pain flared.

"The female is mine," Coal snarled.

"I was bringing her back!" Torrent shouted back, despite the pain of trying to talk.

Coal's eyes were wild. He still wasn't listening. Fuck! Torrent had to work hard to keep from retaliating.

You deserve it!

You hurt Candy.

He clenched his fists, wanting to stop Coal. Wanting to go after his female in the worst of ways but she wasn't his. She didn't want him. He was pathetic. He deserved to be hurt. If Coal incapacitated him, he wouldn't be able to go after Candy. Even if he wanted to. She didn't want him. He deserved everything that was coming his way.

The blow was sharp and so fucking hard that it almost put him on his ass. He both felt and heard his ribs snap. At least two. Fucking hurt! Must be three.

"Stop!" Julie shouted from somewhere in the distance.

"Wait," Torrent growled as Coal advanced. He couldn't see the human. If she tried to intervene she would be hurt.

"Coal. Stop it!" Julie shouted. She sounded far enough away. Thank fuck!

Torrent didn't even see the punch coming. He heard his nose crush and blood gushed down his throat. He staggered but managed to keep his footing. He was the water king. He was damned if he was going down quickly or easily.

Maybe the fire prince had calmed down sufficiently.

"Mine," Coal snarled. He didn't sound any calmer.

Torrent's eyes were almost swollen shut. Coal raised his bloodied fists and pummeled him. It didn't even hurt anymore. Not a good sign.

He heard more bones crack and felt his blood streaming down his face and chest. Hot and thick. It splattered on his feet.

You deserve it!

Lights flashed in front of his eyes, which were squeezed shut. Damn, also not a good sign. He staggered and fell to his knees.

Julie screamed. At least, he thought she did. He felt like he was down a dark tunnel. Deep down. Far removed from everything. He felt woozy and unstable. He felt numb.

The screaming intensified. Yes, it was definitely screaming. There was a loud snapping noise. It rang through him. It banged around in his skull for what felt like an age but was probably only a split second. Then everything went black.

CHAPTER 17

The dragon disappeared into the sky. It moved so quickly that her mind almost couldn't register it. If she hadn't known to look for it as it left, she might not have seen it at all.

She walked to the front of her house and just stood on her porch for a few minutes, taking in her surroundings. Home. It didn't feel like home. It didn't matter, she wasn't staying anyway. Candy pulled the wooden bench until it was in the right place. She climbed onto it. Using the tips of her fingers, she felt across the beam until her finger hit the key. Her spare. The one she had stuck up there almost three years ago when she'd moved out of her apartment and into this house. Just in case. Thank god she had.

She sighed with relief. Now all she had to do was grab her passport and identity document, pack a small bag and she'd be on her way. A shiver of fear ran up her spine. She reminded herself of how Ellis had just lain there on the floor. He'd looked broken. She didn't want him to be dead but she hoped that he was still incapacitated. She prayed hard that she wouldn't run into him. Not now, not ever again.

Please, no!

She took a couple of deep breaths. She was being silly. Ellis wasn't waiting for her. The back of her neck prickled despite the pep talk she'd just given herself.

Candy inserted the key into the lock and quickly let herself in, locking the door behind her. She put her back up against the door. She was safe while she was inside.

Her house was quiet. It smelled musty. "Shit!" she said. Her voice the only thing that sounded in the house. Her plants were brown and limp and dead. On the up side, it didn't feel like anyone had been in her space. She huffed out a breath.

Right, she needed to get packed and to get the hell out of this town. There was nothing left for her here. She felt a pang. If she left, Torrent wouldn't know where to look for her.

Stop it!

He wasn't coming for her. He was a huge asshole of epic proportions. Guys with egos like him didn't ever admit to being wrong. They blamed the other person. They didn't chase after anyone, nor did they apologize. It wasn't going to happen. Even if it did . . . by some small miracle . . . there was no way she could ever forgive him. He'd hurt her too badly. Candy had spilled her guts to him and he'd really hurt her.

To think that he expected her to just jump into bed with him when he presented her with jewelry. She could see he was hurting and angry but it was no excuse. Sky had been wrong, he was never going to be able to get over her past. He was the biggest damned hypocrite alive. She wasn't going to think about him again.

Not ever!

It floored her how he could be so kind and loving and so cruel. Why had he done it? What had gone through his mind?

No!

She wasn't thinking about this. It hurt too much. So much so that she struggled to breathe. A sob left her and she covered her mouth and squeezed her eyes shut. It was done. She wasn't about to cry. Torrent didn't deserve her tears. Asshole.

She pushed off the door and walked to her bedroom. She needed to busy herself with packing. First things first, she opened the safe. It contained her documents and a diamond tennis bracelet that Charles had given to her. She wore it from time to time when she was with him. It hurt just looking at the piece of jewelry. It made her think of Torrent . . . the asshole. She put the bracelet back in the safe. If only she'd thought to leave some money in there.

Her bank cards and cash had been in her handbag when she was taken. The bag that was lying on the ground next to the car. The one she had dropped when Ellis had man-handled her.

She would need to walk into town. She could withdraw money inside the bank and catch the next bus out of town. She'd didn't care where it was headed, as long as she was on it.

The walk into town was a good couple of miles. Best she pack light. She'd think about her future when she was far enough away and able to actually think straight.

Candy pulled out a wheely bag. It was more of an overnight bag but she folded her garments carefully and got three changes of clothes and her toiletry bag into it. She changed into jeans and a t-shirt, tying a sweater around her waist. Then she put on a pair of sneakers. After a quick trip to the bathroom, she grabbed the bag and left, locking the door behind her. She'd get ahold of her landlord and give notice. She'd have to organize for the rest of her things to be removed. Her head hurt.

Not thinking about this now!

One step at a time. Get to town. Withdraw money. Get out of town. Easy. She put one foot in front of the other. Everything was going to be just fine. Candy swallowed hard, trying not to cry. She didn't need anyone in her life. She certainly didn't need an asshole like . . . him. Not saying his name.

Torrent.

She pictured his blond hair, his pale eyes. She pictured his easy smile. Her body could still recall how good it felt being wrapped up in his arms. How safe she had felt. For the first time in her life she'd felt like someone really cared about her. If that was true, he would never have said those things. He would never have hurt her in that way.

She was so lost in her thoughts that she never heard the car approach.

She started when she heard his voice. "Get into the car,

Candy."

She didn't have to look. She knew that voice almost as well as she knew her own. She recognized the convertible. Candy ignored him and kept on walking.

"Get in," Ellis said, louder this time.

"Leave me alone." She kept her eyes on the road ahead. That prickling sensation at the back of her neck. He was watching. How long had he been staked out outside her house?

"Stop being a child and get in the car." He sounded irritated.

"Leave me the hell alone." She glanced his way.

His jaw was set. His eyes hard. Damn! He wasn't going to let her go.

"I don't want anything to do with you. Please, Ellis." She hated to beg but she didn't feel like she had a choice. They were in public, a residential area. Surely he wouldn't hurt her out here. "I told you that I want out. I meant it. Let me go."

"You're my best girl." His voice had a mocking edge. "Why would I do a stupid thing like that? Get in the damn car."

"No." She picked up the pace. Maybe she should head down one of the drives. Too risky, she would cut off her escape route if no one was home.

Ellis huffed out a breath and slammed his hand against the steering wheel. She noticed that his other wrist was in a brace of some kind. "Get your fucking ass in the car."

To hell with it. She dropped the bag and began to run,

going in the opposite direction. Her key was still in her pocket. Maybe if she made it back to her house.

Her whole body shook from both the exertion and the fear that coursed through her. Ellis was a big guy. He was well muscled and he was a psycho. He didn't give two shits about her. He would pump her full of drugs and not give it a second thought. Or he would find a way to coerce and threaten her into doing exactly what he wanted.

Her hand shook as she pushed the key into the lock. *Please. Please.* The hairs stood up on the back of her neck. She yanked the door open and closed it in his face. It was contorted in rage. She just turned the lock in time. Not even a split second to spare.

She sank to her knees. Tears coursed down her face.

Shards of glass flew in through the window and there was a loud crash and the sound of something else breaking. It took her a second or two to register that Ellis had thrown something through her window.

Her mouth fell open. He was crazier than she had first thought. She jumped to her feet and ran for the bathroom. Maybe if she could lock herself in there. The window was too small for him to get in through. She screamed as she ran. Hopefully one of her neighbors would hear the commotion and call the police. She tripped over her own feet and almost fell. Candy staggered and pushed on.

She just got her hand on the doorknob when she was yanked back by her ponytail. She tried to scream but Ellis clamped a hand over her mouth. "You've been a bad girl." He was breathing hard. "Hiring someone to take me out."

He shook his head. "Well, they did a bad job princess and you should've stayed lost. Did I ever mention that some of my clients have rape fetishes?"

She moaned, the sound smothered behind his fingers.

"They pay excellent money for girls willing to pretend. I wonder what they would be willing to put down for the real thing." Ellis laughed and her blood ran cold.

CHAPTER 18

Torrent sat upright and sucked in a breath. It hurt like a bitch. Coming back from the dead was a favorite past time of his . . . not! He pulled in some more air, being careful this time. His chest burned. Everything ached.

His nostrils flared as he picked up her scent. Candy. His female. His. It was her lingering scent on the sheets. She wasn't here anymore. His female was gone.

No, not his. Not anymore. She never had been. Pain flooded him and he moaned. It was internal pain and it was way worse than anything physical he had ever felt.

Torrent slumped back into his blankets and pillows.

"I'm so glad you are awake." It was Sky. The female hovered around him. She tucked in a sheet and poured a glass of water. "Drink this, my lord."

Torrent growled from the pain as he turned over onto his side. "Leave me." He didn't want to see her or anyone else for that matter.

'You need to drink and to eat. You also need to be eased, it will help the healing process. Shall I call Ocean? Another female?" She sounded angry. Her voice was hard and devoid of emotion.

"No," he choked out. "Put the water on the table and go away. I don't want to be disturbed."

"Oh." There was a tapping noise and he realized that it was her foot against the floor. *Tap, tap, tap.* "So you're just going to lie there and wallow in self pity? Whatever you said, or did, to that female, it had to have been really terrible for her to have left."

Torrent grumbled below his breath.

"She was so afraid to talk to you. I told her that you would accept her and forget her past. I was sure you would . . . never mind. I was clearly wrong."

"Do you know then? Did she tell you?"

"No! It was between the two of you." She began to walk away and then changed her mind and turned back. "She was ready to take the next step. That female loved you."

"No, she didn't," he snarled. "She didn't want me as a mate. That much was clear. No wonder I became angry. No one would blame me for my actions."

"What did you do?" There was a rustling noise and when he turned around she had her arms folded. *Tap, tap, tap.* That damned foot again.

"Did you know that Candy sold her body to human males for money?" He immediately felt guilty for divulging something so personal. "If you ever mention this to another soul . . ."

Sky lifted a hand. "I'm Candy's friend. That piece of information doesn't change anything. I still like her and respect her. What difference does it make? We are highly sexual creatures. As long as she is faithful to you going forward, as long as she loves only you. So what if there are others in her past?"

"Money. She took money." He sounded like an idiot.

Sky narrowed her eyes on him. "I'm sure she had her reasons."

She did! He didn't say anything.

"So you are angry that she rutted other males?" Sky rolled her eyes and huffed out a breath. "Do you know how stupid that sounds? What about you? How many females have you bedded? Hundreds? Thousands?"

"Not thousands." He choked out, looking down at the sheet.

"You're jealous. It's as simple as that. I hope you realize it. You were jealous and did something stupid."

"I did not," he mumbled. There was no conviction behind his words. It didn't matter what Sky thought. "My reaction was completely justified."

"I know you did something idiotic, because that human would never have left otherwise, she was too in love with your sorry ass to just up and leave."

"I am your king." He tried to sit up but everything hurt too much. "You will not address me in that way. I'm done listening to your bullshit." He sucked in a deep breath. "Candy didn't love me. She didn't want me."

"Of course she did." Sky gave him a small smile. "She told me so herself. She didn't rut you *because* she loves you."

"That doesn't make sense."

"She wanted things to be right between you first. She wanted to come clean about her past and she wanted you to accept her despite it. You couldn't do that."

"I was so angry. So upset. The thought of her with . . ." he cursed. "Dammit, maybe I was jealous. I've never been jealous. I've never experienced the emotion before. I . . ."

"You love her, my king. You need to make things right with her."

He shook his head. He could remember the look in her eyes. He'd broken her heart. Acted like a complete asshole and had ruined everything. "It's too late."

She shook her head. "You will need to grovel long and hard but I'm sure that she will forgive you in the end."

"How can you be so sure?" He could hear the anguish in his voice but it couldn't be helped.

"Because she loves you." Sky yelled, sounding frustrated. She smiled. "Don't make me keep repeating myself, my lord."

"You're right." A huge load lifted off of him. Even if it took years. He didn't care. He would win Candy back. He would make it up to her. Torrent moved into a sitting position. His head spun.

His neck hurt. Coal had snapped it, no doubt. His face blossomed with pain, as did his chest. The fire prince had done a number on him. That was for sure. *Little shit!* He was lucky Torrent hadn't fought back.

Sky touched the side of his arm lightly. Pain blossomed there also. His flesh was still healing from the burns.

Torrent groaned.

"Lie back down." Her voice was soothing.

"No! I need to fetch my female," he growled.

"Coal sends his deepest regrets, he is sorry he did this to you. He publicly acknowledged that you allowed him to win and has already sent a male to fetch Candy. He said that it was the least he could do. He may have mentioned that Candy might feel sorry for you in your current state. It would be wise to allow him to bring her right away."

The fire prince was lucky Torrent was a forgiving male. "Fine," he said. Torrent could feel sweat bead on his brow. "Okay." He fell back. "I'll have some of that water now." He needed to try and heal. After the beating he'd received, he probably looked grotesque. He didn't want to scare Candy. Especially since she couldn't handle the sight of blood. He needed to look banged up but not hideous.

It was important that he start thinking of ways to win her back. Candy had been right to call him an asshole. Sky and Julie were right on the money as well. Torrent would prove himself worthy. She would forgive him. She had to. He drank some of the water and then closed his eyes. The sooner he healed, the better.

Her hands were bound at the wrists.

"Your first client is on his way." Ellis winked at her. "Are you sure you don't want to change your mind? The good senator was most upset when he heard that you weren't taking on any new clients after all. He offered more money." He paused. "More than we'll get from this pretend rape."

"It won't be pretend. I can't believe you're doing this." Tears caused her throat to clog but she refused to let them fall. A guy like Ellis would get a kick out of seeing her upset.

"Believe it, baby. Do you really think I'd just let you walk away?" He walked to the other side of the room. "You're a damned gold mine, Candy." He snorted out a laugh. "Even your god given name is a hooker name for god sake."

"I can't help it my mom is a hippy."

"I can't help it you're in such demand. By the way, Charles died."

"What?" Her voice was laced with shock. "Don't lie to me, Ellis." Charles was her longest client. They had sex on occasion but he mainly just wanted to spend time with her. He'd cried the first time he had been intimate with her. The old guy still loved his wife. He spoke of her all the time. Charles was gone?

"How? When? You're lying, Ellis."

"I'm not lying. He died in his sleep. Someone called looking for you." Ellis laughed. He looked more relaxed. Maybe she could negotiate with him. She didn't believe that Ellis would really go through with this whole rape thing. He was just trying to scare her into doing what he wanted. "Looks like the old geyser left you something in his will."

Candy bit down on her lip. Charles was a really sweet man. A gentleman. He and his late wife didn't have any children. His wife, Beatrice, was unable to conceive. It didn't change the way he felt about her. It did mean that he didn't have anyone to leave his fortune to. Surely he didn't leave it to her. That would be crazy. No way!

"We're going to go to the lawyer's office first thing in the morning. I knew you were going to make me a rich man." He rubbed his hands together.

"You can't be serious. I'm sure Charles didn't leave me much."

Ellis looked thoughtful. "I think he left it all to you. His tight piece of ass. If that's the case, we're getting hitched, baby." He winked at her.

"What?" She looked at him in disbelief. "You're crazy."

"Crazy for you." There was a knock at the door. "It's show time, babe." He opened the drawer and rummaged through it, pulling out some tape.

Shit! Maybe he did mean it or was this another ploy. Him taking it a step further. "Don't do this, Ellis. If Charles left me anything . . ." She felt desperation set in. "I'll give it to you. I don't care about the money. I have enough." She was breathing hard, trying not to lose it. "Just let me go, please."

"There's no such thing as enough money." Ellis nodded, looking thoughtful. "I've made up my mind. I think I'm going to enjoy watching you get broken in . . . for me." He winked at her. "My soon to be wife."

"You're crazy." He was. She could see it in his eyes. Ellis was evil and not all there.

"Just so you know upfront, our marriage won't be

exclusive. I get to fuck other women and you are definitely going to fuck other guys." By the bulge in his pants, she could see that he was hard. Not only evil and crazy, it turned out he was sick as well.

He pulled the tape and broke off a piece using his teeth. Then he kneeled beside her. Candy turned her head away, trying to avoid him but Ellis gripped her by the jaw with his good arm and slapped the tape over her mouth. He pushed down hard.

"Just remember," he whispered against her ear. "The harder you fight, the more he'll enjoy it. This guy is a freak."

Pure terror gripped her. Her nostrils were wide as she struggled to breathe. She fought against her restraints until her hands felt raw.

Ellis opened the door. She heard him greet someone. Then footsteps. "She's ready for you," he said.

"Do you have a pair of scissors like I asked?" she heard the guy say.

"Yeah, but"—Ellis paused—"I'm not so sure . . ."

The stranger laughed. "Don't worry, I won't hurt her . . . I like to cut off their clothes."

Oh god! This wasn't happening.

"No hitting or biting." Of course not. Ellis would hate to see one of his merchandise items broken.

The guy chuckled as they entered the bedroom. Candy was on the floor. The guy was really short, and skinny. His hair was thinning on the top. His whole look screamed nerd. His eyes widened as he spotted her. She read excitement in their depths.

"Shit!" He sighed. "Her eyes. Oh man!" He put a hand over his mouth. "Look at that fear. I could almost swear this was real."

"You paid good money so you got my best." Ellis leaned against the door and folded his legs across each other, looking so relaxed. "Oh, I need to give you this." He threw the guy a bottle and she realized that it was lube. Then he handed the guy a string of condoms.

Candy felt ill.

"I know you're going to be rough and I wouldn't want you to tear or bruise her. You have to wear a condom. No glove no love." He laughed at his own joke.

The guy nodded, looking enthusiastic. "Sure thing. I'll use the lube and the condom. No problem."

"One last thing." Ellis smiled. "I'm staying . . . just to be sure."

"What?" The guy didn't look happy.

"I'm staying," Ellis repeated. "I'm watching."

The guy shook his head. "I don't know if . . ."

"I can't leave my best girl with you, like this." He pointed up and down the length of her. "You wanted her tied up and gagged. No problem but I wouldn't be able to hear her shout for help if you got a little rough. I need to stay and watch."

Sick bastard! They were both sick but Ellis took the cake.

"You can pretend we're a tag team or something."

"I don't like to share." The guy sounded whiney.

There was a tic in Ellis' jaw and for a second she thought he might throw the guy out. *Please, please.* Then he smiled. "I don't want in on the action, I just want to watch. Forget I'm even here. I'll give you a discount for the inconvenience."

The nerdy guy seemed agreeable and they haggled over price. Candy swallowed hard, trying not to puke. Maybe if she peed herself. The guy put his beady eyes on her and she realized that nothing would deter him. In fact, if she fought him or peed herself, it would probably turn him on more.

"I like to play a bit with them first. I won't hurt her though." He picked up the scissors and tested them. The blades flashed as they opened and closed, making slicing noises.

"Knock yourself out." Ellis took a seat. "Touch a hair on her head though and you will regret it."

"I would never hurt her."

The nerdy guy turned towards her. "It's time to play." He smiled. His eyes looked dead. She couldn't help but notice that he wasn't in the least bit turned on. This guy was sick with a capital S. He took a step towards her and she couldn't help herself. She screamed. The sound was held back by the tape.

Then she wriggled and tried to get up onto her feet, which were tied with a cable tie. The sicko's eyes gleamed and his smiled widened. To her horror, the start of a hard-on lined his pants.

CHAPTER 19

I t felt like the walls were closing in. That everything was spinning. "What?" Torrent roared.

"Lie down, my lord." Sky tried to push him back down. "You are in no condition."

"I have to agree with Sky," his brother boomed. "I will take a team of males. I will find her."

"No." Torrent lurched to his feet. He felt like a day old lamb. "I will find her myself. She is mine." The world spun harder, he gripped his brother's shoulder to stay on his feet.

"You won't be able to shift. You were dead a couple of hours ago." Tide looked at him with concern. "Even if you do make the shift, you might not be able to stay in dragon form for the flight. If you shifted at thirty thousand feet, the fall just might kill you for real."

"It won't happen." His head cleared somewhat. "Not with this amount of adrenaline in my veins." He pulled his shoulders back and locked eyes with Tide.

His brother shook his head. "It's a bad idea."

Torrent grit his teeth. "I have to go. She is my female.

Mine."

"I understand your—"

"No you don't. You have no clue. We're wasting time arguing. Bring the fire dragon to me. I want the details first hand." When no one moved, he shouted. "Now!" Smoke wafted from his nose and mouth. If he had been a fire dragon, there would have been flames.

"Maybe you're not as weak as I thought." Tide turned and left.

Torrent was still royally fucked up. His bones were only half knitted and his skin was still pink and even still raw in places. The biggest problem was the lack of energy. It was a pity Coal had killed him. It always sapped a male and made the healing process that much slower. He would deal. His female needed him.

Within minutes, his brother returned with the fire Dragon. "Good day." The male nodded. "I am Heat. I was the male tasked with fetching your female. I was given her address, a description and was told to bring her back here to the water lair."

Torrent grit his teeth, having to work hard at remaining patient. He wanted to grip the male by the throat and demand answers. Since he knew that this wouldn't help, he kept silent, at least for the time being.

"When I arrived at Candy's house, the human protectors were there. There was a vehicle parked out front, lights flashing. There were two protectors inside of her house. One of them held a suitcase and was talking with an older human female."

"Go on." Torrent growled, patience waning by the second.

"The older female lived across the road. The human protector was busy questioning her. The suitcase belonged to your female. She was walking on foot, with the suitcase when a male pulled up in a vehicle next to her. He was driving one of those roofless cars, I can't recall the name of such a vehicle . . ." He lifted his eyes in thought.

"It doesn't matter," Torrent snarled. "My female is in danger. Give us the facts and do so now."

The fire dragon nodded. His throat worked and there was a sheen of sweat on his brow. It was the only outward indication of fear. "It seems that the human female that lives across the road from your female is very interested in what goes on in the area. She heard Candy's house door slam and watched her leave her home. The human male chased Candy soon afterwards. She dropped the suitcase in her attempt to get away. He broke into her house and physically removed her. At this stage, her hands were tied and it looked like he was threatening her as he pushed her into his car and sped off. The window to her house was smashed. She did not seem to be injured in any way. The human was too afraid to intervene but she called the protectors immediately. She—"

Torrent could not withhold his rage any longer. He roared. His fists were clenched so tight that his nails dug into his skin. Adrenaline coursed through him. It felt like his scales were rubbing him raw and his teeth erupted.

The fire dragon took a step back. "I would be happy to

assist with any rescue operation."

"The female was unharmed and very little time has passed since she was taken. We need to assemble a team." Tide was the vision of calm. His brother's demenor and words helped calm him as well . . . somewhat.

Torrent nodded. "No more than two males, as well as yourself and the fire dragon." He glanced at the male.

The fire dragon nodded. "It would be an honor."

Torrent clasped his hands in front of him, he looked his brother in the eyes. "There is no time to waste. I'm going to leave ahead of the team. The male's name is Ellis. Candy used to work for him at a place called Kitty's. I'm not sure where it is but I plan on finding out. Sky . . ." He called to the she-dragon who came running.

Her eyes were wide, they were filled with tears. "Yes, my lord."

"Do not concern yourself." His voice shook but it couldn't be helped. Torrent had never experienced fear before. Not like this. To his very core. Like a living and breathing thing. "I will bring Candy back." He touched the side of her arm. Her lip quivered but she pulled her shoulders back and nodded. "Where is my cell phone? I'll need to research this male, this Kitty's establishment. Brother?" A low bark.

"Yes." Tide stepped in beside him.

"Take your cellular device. Call me when you reach Walton Springs." He huffed out a breath. "I should have all the details by then."

"I would urge you to wait the ten minutes that it will

take me—"

"No!" He snarled. Torrent had waited long enough. His female's life lay in the balance. He could feel it.

Sky returned moments later with his phone. It had been placed in a ziplock bag. He would thank Sky properly later. Phone in mouth, he erupted into his Dragon form and left without a second to spare

"We'll be right behind you." Tide bellowed as he flapped his wings.

Everything ached but he didn't give a shit. He tried to clear his mind. The only thing he could do was concentrate on his female. On her face, her eyes, her lovely smile . . . the one she saved just for him. It was because she loved him. Sky was right. What a fool he had been. What an utter fool. He only hoped he got the opportunity to apologize.

Hang on, Candy.

I'm coming for you. Just hang on!

An anguished wail was torn from him. She had to be okay, she just had to be. That male was going to wish he had never been born.

CHAPTER 20

The freak leaned in next to her, still holding the scissors. His breath was coming in tight gasps. His eyes were wide and his cheeks flushed with excitement. She tried to worm away from him but he grabbed her by the leg and yanked her back. His grip was surprisingly strong for such a scrawny guy. "Stay still. I don't want to cut you." His voice was unnaturally feminine sounding with a nasal edge. It made her skin crawl. Everything about this guy made her skin crawl.

He moved to her ankles, bringing the scissors down to the bottom of her jeans. He obviously planned on cutting them off. As he brought the scissors further down, she kicked out with both legs and knocked them from his hands.

"Owwww." A long drawn out whine. "Quit doing that." He gave her a wink, like suddenly it was okay for her to play along with him or something. He thought that this was all an act. He expected her to play along. Tough freak'n luck. This might be a game to him but it sure as hell wasn't to her. The nerd leaned over, grabbed the scissors and moved back to her ankles.

As he got close, she kicked him again, harder this time. He narrowed his eyes. "I said to quit it." His voice was even more nasally this time round. "Tell your girl to stop messing around." He glanced at Ellis who had made himself comfortable on one of the chairs in the corner.

Ellis held up his hands. "Hey, I'm not even here remember? You said you wanted authentic. That's about as authentic as you're gonna get." He pointed in her direction. "No rape victim is going to just play along."

The nerd huffed out a breath. "But you said I can't hurt her. If this was a real rape, I'd punch her or cut her a little. I'd get her to cooperate."

"You can't break or damage the mechandise. I don't want you bruising or tearing her pussy either but you can hurt her a little." Ellis shrugged.

Bastard! She made a moaning noise which made Ellis smile in her direction.

The nerd didn't even notice the exchange, he was too busy getting all excited for that. "I can?" His chest was heaving now. He was clenching and unclenching his fists. His voice was singsong.

Ellis smiled. "That's what I said."

He was such a dick! What was wrong with people? It was a question she asked herself more than once. What the hell was wrong with society?

This was a world in which children were abandoned, abused and murdered. Ghandi had once said that you could tell the quality of a nation by how it looked after its animals and she'd been to the shelters. Cages overflowing with unwanted pets. All of those innocent eyes staring back at her, begging for some sort of affection. For love of any kind. Many of them would never leave. Not alive anyway. It was heartbreaking.

Tears were streaming down her cheeks and she shook her head as the freak moved back to her ankles. "Now . . ." His voice vibrated with excitement. "Are you going to be a good little girl or am I going to have to teach you some manners?"

There was no way she was going to just lie there and take it. She gave a nod, feigning acceptance.

"That's a good, little—" He began to say, but at the last second, she kicked out. He yelled out in pain and anger. The guy moved much quicker than she expected. He gripped her hair and pulled hard. He pulled until she was sure it was going to come out by the roots. He pulled until pain surrounded her and filled her. Until she became one with it.

Her head thudded softly against the wooden floor as he released her. She could feel him tugging on her pants, could feel the cold steel from the scissors as he worked his way up her leg. She was too afraid to move in case a sharp edge caught her.

Her scalp throbbed with every beat of her heart. Unfortunately, her heart was beating fast so her head hurt badly. Then his hands were on her. He rubbed up and down her leg and squeezed her thigh. He'd cut most of the way up her thigh but had stopped just short of going all the way.

She forced herself to open her eyes and moaned in frustration and irritation. This seemed to egg him on. He squeezed her thigh harder, almost to the point of pain. "I can't wait to fuck you real good. Show you what a real man can do."

Right. If he was any type of real man he wouldn't be doing this. He might be 'playing pretend,' but he was sick just the same. That much was apparent.

He moved up, his eyes glued to her chest. No you don't, asswipe! When he leaned forward, intent on cutting her T-shirt, she head butted him in the face. There was a cracking noise and his nose began to gush.

"What the fuck!" He cocked back his fist, his face pulled into a sneer.

"Don't you dare." Ellis warned, trying to make himself sound gruff, even though she could hear he was smiling. He was loving every minute of this. Sick son of a bitch that he was.

"She broke my fucking nose," the guy whined.

"You told me you wanted authentic. Are you changing your mind? Is a tied up woman too much for you to handle?"

The freak narrowed his eyes on her for a long while. His jaw tightened and he nodded once. "No! I'm game."

Her heart sank.

"Get cleaned up and rape the bitch already." Ellis sounded bored.

The guy nodded and disappeared into the bathroom.

Ellis chuckled once the freak was out of earshot. "This is the most fun I've had in a long while. I'm actually rooting for you, Candy. I'm not sure this loser can even get it up." He shook his head.

All too soon, the guy was back. His nose was a little puffy and he plugged it up with some wadded up tissue paper to stop the bleeding. He looked pathetic.

"I'm done playing." His voice was cold, his eyes hard. Before she could do anything, he gripped her throat, holding her down. She felt a weight on her middle. His knee maybe? She struggled to take in enough air. Candy could feel the cold of the blade as it glided up her torso. She could hear the snip, snip as it cut her t-shirt. Her arms hurt because they were being crushed beneath her body.

Her eyes were wide. Her nostrils flared as she tried to take in air. Her vision became blurry. She needed air. Needed it now. Black patches danced in her vision. She struggled to see, to think. Needed air.

His hand came off of her neck and his knee lifted. Candy sucked in a deep breath. Her legs fell open. No, he'd cut the cable that bound them. She sucked in another hard breath. Her zipper was being yanked down and he was pulling on her jeans, making groaning noises from the exertion.

She was fighting to get enough air into her lungs so that she could move. So that she could fight. Her vision was still blurred and her body felt so weak.

She kicked at him but he slapped her leg away. Her pants were about halfway down her thighs when her vision began to return.

"No fight left, girly." He said, his voice even more nasally than before. He stroked his fully erect dick through his pants. "I'm looking forward to this." He sickend her. As in, a wave of nausea rolled through her and she had to suck in air to try and quell it. The last thing she needed to do was vomit with her mouth taped shut.

Candy kept on sucking in air through her nose. The worst of the nausea subsided. She was biding her time. If this dickhead thought that she was done fighting, he was dead wrong.

He grabbed ahold of her jeans and gave another hard tug. Thankfully, her underwear was still in place, as was her bra. Candy bent her knees to stop the garment from going down much.

"Stop that." The freak moaned. "I'm done playing." He gave her pants another yank and she twisted her body, bending her knees again. His entire focus was on getting her jeans off. The freak moved in close, his legs splayed. If she could just move a little to the right, then she'd have a clean shot. One well placed kick to the balls would put him down for a while. He might not feel like sex anymore. At least not today.

Just a little more. She twisted . . .

There was a loud crashing noise. It was like one of the walls had fallen down or something. The crash was followed by a loud roar. It shook the walls, the very foundation. The door to the room they were in was next. It splintered inwards, a couple of shards landed on her.

The freak brought up his arm to shield his face.

"What the fuck!" Ellis leapt from the chair. Shards of wood splinters were in his hair.

The freak's eyes widened and he sucked in a deep breath.

That's when she saw him. It was Torrent. Oh god! She'd never been more happy to see someone in her whole entire life. His eyes were bright blue slits. His teeth sharp and deadly looking. His lip curled away from them as he snarled. Although he was mostly man, it was easy to see the animal in him. His muscles bulged. His skin looked like it might burst from trying to contain him. In this moment, Torrent looked larger than life. He looked completely savage.

The freak turned all the way around. Still on his knees. He made a whimpering noise. He probably didn't know what he was seeing. A huge, pissed naked guy had just broken his way into the room. He whimpered again as Torrent picked him up by his neck in an almost gentle hold. The freak kicked his legs, like he was running in mid air. It reminded her of a puppet. His actions jerky.

The hold Torrent had on him was anything but gentle judging by how the guy began to choke. Loud gagging sounds that would've sounded revolting had they been coming from anyone else.

In an almost casual fashion, his eyes still locked with the freak's, Torrent reached between the guys legs and he squeezed . . . hard.

There was a strange popping noise. It was a sound she'd

never heard before. One she hoped never to hear again. Torrent dropped him and he fell into a screaming heap. His hands clasped between his legs. The screams spoke of a depth of agony she never knew existed.

She wanted to feel sorry for him but couldn't muster even the tiniest bit of sympathy. The guy was sick and depraved and in the worst of ways. From between his clasped fingers, blood blossomed, the stain spreading across his cream coloured chinos. His face was a bright red.

Ellis had his back against the wall, his hands in front of him. "Name your price." When Torrent took a step towards him, he began to beg. "Don't hurt me. Please. Do you want the girl? She's yours. Anything just—"

"She is not yours to give." Torrent growled, not sounding quite human.

"What do you want then? Anything. Name it." He was crying, snot ran from his nose and spittle flew from his mouth. "Please . . . just . . ." He shook his head, holding his hands out like a shield. Like they could somehow keep Torrent back. Ellis glanced to where the freak lay, then moved back to Torrent and then to Candy. "Help me! You owe me. You owe me, Candy."

She shook her head, trying hard to convey her thoughts. *No, I don't!*

He looked back up at Torrent. "What do you want? Surely there's something. Everyone has a price."

"I want you dead." There was no warning. No more talking. No discussions. Torrent smashed his fist through

Ellis' chest. She could hear his bones crack and break. There was a slurping noise and Torrent pulled back, Ellis' heart was clasped in his hand. It was still beating.

Ellis looked down at the heart. There was a look of shock on his face. He looked back up at Torrent. He tried to speak but his mouth would only open and close, blood trickled from between his lips. The heart in Torrent's hand gave a shudder and stopped. Then Ellis fell to the floor . . . dead.

Torrent dropped the heart and turned towards her. His face suddenly looked ashen. For the first time, she noticed that his nose was swollen with black bruises beneath his eyes. His chest, parts of his stomach and arms had peeling skin. Some parts were pink and puckered, others raw and open. He fell to one knee. "Candy," he groaned her name.

Not for the first time today, she fought against the rope that bound her arms behind her back. She moaned against the tape that covered her mouth.

Torrent fell face first onto the hard floor. The only thing that kept her from losing it completely was the sight of his chest as it rose and fell.

Early hours of the next morning . . .

Torrent tried to open his eyes for the umpteenth time and failed. He felt a momentary panic that quickly subsided. What was wrong with him?

Nothing.

Everything was fine.

The voices had woken him. Although woken was not the right word since he wasn't truly awake. Roused—yes, better, there were voices that had roused him. Females. He tried to make out what they were saying. "I need to see him for myself." Her voice was far away. Like it was being projected through water or even something more viscous. Like molasses or syryp. Who was the female that spoke? He knew that voice. Just as an image began to form in his mind he lost it. It wafted away like smoke and a light breeze.

Torrent felt warm. He was so tired. More tired than he'd ever felt before.

There was more chatter but it was too far away. He buried himself deeper in the covers. Breathed in her sweet scent and allowed himself to be drawn back into sleep. There was a scratching on the edge of his mind. Something his subconcious was trying to make him remember but he was too exhausted to even try and think what that something could be.

"Let me in." More insistant.

"He needs his rest." A mere whisper but closer this time.

"I won't disturb him. I saw how he looked when he"— her voice broke—"saved me." The nagging redoubled. The prickling sensation grew. It made his head hurt. It made his gut churn.

Candy.

If she was speaking to someone then she wasn't in bed with him. Why wasn't she in bed with him?

"The healers said that he needs his rest. Try to understand." The voice was laced with concern, it held a soothing tone.

"Please." His female. It was her. His Candy.

Torrent tried to call her name. He made a croaking sound and his hands gripped the covers.

"Oh no!" The female whispered. "You must go. You can come back later."

No! He needed his female. Something bad had happened. Something terrible. He couldn't remember what. Calling on all his strength he possessed, he tried to will his eyes to open, to make his body move. His legs jerked and there was a ripping noise.

"I'm not going anywhere. I need to be sure that he's going to be okay." Candy whispered. "Let me sit with him a while, at least until he calms down."

"You're aggravating him. Just look at him." It was Sky.

"Candy!" Torrent roared her name as he finally managed to break from his deep sleep. He felt groggy. Every muscle ached. His chest burned with every breath and it hurt to turn his head.

It took a few seconds for his eyes to adjust to the dim candle light.

"No. Let me go." Sky was in the process of dragging Candy out of the room.

"Let her go." His voice was a dry rasp, hardly recognizable as his own.

Sky turned her head. "My lord," she all but whispered. "You should be sleeping. The healers gave you a draught."

Ah, the reason his head was so groggy and why he felt so woozy. It didn't account for his pain.

"You were badly beaten and expended far too much energy saving Candy." The she-dragon hugged his female tightly around her shoulders. Her eyes filled with tears. "I'm glad that you did but the healers have given strict instructions that you remain asleep for at least twenty-four hours. That was sixteen hours ago. It's far too soon for you to be awake."

"I don't care." He pulled the covers to the side and got as far as throwing a leg over the side of the bed. When he tried to lift his torso, the world seemed to turn on it's axis. Torrent groaned. He locked eyes with Candy who was openly crying. She didn't make a single sound but tears coursed down her cheeks. It made him sad to see her so upset.

He called her name and held a hand out to her. He had no energy. Memories of what had happened threatened to overtake him but he pushed them down. He couldn't deal with it right now. His brain was fogging over and he struggled to stay concious. He sucked in a few deep breaths and began to feel a bit better.

Sky rolled her eyes and shook her head, she tsked like a mother hen but she also let Candy go.

His female walked to him, taking small tentative steps. When she was close enough, he pulled her into bed with him. She came willingly, curling her small body against his side. Torrent wrapped his arms around her. "Are you hurt?"

"No." Her body shook and shuddered.

"Are you sure?" His limbs felt heavy. Now that she was in his arms, he was struggling to stay awake. The medicine the healers had givem him was taking its toll. "Are you okay?"

"I am now."

"You're safe." He managed to push out just before sleep took him.

CHAPTER 21

C andy struggled to sleep. It felt so good to be in his arms again. It would be so easy to just forget everything that had happened. Every hurtful word he'd said to her and just go on as if nothing were wrong.

Soon after Torrent had saved her and subsequently lost consciousness, a small group of dragons had arrived. There was a big guy amongst them, he had ash-blond hair and the same pale blue eyes as Torrent. It was easy to see that he was in command. His chest markings were golden with green streaks. He barked orders and saw to Torrent himself, carrying him back to the water castle. She later learned that his name was Tide and that he was Torrent's younger brother. Only one year his junior. Aside from their hair color being slightly different, they were carbon copies of one another. The news came as no surprise. He was polite to her but didn't speak much with her either.

She was taken to her original room. The one she'd stayed in her first few days there, before moving in with Torrent. Sky came to see her. She'd filled Candy in on the events that had taken place.

Candy was torn. On the one hand she was still very upset with Torrent and had still wanted nothing more to do with him, yet on the other, she needed to make sure that he pulled through okay. Sky assured her over and over again that he would be fine but she needed to see it with her own eyes. The thing she needed the most though was to thank him for rescuing her.

Her eyes filled with tears and she blinked them away. Bad things had happened in her past, she was uncertain about her future but she was sure that she would rise above it. If nothing else, she was strong and resillient.

Torrent sighed, he pulled her closer. Flush against him. His chest was against her back. Her butt cradled against his abs. Even his legs were curled up around hers. So safe. So warm. He wasn't well. She needed to stay with him until he recuperated. Just a couple more hours and then she could be on her way.

No biggie.

She must've fallen asleep, because when she woke up, it was to Torrent's pale stare. His eyes locked with hers and he gave her the ghost of a smile. "You're awake," he said unnecessarily. He touched her cheek with just the tip of his finger. He was looking at her with such intensity, such . . . emotion that it threatened to take her breath away.

"I almost lost you." He clenched his jaw and his throat worked. "I'm an idiot. You were right to call me all of those things. Asshole being on the top of the list." He sucked in a deep breath.

One of his arms was around her waist. She was lying on her back. Torrent was on his side "Um . . ." She didn't know what to say. How did she respond?

"How are you feeling? Are you okay? Fuck . . ." he half growled the last. "I did this to you. I put you in harm's way. I'm so sorry."

"It's not your fault." She shook her head.

"If I hadn't said those things . . . hadn't driven you away." He shook his head. His voice was raw. His eyes glinted. "It's all my fault."

She hadn't expected this and was ill-prepared. "No. Wait."

He shook his head. "I'm a fool, an idiot." He made a rumbling noise and covered his face with his hand.

Candy turned onto her side, facing him. She touched the side of his arm. "It's not your fault that Ellis is . . . was a pshycopath. You didn't do any of it. Yes, you acted like an asshole and I'm still very angry with you but I'm also thankful." She swallowed hard. "You saved me." Her voice cracked.

Torrent swore. He grabbed ahold of her and pulled her to him. He held her for a while. "It should never have happened. If I could kill him again I would. I should've ripped off his arms, ripped off his fucking legs and left him to bleed out . . . he got off too easily." His whole body shook and his voice sounded strangled.

"You got there in time. I'm okay. I swear. I'm fine." Her heart would break when she walked away again but she would hold her head up high and she would manage.

She would. She always had.

He pulled away. His face was damp. Oh flip! Torrent wiped a hand across his eyes and aside from some residual moisture on his lashes, the wet was gone.

Shit! It hurt her to see him so cut up. His soul laid bare. "Shhhh." She buried her face in his chest and hugged him to her. "I'm fine." *Mostly. Still cut up over you.* She couldn't say it.

"Are you sure?" he cupped her cheeks in both his hands. "I'm so sorry, Candy."

She felt herself tense. She wasn't ready to discuss this. Not now, maybe not ever. "It's okay. We're good." *Drop it!*

His eyes hardened with determination. He wasn't going to drop it. "It's not okay and I can see that we're not good." He shook his head.

"We're good, we're just fine but we can't be together." There, it was out. The old elephant in the room.

Torrent nodded. "Shit. Forget I said anything. I wasn't supposed to even bring this up. I promised myself I was going to give you some time. It's too soon isn't it?"

She shook her head. "It's not too soon." Candy sat up and crossed her legs. She was wearing one of those god-awful baggy sweaters and a pair of leggings. He was wearing . . . just a silk sheet that barely covered his midsection.

Sure to keep her eyes on his, she carried on. "I don't think that I can get past the things you said. You hurt me."

Torrent sat up as well. She had to crane her neck to

maintain eye contact. She prayed the sheet was still in place since he didn't seem to give much of a shit.

Why did he have to be so damned big? It irritated her how sexy he looked. His skin was still pink in places, though otherwise he didn't look any worse for wear. His hair was mussed, yet it made him look even more attractive. Go figure.

Candy was not going to allow herself to be sidetracked. No way! She couldn't let him sweet talk her either. He tried to pay her for sex. Even after working for Ellis. After all her years as an escort, she had never felt as degraded as in that moment.

She must look like a complete mess but he didn't seem to notice or he pretended not to. It didn't matter though.

Torrent scrubbed a hand through his hair. It messed it up some more. He didn't look any less handsome though. "I was jealous and angry and so damned jealous." He paused. "I know I'm repeating myself but I couldn't see straight. I've never been jealous before in my life." He looked distraught. "How do I make this up to you?"

"I told you that I forgive you." She left it at that.

"But you still can't be with me?" That distraught look was back.

She shook her head. "I don't know what to say." Tell him no. Tell him to go to hell. She couldn't.

"I freaked out. I lost it." He grabbed the back of his neck and squeezed. "I should never have done that . . . offered you those jewels. I felt so jealous of those human males. I couldn't see straight. I didn't realize what I was feeling at the time. I didn't realize how jealous and pathetic I was. I was angry at you for making me feel that way. I was angry at myself for letting you get under my skin like that. I'm a king . . ."

"Yeah, yeah, so strong and great and fierce." She tried to use a joking tone but it came out sounding like an accusation.

He shook his head. "I am a king and yet I am nothing"—he paused—"I am nothing without you."

Her heart melted a little.

"I am a great king and yet I was reduced to behaving like a small child. I acted like a little boy. My grandmother would throw me over her knee if she found out how I treated you, and rightly so." He seemed to speak more to himself than to her. His eyes moved back to meet with hers. "There is nothing that I could say or do to make it right. There is no turning back the clock. When I heard about those other males, I freaked out. I let jealousy overtake me. I allowed myself to fall in love with a female who wouldn't allow me to claim her. No female has ever turned me down before. I was . . . am so in love with you that I can't think straight. I'm a jealous asshole . . ." He shook his head. "Like I said . . ." He grabbed her hands in his. "There is no turning back the clock but maybe you would agree to us starting over. A new beginning."

He was in love with her.

In love.

With her.

She could hardly breathe. She felt light headed. She

hadn't expected this. She wasn't sure what was going to happen but this wasn't it. Firstly the emotion. The tears. A grown man . . . shifter—eek—crying because of what had happened to her. Then this. She'd expected him to be pushy about getting back together but starting over and love and apologies. He was opening up to her and admitting to his feelings.

Torrent was frowning, his face filled with concern. "I know." He gave her hands a squeeze before letting go. "Too soon. I'm sorry."

More apologies.

No pushing at all.

Her hearted melted some more.

"I'll get out of your hair. I'll—"

She grabbed his hand. "Okay . . ." she hadn't just said that. She realized that she was smiling.

Torrent looked unsure for a second and then he smiled back. "Okay, as in yes?"

"Yes, but we start over and not where we left off. We start at the beginning."

"The beginning?" His frown deepened. "Should I hunt you again? I might have to kill others if they—"

Candy laughed. "No, we'll skip that part but maybe we can be friends and see where we go from there. You hurt me really badly. You made me feel cheap and worthless."

Torrent swallowed thickly, his throat worked but he didn't say anything.

"We can try but I can't make any promises." She was such a liar. Her heart was a puddle inside her chest. The question wasn't if she could take him back, it was how long before she did.

He nodded. "I will strive every day to show you what you mean to me. To prove to you how much I value you. You are more precious than gold or diamands. I hope you know that."

"I might, but I guess you need to prove to me that you feel it. You need to show me. I'm not interested in gold or jewels or fancy titles or any of that other stuff."

"I know. I'm so glad you are agreeing. You need to know that I lo—"

"Wait." Her voice came out sounding a tad panicked. "You can't say the L word. It's not fair."

"It's going to be difficult but I agree to everything."

"There's more." She raised her brows.

Torrent smiled. "Why am I not surprised?"

"I want to meet your people and explore your lair. I want to get to know your way of life. We need to stay in separate chambers and we're friends, so no sex."

He choked out a laugh. "Because we were having so much sex before?"

She couldn't help but to smile. "Oral sex is still a form of sex."

His eyes glazed over and he made a low growling noise. "I may die by the time you finally allow me into your body, but I agree."

She felt a zing of need as he spoke of being inside her. Shit! She wasn't going to last. Not at all. "Are you sure?"

He nodded.

"I wouldn't expect you to be exclusive." Her voice squeaked. She couldn't believe she was even saying this.

"Do you want other males?" His muscles tensed.

"No. Not at all but at the same time . . ." she shrugged. "I'm asking you to dial our relationship back. I'm asking for friendship, it wouldn't be right to demand exclusivity." As much as I want to.

"Do you want me to fuck other females?" His nostrils flared, his body tensed.

She grit her teeth. Anger and—yes—a good dose of jealousy raced through her. "No. I would hate it." She grit out. "It would kill me but I can't expect you just to wait for me." Softer this time. "Sky said that you would get weak." If he so much as looked at another woman she would kill him. Why had she even said that? Why? She had to be fair though.

His eyes blazed. "I don't want anyone else. I made a mistake. I will prove myself to you and, Candy . . ."

Thank god!

"Um." More of a sigh.

"When I put my mind to something, I give it my all. My everything. My undevided attention." He licked his lips. "You will be mine."

A shiver raced up her spine. It was of excitement, anticipation but also of fear. Torrent was everything she'd always stayed away from. He was too good looking, rich and arrogant. He was also really sweet and kind when he wanted to be. He could hurt her. He could crush her.

He leaned forward and she realized that his focus was

on her lips. "We're friends." She blurted before he could kiss her. Thing was, if he kissed her, all out went at it, she would be putty in his hands.

He gave her a smile that made her want to groan. Then he kissed her on her forehead. It was so tender. So sweet. Torrent let his lips linger for a moment before pulling her into a tight hug.

The next day . . .

"What did you say to him?" Sky asked.

"What do you mean?" Candy put her book down. It was the second in the series—The Demon Prince's Love Slave—Torrent was going to tease her when he got a look at the cover.

"Torrent made a public anouncement. He has renounced his claim on you, stating that you are just friends. Just friends?" She frowned, looking shocked. "Torrent has never been friends with a female before. Maybe me but that doesn't count because I'm family. Then again, he's never been in love with one either. Anyway, he also pointed out that if a male so much as touches you, and I quote—I will disembowel the bastard myself. He smiled while he said it." Sky visibly shivered. "The male is besotted."

"He said that?" Candy couldn't believe what she was hearing. Part of her felt hurt. He renounced her.

"Yup. You are free to go whereever you want. You are quite safe. Just don't be too surprised if any of the guys turn around and walk the other way if they see you coming."

"He wouldn't really hurt anyone though." She shook her head. "I'm not sure I like this jealous side. It's what caused the problems between us in the first place."

"Yes and no." Sky widened her eyes. "He is in love with you. Normally a couple would mate and be done with it. With you two, everything has been up in the air indefinitely. On the one hand it's good for Torrent, he needed to learn to work for a female. He's had it too easy but on the other hand, it's not natural for a shifter. He is driven to mate you and to keep other suitors away. He is hardwired this way. Doing anything else will demand huge strength and patience. It will go against his grain. I need to give you some advice."

Candy smiled. The other woman was a mother figure and a friend all rolled into one. "That's fine. Go ahead."

"I can see that you weren't happy when I mentioned that Torrent had renounced you. I know your feelings run deep for him." She paused. "Here goes, don't make him wait too long. I don't know what he did or said to make you so angry with him but please, take my advice on this one."

"It's not about making him wait. I can't help my own feelings."

"Do you love him?"

Candy bit down on her lip.

"Do you?" She used a more pressing tone.

Candy nodded. "I do."

Sky smiled. "Let him pay for being a prick and then take him back. He is a shifter and he loves you. He will never want another female . . . you are it for him. I'm not saying he won't be an idiot or do the wrong thing from time to time. He is a male." She sighed and rolled her eyes. "It's bound to happen but you need to trust that he will ultimately do right by you."

"You're right." Candy smiled. "I'll try really hard to let this go." A big part of her already had. It was important though that he never do anything like this again. He needed to accept her for who she was. That meant every part of her, the good, the bad and yes, the ugly. She was who she was. "And . . ." She raised her brows. "Any sign of your pregnancy?" It was a shameless change of subject but she was also really curious.

"Not yet." Sky beamed. "It's still a bit early though."

"I'm sure that all of the signs will be there in no time." Then she frowned. "What are the signs anyway? I'm sure it's different from a human pregnancy."

"I don't know much about human pregnancies. Dragons are different, even amongst our own species. Air and water dragons are similar in that we give birth to live young."

Candy felt her mouth gape for a second. "As opposed to?"

"Fire dragon females lay eggs."

"You're shitting me?"

She shook her head. "Nope. You can count your lucky stars that you weren't nabbed by one of the fire dragons.

It's the male that dictates the pregnancy. I'm an air dragon but my son or . . ." She looked wistful. "My daughter, will be water because my mate is a water dragon."

Candy could feel that her eyes were wide in her head. "Okay, so you'll actually give birth to a baby, not a dragon or an egg?" She couldn't help but to pull a face.

Sky smiled. "Yup." She probably didn't know she was doing it, but her hand was touching her lower belly. "In about six months or so, if all goes well, I'll give birth to a baby. If not . . ." She pulled her hand away like she had been burned. "It'll be at least six months before I go into heat again." Her eyes clouded.

"Wow . . . so long?" Candy gave Sky a shoulder bump. "I'm sure you must be . . . you know."

She looked horrified for a second. "Don't jinx me." Then she nodded. "It's fine, I'm one of the lucky females, at least I am fertile. If I'm not with child, there's always next time." She tried to sound like she didn't mind either way but Candy could see the longing in her eyes.

"What happened to your species?"

Sky shrugged again. She looked sad. "Females just stopped being born. Simple yet devestating. A female birth is a rare occurance. She-dragons that go into heat, are even more rare at that. And here we are"—she waved her hands about them—"surrounded mostly by males. Most of our remaining females are elderly and already mated."

Candy nodded. She tried to lighten the mood. "Hopefully us humans can help out, for a while at least. Who knows, if enough she-dragons are born in the coming years, there'll be no need for any future hunts."

Sky laughed. "Firstly, the hunt is a dragon tradition that was started because there were not nearly enough females to go around. Male dragons have hunted she-dragons for many years. It's considered exciting and fun. Only the strongest, most resilient males win and continue the bloodlines. Then . . ." She hesitated. "You really weren't told anything before being hunted?"

Candy shook her head. "We were fed bullshit, remember?"

Sky made a humming sound. "Right. Human females will only birth males. At least, it is most likely that you will birth males."

"How can you know that?"

"It is twofold. Firstly, the two human females that have birthed dragons both had males and then, the other shifters species that interbred with humans also all had males. It's the same with the vampires. There has yet to be one female offspring from a non-human with a human, and this being true across the species."

"Okay." She licked her lips. "I haven't given kids much thought. I guess I wouldn't mind either way. It's good to know I won't have to push out an egg though."

Sky pulled a face. "The only downside is that we are pregnant for much longer. It's only six weeks incubation time for the egg layers and then it takes about six weeks for an egg to hatch. We have to carry for a whole six months. It's back breaking. Labor is much longer and—"

"Only six?" Candy laughed. "Try nine on for size.

That's how long humans are pregnant for."

"Nine." Her eyes were wide. "I won't complain then. Labor lasts about six to eight hours. Our young are pretty small and weak when they are born, normally around four and a half pounds."

"That's tiny. I'm beginning to think that human women got the short end of the stick."

"Nah, the vampires did," Sky raised her brows. "They're pregnant the longest and give birth to huge babies. Rumor has it that their females have narrow hips. Most of the females are too narrow in the pelvis to birth young." She lifted her head and cocked it to the side. "We'll talk about this later."

"You still haven't told me how we'll know if you're pregnant or not."

"My scent will change. It's even more noticeable since I'm a an air dragon and Lake is a water dragon. You might end up being the first human pregnant with a royal, dragon child." She lowered her voice to a whisper. "How exciting would that be?" She gave Candy's hand a squeeze.

Candy shook her head. "Not happening. I'm not ready for that."

Sky shushed her. "We'll chat later. I still haven't told you about the earth dragons." She giggled. "Your date is almost here." She practically ran from the room.

Candy could hear her call out to someone. A deep voice answered. It was Torrent. Her heart beat a little faster.

It took about a half a minute for him to knock on her door.

She smoothed a hand down her dress. "Come in."

He walked in and her eyes widened with surprise. Torrent was wearing jeans, a faded baseball shirt and sneakers. The jeans pulled tight around his thighs, as did the shirt around the span of his shoulders and the breadth of his biceps.

"You look amazing," he growled. She forgot for a second that she was wearing a summer dress. It was pink, of all colors. It was one of the items he'd had his men purchase for her not so long ago. There were sandals on her feet and she wore her hair in a loose ponytail.

He pulled a face. "Am I allowed to say that? Surely I am? I can tell my friend"—he emphasized the word— "that she looks amazing, can't I? Now . . ." His eyes turned up towards the ceiling. "If I said that you were sexy or just about the most ravishing creature that I'd ever seen, that would probably be pushing it . . . for a friend."

She had to smile. "That might be pushing it . . . yes. You look pretty amazing yourself."

"Yeah . . . um . . . I ran a little errand earlier. I got you something."

"I don't need anything. I told you that earlier."

His face fell. He suddenly looked really unsure of himself. More like a little boy than a grown man . . . a king. She felt guilty. "I didn't mean it like that. I'm sorry."

Torrent grinned. "Okay well . . . I'm a little nervous now that I'm here . . . I had this all planned out. Shit!" He ran a hand through his hair.

"What is it? Now you have me all intrigued. I'm sure

I'll love it, as long as it's not jewelry. No more jewelry." She smiled.

He seemed to relax. "No, it's nothing like that. If you're not happy . . . I'll make a plan." He walked towards the door and then back towards her. "I'm sure you'll like it." Only, he didn't look sure at all.

She smiled at him. Torrent turned and disappeared behind the front door.

When he came back, he had a sheepish look on his face and the cutest little puppy under his arm. It was a mix breed of some kind. The little thing had long hair and a long nose and the biggest brown eyes. The puppy reminded her of a teddy bear. Okay, not quite a teddy bear, maybe a dog mixed with a miniture bear. "Oh my word." She gushed. "That's the cutest little thing I've ever seen in my life." The little guy . . . She didn't know how she knew but it was definitely a boy . . . had to be a few months old already. His tail wagged like mad.

"I didn't name him. I thought you could do the honors. He's yours." Torrent smiled, it was shy and so sweet. "If you want him."

Her heart melted a whole lot more. The dog began to squirm in his arms as she drew closer. He began to whine a little as she put her arms out towards him. Torrent spoke as he handed the bundle of fur to her. "I rescued him from the pound. They wanted to do a home check but when I told them that he was for you, they said it was fine. The check I wrote probably helped too." He smiled. "Don't get mad. This had nothing to do with money."

She had to laugh. "I know that."

Candy felt teary. She sniffed and widened her eyes to try and keep any tears from falling. She was so ridiculously emotional, which wasn't like her dammit. She was just so happy. Her mom would never let her have a pet and her erratic hours made keeping a pet difficult after she left home. She'd always wanted a dog. The little one wriggled in her arms he was wagging his tail so hard. He licked her neck and her hands and tried to reach up to get at her face. He had puppy breath and everything. "You are the cutest little guy. Just the cutest."

"Um."

When she looked up Torrent was rocking on his heels. He looked nervous all over again.

"What's wrong?" She licked her lips. "I'm thrilled. I couldn't be happier."

"There's more." He blurted.

"More?"

He nodded. Then he opened his mouth and thought better of speaking. He held up a hand, signalling for her to wait. Torrent walked out, the door clicked softly behind him. He returned holding a pet carrier. It was small and purple. The animal inside was growling.

"What have you got in there?"

Torrent put the carrier down. "Um . . . I couldn't leave her there." He chewed his lower lip. "I struggled to leave any of them there." His expression darkended. "No creature should have to live behind those bars, in tiny cages. It's not right." He shook his head. "I don't know why I bothered though . . ." Then he grinned broadly and shrugged. "She's not very grateful for the rescue." As if on cue, another grow sounded.

Torrent opened the door to the carrier. It took about a half a minute but a tiny dog finally emerged. It looked like a chihuahua cross. She was almost black with dark eyes. There was grey fur around her mouth, which idicated that she was already quite old.

This time a serious lump formed in her throat and she had to really fight the tears. The older animals hardly ever found new homes. Torrent went down onto his haunches, he spoke softly to the small creature. The little dog wagged her tail but she also growled at poor Torrent. The growling got worse as he put a hand out towards her but then again so did the tail wagging.

Torrent chuckled. "I'm not sure what to make of her." He shook his head. "I hope you don't mind but I named her already."

"Oh yeah?" Candy put the puppy down. The little one bounced around. He ran over to the black female and bounced around her but she remained indifferent.

Torrent nodded. "Yeah. It's on account of her love hate relationship for me. You see, I know she loves me. I can tell these things."

Candy made a sound of aknowledgement.

"But, she growls if I come anywhere near her. She snaps at me if I try and touch her."

"I see."

"I've decided that I have to call her Candy. Candy the

Second." He gave her a shiteating grin.

"You can't name our dog after me."

Our dog.

Our. Her heart raced.

"Want to bet? Watch this . . . Candy . . . Candy . . ." He called the dog, who turned towards him. The animal wagged her tail even harder. The moment Torrent moved a little closer she growled baring her little teeth. "See, she knows her name."

Candy couldn't help but to smile. "You can't call her that."

"It's already done."

She reached out and scratched the old girl behind the ear. There was zero reaction of any kind. No aggression, but neither was there any show of happiness. Pure indifference.

Torrent leaned in. "Your name is Candy. Am I right, girl?" The little dog wagged her tail. "See."

"We'll think of something else . . . together."

He nodded. "Only if Candy the Second agrees." He smiled.

"Whatever." She gave him a swat on the side of the arm. "And Torrent."

"Yeah."

"Thank you. This is the sweetest thing anyone has ever done for me."

He nodded. "I'm going to start an adoption program and I'm hoping you'll help me, since your medical career is out the window, on account of you being squeamish about blood."

She had to laugh. He was right. "What did you have in mind?"

"These guys"—he pointed at the dogs who were exploring the apartment—"sparked a ton of interest amongst my people. I want to try and find homes for some of those animals at the pound. Why not here with us? Maybe even with some of the other species."

"You mean the vampires and the other shifters?"

He nodded. "Why not? I thought the animals might be afraid of us but they're not."

"What about Candy the Second? She doesn't seem to like shifters." Candy laughed. "We'd better think of another name really quickly before that one sticks." She added.

"I think it's too late for that." He choked out a laugh. "She only reacts to me. She didn't mind any of the others touching her, holding her. She doesn't seem to care either way." He smirked at her.

"Love and hate."

"Not hate exactly." He winked at her.

"More like extreme irritation."

"I'm hoping if I try hard enough, she'll come around." He kissed Candy on the temple. "Let's take the dogs for a walk."

"That sounds like a really good idea."

It felt weird to walk out of the room together. Torrent had Candy the Second on a leash and she had her puppy. She needed to come up with a name and soon.

Torrent grabbed her hand. It was like the most natural thing ever. It felt right. "Is this okay?" He touched his shoulder against hers.

"Yeah." She squeezed his hand.

They passed some big burly warrior types. They glanced their way and greeted them but otherwise kept on going. They made their way through a maze of vast hallways. They were huge. Torrent explained that the areas within the lair needed to accommodate a dragon in full shift. Dragons hated cramped spaces. They were claustrophobic. Which made sense.

They walked and talked. It was nice. It was really nice. It was also really comfortable. Underneath all of that niceness and comfort was a raging inferno that was her libido. And by the huge bulge in Torrent's jeans earlier, she would say that he was feeling the same. Candy needed to find some serious resolve. She needed to make him wait just a little bit longer. They had a long future ahead of them and she needed to be sure that he never pulled that kind of shit again.

CHAPTER 22

The next day . . .

Torrent felt nervous. Ever since meeting the human female. Since bringing her into his life and falling hard for her, he'd experienced a range of new emotions.

Jealousy. Blinding fear. Fierce love. A need to protect like nothing before and then there was nervousness. He didn't like this new emotion at all.

His mouth felt dry. His hands clammy.

"Do I look okay?" Candy turned to him. Her eyes were wide and her skin pale. Too pale.

"You look amazing."

"You're not just saying that?"

He gave her the once over. Candy was dressed in a navy blue dress. It was . . . what had she called it, a knitted fabric or something. It had a conservative neckline and ended just above her knee but somehow it still made her look sexy as fuck. Maybe because it fit her perfectly, accentuating her curves perfectly. "I swear." His voice had turned a bit growly. "It's perfect."

She played with the string of pearls around her neck. He had some of the males fetch her things the day before. "I guess I'm a bit nervous about meeting your family."

"They'll love you." The pearls added to the appeal. The way they lay between her breasts. Drawing the eye. Shit! Eyes up. *Friends*. They were friends. Just friends. At least for now.

"I broke off our engagement . . . our mating thingy. They might be upset with me."

He stepped towards her. He clasped her elbow. "I was the one that lied. I'm the one taking the flack for it. It's not your fault. I was very clear about that."

Her eyes looked clouded in thought and maybe with a tad of concern. She nodded. "Will the dogs be okay?"

"It's dinner." He tilted her chin up. "We'll only be gone for a couple of hours at most. They'll be just fine. Look at them." The furry pup lay on his back, legs in the air. He was snoring softly. Candy the Second lay with her head resting on her paws. There was a knocking sound as she wagged her tail when she caught him looking her way. The wagging was quickly followed by a soft growl.

"Still wary of you."

"Mmmm." He allowed his gaze to move to her lips for a moment. "It looks like it."

She gave him a nervous half smile and thread her fingers through his. "Let's do this." Then she held back. "Do you know who I'm most nervous about meeting?"

His stomach felt like it contained a lump of lead. "My grandmother."

She nodded her head. "I think your brothers will be okay. I already feel like I know Lake because of everything Sky has told me about him. I already met Tide and your youngest brother. Tide at the rescue and Storm was the guy who dropped me off when . . ." She let the sentence die.

He felt his scales rub at the thought of what had happened. Of those human males. How they had hurt his Candy. Torrent regretted not killing the small one. The one who had dared to put his hands on his female. Torrent had paid the male a visit. Intent on finishing the job. The prick was in a hospital. At least the male would never have young and would most likely never gain full function of his dick again. He would require several corrective surgeries. Good! Torrent had crushed both his balls and his cock. It served the fucker right.

The male had begged and pleaded, and had looked so pathetic. He had peed himself. Bloody urine had flowed from a tube between the bandages. He'd almost felt sorry for the human. Torrent had let him go with a severe warning. One he would make good on if need be. Besides, he figured that leaving the male to live might be punishment in itself. He would keep an eye on him though.

"Hey," Candy said. "Are you okay?"

"I'm just glad you're here and that you're giving us another chance."

"Me too." She brushed her lips against his. It was quick but it made his heart race.

"A friendly kiss." He was a total pussy but found that he didn't give a shit.

She nodded. "Mostly."

"Mostly?" He raised his brows. He'd take anything . . . anything.

She gave his hand a tug. "We're going to be late." Her eyes widened. "Are you sure I look okay? I could change."

"Don't you dare. I don't want you changing anything."

Her throat worked and she gave him a single nod of the head. "Thanks. Let's do this thing." She sighed.

"They are going to love you. I promise."

Minutes later they walked into a large dining room. The long table had been set. He heard Candy suck in a breath. It was a sight to behold, hundreds of candles had been lit. The lighting had been set to dim. A fire blazed in the hearth.

She held onto his hand like a lifeline.

"Hi." Sky smiled from ear to ear. Lake clasped the female around her waist.

"Hi." Candy trembled against him. She really was nervous to meet his grandmother. The lady in question with talking with Storm, Lake and Sky. Tide wasn't there yet.

His grandmother smiled. Crinkles appeared around her eyes. She still looked relatively young except for her shock of white/grey hair.

"Well." His gran raised her brows. "Aren't you going to introduce me to the female that has stolen your heart?"

He choked out a laugh. "Of course, Gran." Trust his

gran to put it out there. He let go of Candy's hand, putting it to her lower back instead.

She moved forward and put her hand out. "I'm Candy."

His grandmother took the outstretched hand, her eyes on his female. "I'm Rain. It is a pleasure to meet you. You have a lovely name."

"So do you and it's a pleasure to meet you as well."

"This is Lake." Sky interjected.

Candy turned towards his brother. "I feel like I already know you. I'm very excited for you guys with the pregn—"

Lake growled. It didn't matter that the male was acting on instinct. It pissed Torrent off. He stepped forward and growled back.

"Now, now." His gran tsked. "Enough of that."

"My female is not familiar with our ways." His voice was deep and threatening. It couldn't be helped.

Lake nodded. His shoulders dropped as he relaxed. His brother locked eyes with Candy. "It is considered bad luck to talk of such things."

Sky put her arm around her mate. "It's okay, love." She looked up at him with such love and devotion. "Candy is a human so it doesn't count."

Lake dropped a kiss on her brow. "You are right, sweets." He turned his gaze back to Candy. "I'm sorry for overreacting."

His female put her hands up. "I really need to learn the traditions and what nots. It's my fault entirely." She was talking too quickly. "It won't happen again." She mouthed *sorry* to Sky when Lake wasn't looking.

"It's one of those really touchy subjects." Storm interjected. "Better to not say anything." He winked at Candy. The little shit. "We can talk about other things. More fun things."

Torrent gave a small shake of the head. Storm grinned at him and gave the tiniest little nod. This was going to end in blood shed. He could tell.

His grandmother had always been good at intercepting a conversation. More like hijacking one. "So, dear . . ." she directed her attention to Candy. "Tell me about yourself. Wait just a minute." She glared at Storm. "Why haven't you offered our guest a drink?"

"She's Torrent's date." He smirked.

Gran gave him a hard glare. "Exactly, he needs to stay at her side. You're being rude."

Storm took a step back and seemed to cower a little under their gran's death stare. "What can I get you to drink?" Storm smiled at Candy. His look and demeanor was a little too friendly for Torrent's liking.

"Some fruit juice would be great." Candy seemed oblivious to the tension.

"I'll have a glass of red wine, brother." It was Torrent's turn to smirk at Storm who scowled at him as he handed him his glass moments later.

Torrent might be the king, but at family gatherings, they were a family like any other. At least Candy looked more relaxed. Gran was telling stories about when they were kids. He'd given his brothers strict instructions not to give him any shit. Not tonight. Not while Candy was here. The problem was that he'd asked them as a brother and not as the king so all bets were off. If they started in on him, it would make her uncomfortable.

Things were going well. They all laughed as Torrent's grandmother recalled another story about one of her grandkids.

"The best story is of Tide, when he first found his dragon."

Torrent turned to Candy. "Dragons don't shift until we're about twelve."

Torrent's gran laughed. She was remarkably beautiful. Her hair was snowy white. She looked like she had the same coloring as Torrent and Lake. Her white-blond hair had turned grey-white with age. Aside from the hair and maybe a look of wisdom in her eyes, she was still young looking. "Tide couldn't wait to change. He used to practice every day."

"It was so funny. He'd meditate and actively try and bring on the change." Lake laughed.

"Well, one day"—the older lady continued—"he managed to somehow get it right, only, it didn't go quite as planned." She turned and whispered to Candy. "The process should not be rushed or forced."

Storm laughed. "No it shouldn't."

"You wouldn't even remember," Lake said. "You were too young."

"I do remember." Storm pulled a face of irritation. "How could I forget something like that?" He was the only brother with brown hair. He had the same pale blue eyes. They all did, including Torrent's grandmother.

"He shifted but only got half way." Torrent chuckled.

The older lady nodded. "He had a long tail, wings instead of arms and a whole lot of scales. Everything else was still very human."

Candy covered her mouth with her hand and laughed. "I can picture it."

"No need, dear." The older lady winked at her. "I have pictures. He was like that for a day or so before finally changing back. Come for tea and I'll show them to you."

"I don't even want to know what pictures those would be, Gran." Tide walked in. He strode over to his grandmother and gave her a kiss on the cheek. "Although I can guess." He looked up at her. His blue eyes filled with humor. "Candy." He smiled. "It's good to see you."

"You too."

Torrent growled.

"Relax, brother." Tide gave Torrent a slap on the back. "I like my intestines where they are . . . thank you very much."

"Ah." Rain, gestured to the table. "The first course is being served. Please try and behave boys." She looked at each of them in turn. "No swearing or fighting."

"Wouldn't dream of it, Gran." Tide's grin looked mischievous. He glanced at Torrent and his grin grew wider. There was something going on between them,

Candy wasn't sure what it was. Sibling rivalry, good humored teasing? She didn't know.

Dinner comprised of five courses. Candy felt like she might burst by the time they finished the dessert round.

"Let's take our tea in the living room." Torrent's grandmother gestured towards the overstuffed leather sofas.

The evening had turned out to be fun. It was easy to see how much this family loved one another. How much they respected each other.

Rain put her cup down. "It's time for me to take these old bones to bed." Each of her grandsons gave her a kiss on the cheek.

"I'll walk you." Torrent held his hand out to his grandmother. He helped her to her feet. In this moment, he wasn't the king, he was the grandson, the brother.

Rain smiled and gave him a tap on the arm. "Such a good boy. I'm fine. Candy . . ."

Oh shit! "Yes?" She stepped towards the older woman. "You can take me to the door and see me out if you will?"

She nodded. "Yes, of course."

Rain linked her arm with Candy's. "Good night, all."

They wished her a good night right back and then Candy heard Lake suggest whiskeys.

"I've enjoyed meeting you." Rain looked down at her to maintain eye contact. These dragon women were huge. Even the old ladies of the species.

"Thanks for being so nice and for making me feel so . . ." She wanted to say part of the family but that didn't quite gel. Not yet anyway. "Welcome."

"Walk out with me."

Candy nodded, feeling nervous. This was the part where she got into trouble for breaking Torrent's heart.

Rain led her into the hallway and shut the door behind them.

"I do care for your grandson . . . I swear . . . I . . ."

"Of course you do, dear. You love him," she stated. "It's easy to see that the two of you are crazy about each other. My grandson explained that he did something out of jealousy. He said that"—she looked up in thought—"ah yes, he said he was an arrogant asshole."

Candy burst out laughing. It was partly because she had been so tense. "Is that what he said?"

"Yup, and I believe it too." The older woman took ahold of both her hands. "I also married the king, it feels like just yesterday." Her eyes clouded in thought and a small smile took residence on her face. "I know all about it. It takes a certain kind of male to lead a kingdom and they really do need to be taken down a rung or two early on in the relationship. They try and rule everything, including their relationship. It should be a partnership, but you know that don't you?"

Candy nodded. "I'm glad you understand. I was a bit worried about what you would all think."

"Well, I do understand and it doesn't matter what we think. It only matters what you and Torrent think and feel." She paused. "My mate respected and loved me all the more in the end and so will Torrent. I've never seen the boy smitten." She shook her head. "Of all the boys, I never expected him to fall the hardest."

"Tide and Storm don't have mates yet."

"There is no way they're beating that boy." She squeezed Candy's hands in both of hers. "He really does love you."

"I know."

"Don't do that. I can see the guilt. You take the next step when you are ready. He'll wait for you."

Candy nodded. "Thank you."

They said goodnight and Candy went back inside. The atmosphere was tense. Or, at least Torrent was tense. The others were laughing.

"Stop," he said, his voice had a hard edge. He shifted on his feet, his abs were so ripped. His chest broad.

They all stood by the fire. Except for Sky who was sitting on the nearby sofa.

"You should take your female home now," Tide said. He took a big swig of his whiskey and chuckled. "Oh yes, I forgot, she's your friend."

Storm laughed before turning serious. His mouth twitched. "What's it like anyway, having a female that's a friend?"

"Stop your shit," Torrent spoke under his breath. "She'll be back any minute and you'll embarrass her." He glanced towards the door. His eyes widened as they landed on her. "Hi . . . you're back. Can I get you anything? My brothers were about to leave."

So they were all giving him grief about the fact that they

hadn't actually mated.

"We're not going anywhere." Tide swirled his drink. "We were just talking about—"

"Nothing." Torrent narrowed his eyes on his brother.

"Uh oh." Sky rolled her eyes. "I can see where this is going." She locked eyes with Candy and pulled a face. "They're about to fight. It won't take long and they'll be beating the scales off of one another."

"There will be no fighting." Torrent folded his arms across his chest. "My female might get hurt."

"Except, she isn't your female." Storm smirked.

"She's your friend." Tide choked out a laugh. "There was no sealing of any deal."

"Should I get some of those human pills for you?" Storm asked. "The ones that . . ." He pointed to his . . . man part.

"I don't need any goddamned pills. Shut up already."

"Yeah, because then he'd have a hard dick and a best friend. How awkward would that be?" Tide took a sip of his whiskey, smacking his lips.

"I don't need pills." Torrent spoke carefully, like he was using every bit of resolve to stay calm. "I'm"—he cleared his throat—"very happy to be friends with Candy." He gave her a tight smile. "So much so that I could be friends with her for . . . a very long time and be happy with it. No, thrilled."

All three of the guys laughed. Tide doubled over, spilling his whiskey. He wiped at his face and had to sit down. Sky rolled her eyes and mouthed *ignore them* to

Candy.

Torrent clenched his jaw so hard Candy was worried he might end up cracking a tooth. He looked like a lost little boy. He was sucking it up for her. She knew in that moment that he would crawl through hot coals for her. He would do anything for her. All of her. The good parts, the bad parts and the ugly parts.

Candy cleared her throat and stepped forward. The guys stopped laughing. The room became so quiet. The only sound was of the crackling fire. "I think we should go now."

"Your *friend* is tired," Storm said. Tide chuckled, as did Lake. Sky hit her mate on the arm so he stopped, looking guilty.

"Actually, I'm not in the least bit tired." She looked at Torrent who was frowning. "I was thinking that maybe we could go back to your place."

The frown deepened, turning to more of a confused look than an angry one.

"I don't know." She twirled the pearls between her fingers, his eyes dipped to her cleavage. "Maybe we could have hot, sweaty sex." They flashed back to lock with hers.

His mouth fell open. All of their mouths fell open.

"All night, bed-breaking, sheet-tearing sex." She whispered, knowing full well that they would all hear her perfectly.

Sky giggled.

"That would be great." He yelled. Then he turned serious. "Um . . ." He swallowed thickly. "I mean, yes, definitely. Only if you're sure that's what you want?"

"Pussy." Tide coughed the word into his fist.

Candy turned her gaze onto Torrent's brother. She gave him what she hoped was a seriously dirty look. The guy had the good grace to look sheepish.

"Further more." She closed the distance between them and looked into Torrent's eyes. His beautiful pale blue stare. He took her breath away. Made her feel tingly all over. "I don't want to be your friend."

"You don't?" The look on Torrent's face was almost humorous. "No. People who have hard sweaty sex can't be friends . . . not really."

Torrent made a choking, growling noise.

She licked her lips and his eyes tracked the movement of her tongue. "I want you and I choose you and . . ."

He put his hand over her mouth. "You're publicly choosing me . . . again."

She nodded.

He leaned forward until his mouth was hovering over her ear. "If I choose you back, then us having sex would mean . . ." She had to strain to hear him. So sweet. Torrent was trying to give her a way out.

She pulled his hand away before he could finish. "I know exactly what it would mean."

He smiled. "We would be officially mated if that happened."

"I know, Torrent, and I choose you and I want you." She threaded her hands around his neck.

"I'm going to be sick." One of Torrent's brother's

announced. Someone else gagged and Sky sighed.

"I'm so damned happy right now." Torrent's chest heaved as he pulled her against him. "I choose you, Candy. I love you so damned much . . ."

There were more gagging noises behind them.

"Excuse me, just a second." He turned and there was a slapping noise.

"Owww!" Tide complained. "It wasn't even me."

Torrent turned back to her. "Where was I . . . oh yes . . . I love you and I can't wait to . . . spend forever with you and . . . I can't wait to have all night, sweaty sex with you." He picked her up and she wrapped her legs around him.

"Tide." He growled as he strode towards the door, his eyes were still locked with Candy's.

"Yeah, yeah . . ." Tide said. She looked over Torrent's shoulder and saw that Tide was smiling. "I'll take care of things. Go and claim your female. It's about damned time."

"Lucky bastard!" Storm muttered.

Torrent nuzzled into her neck. "I am. I so am. Tide . . ."

"Yes." Bored sounding.

"You might not see me for a few days."

"Go already."

"Inform me if anything . . ."

"Go," Tide growled.

Sky laughed. Candy struggled to breathe, she could feel Torrent hard and ready between her legs.

CHAPTER 23

They'd first gone to his place and then realized that the dogs were at hers. "You're moving back in with me." He said, as he picked her up and practically ran to her chamber.

The moment he put her down, Candy pulled her dress over her head. She was wearing human coverings. White lacy material that was completely see-through. His dick lurched in his pants. Her nipples were so pink. They pushed hard against the thin fabric like they were trying to cut free.

He growled as he suckled one of her nubs through the lace. He cupped her other breast, feeling its weight in his hand. Then he pulled back so that he could look at her sex. A thin strip of thatch beneath a small white triangle. "I don't know where to start." Then he took a step back and licked his lips. "Are you sure about this?" This was all so unexpected. He needed to be sure that she was really ready, that she was doing this for the right reasons.

Her heart rate kicked up a notch. "Why? Aren't you?" She frowned.

"I'm more sure than I have been about anything ever . . . as in ever before." He tripped over his words but he didn't care. He was so wound up it was scary.

She huffed out a breath. "Good." She nodded. "I want you and I want us. I'm very sure."

"We agreed to a cold shower before . . ."

She narrowed her eyes. "We've waited long enough dammit. Take me already."

"Thank fuck." Torrent groaned as she gripped his cock through his pants, and fisted him from base to tip. He had to grind his teeth together to keep from swearing.

"I think we should forgo foreplay and skip to the main event. We've waited long enough." She dipped under the elastic and circled his tip with her finger.

Torrent squeezed his eyes shut and groaned. "I'm so damned wound up. I can only make you two promises . . . no make that three."

"What promises?" She licked one of his pecs.

"Fuck, Candy. You need to stop touching me or all bets are off. I'll come like a teenager."

"That's fine." She reached up and kissed him. "I wouldn't mind."

"This is our first time and I'm feeling the pressure. I've never been this turned on before."

"You have nothing to feel pressured about and I'm so turned on it's scary." She kissed him again. "Do you want me to take the edge off." She bobbed her eyebrows and fisted his dick, this time skin to skin.

He cursed under his breath. "Stop that and no. I want

to be inside of you. I promise to take you slowly and carefully the second time around."

She smiled, looking like a naughty vixen. "What about this time?"

"It's going to be hard and fast but you'll come hard. Those are the three promises but only if you stop playing with my cock."

"Ohhh! Sounds good." She jumped into his arms and he caught her. Her pussy came up flush against his dick. "By the way."

"Yeah." Shit he was barely holding it together. His balls were already up. Locked and loaded and ready for release. Once he started he didn't think he could stop.

She pulled her bottom lip between her teeth. "I just wanted you to know that I love you too."

It filled him with joy to hear her say it. "You're mine now."

She nodded. "Yes, I am."

It was a relief to hear her admit it. To hear her declaration of love. Something eased inside him. "I am yours, Candy. All yours. You can tell me anything. Ask me anything."

She leaned forward and kissed him, pushing her lush breasts against his chest. He walked over to the bed and put her on it. Then he pulled off his pants and watched as her gaze dipped. As her eyes turned greedy. She probably didn't know that she was doing it but she opened her legs. A silent invitation and he was taking it.

Her lacy panties were soaked with her juices. The scent

of their intermingled arousal filled the chamber.

"I'm so sorry." He growled as he pulled himself between her legs. He couldn't wait any longer.

"Why are you sorry?"

"I had planned on making love to you but our first time is going to be fucking."

Her pupils dilated. She liked a bit of dirty talk. Thank fuck because there was more where that came from. Plenty more.

"And I'm sorry for this . . ."

"What?" She squealed when he ripped off her panties. "You didn't just . . ." She moaned as he put his cock in line with her opening. Then her eyes widened. "We need a condom."

"No we don't." His voice was so deep.

"It's a rule . . ." She licked her lips.

"No rules with me."

She shook her head. "No rules." He could see that she was still unsure.

"Good." He paused. He couldn't believe he was about to say this on account that he just might die if he didn't come inside her. No barriers. "You're not in heat but I will get a condom if . . ."

"Okay, you can come inside me then. I trust you"

Yes! He felt like fist pumping the air. "You're sure?" It came out sounding strangled.

She nodded. "Yes," breathless.

"I'm going to go ahead and fuck you now."

"Please do." Her head dropped back and she moaned

as he thrust all the way into her, in one hard move.

"God," she choked. "You're big."

"Am I hurting you?"

She shook her head. Her eyes glassy. Her breaths were coming in pants. "Just so full. Good."

"Thank fuck because I'm never leaving. Never." He was panting just as hard.

She gave a laugh. It squeezed his dick. It felt amazing. He thrust into her a couple of times, keeping his eyes on hers. Their breaths intermingled. "I was right," his chest rumbled.

"About?" More of a moan than a word.

"About your g-spot."

Her eyes widened. "Oh," forced out.

"It's big."

Her eyes struggled to focus on him. "Really?" More hard panting as he kept moving in and out of her.

He nodded. "It's right here." He angled his body slightly and felt her pussy instantly pull him in deeper, her wet channel closed more tightly around him, squeezing the hell out of him.

Her eyes rolled back and she groaned. All out groaned.

"Receptive." He pumped into her. "Fucking amazing." He kissed her hard. Part of him couldn't believe that this was even happening.

He didn't deserve her. He would spend his life making sure that she didn't regret this. Torrent couldn't hold back anymore. "I love you" He ground the words out as he gripped one of her thighs and pulled it up higher on his body so that he could plough into her.

Oh god.

Oh god.

The bed shook. It hit against the wall with each hard thrust. *Bang, bang, bang.* In quick succession. Her body hummed and buzzed. She struggled to take in enough air even though Torrent leaned on an elbow to keep most of his weight off of her. He used a hand to open her more to him, to pull her higher so that he could take her deeper, more completely.

Sweet Jesus.

She'd never felt so full. Every stroke took her higher. Every thrust caused her nerve endings to flare more vividly to life. Her heart raced. Their bodies were slick, sliding against one another in a frantic, all consuming race. He'd said that he would take her hard and fast, that he would fuck her and he was, like an animal. Like a man possessed. She could feel his pent up need for her. It was strange because she could even feel his love for her as well. Right now and in this moment. She'd been fucked many times, but not like this. Never like this. Love fucked.

Her channel fluttered. Her breath caught in her throat. Everything stilled for an instant as her whole body tightened to snapping point and then she was falling, falling into bliss, falling into him, Torrent, her mate. She cried out his name.

His body tensed and he seemed to swell a little before he groaned, jerking into her. She felt hot spurts and he thrust harder. *Bang, bang, bang.* The bed may or may not have lifted completely from the floor. He kept pushing into her. He moaned and mumbled garbled words. His movements slowing but they were no less hard. He finally stilled, Torrent was breathing quickly. His chest lifting and dropping in quick succession. He put his forehead to hers. "We're doing that again."

Before she could answer, there was a whining noise next to the bed. They both looked down. The puppy had his paws up on the side of the bed, tail wagging. Tongue lolling. Torrent kissed her nose. "I'm going to take the dogs out for a walk and then I'm making sweet, passionate love to you. So . . ." he paused. "When I get back, you can tell me exactly what you want and how you want it."

Her heart swelled with love. "I just want you. The rest doesn't matter."

Torrent got off the bed, he pulled on some pants and went to fetch the dog leashes.

"Do you want me to come along?" She asked, stretching out on the bed.

Torrent moaned, his eyes on her butt. "No, I want you to stay right there, just like that. Don't move a muscle."

She heard him talking to the dogs. "Candy." He called to her, his voice was filled with awe. When she turned, she saw the little black dog wagging her tail, the little girl was licking Torrent's hand. "Candy the Second might like me after all." He was grinning like a crazy person.

"Hey, look at that." She smiled at him. "You must've grown on her."

Torrent grinned. He clipped the leash onto her collar. "She loves me after all."

"I think that maybe she always did."

He cocked his head. "I'll be back. Don't you move." He walked to the door and turned back. *What was he up to?* "Don't worry, I haven't forgotten about your little, hot button." He looked pointedly as her ass.

Candy threw a pillow at him but it missed by about a mile. She could hear him chuckling like mad as he left the room.

CHAPTER 24

Two and a half months later . . .

C andy watched as the two specks completely disappeared. She smiled to herself. A couple of weeks ago she wouldn't have been able to see anything on a cloudy night like tonight. Her senses were slowly improving and not just her eyesight, all of them. She could hear better, smell better, even her sense of touch was . . . better. Off the charts was probably a better description.

While some things had improved though, others were . . . not as good. At least, she didn't think so but she couldn't say for sure.

She suppressed a sigh as they walked back inside, closing the balcony door to the chilly breeze.

"Are you sure you didn't want to go with them?" Candy asked. The guys had gone for an after dinner flight, to try and work off some of the copious amounts of food. Sky had gone out of her way to prepare an amazing meal.

"No, thanks. Those two will spend the entire flight behaving like children." A look of hurt crossed her features for a second or two. Then Sky schooled her emotions and stoked the fire, adding a couple of logs to the embers.

Candy knew exactly where her friend's thoughts had wandered to. "So, how are you doing?" She took a sip of her wine before putting it on the side table.

Sky looked back over her shoulder and the she-dragon smiled, but she could see some of that residual sadness cloud her face. "I'm good. Lake has been so supportive. He is"—she sucked in a breath—"he's wonderful. I'm lucky to have him in my life."

"He's just as lucky to have you as well." Candy moved closer to the other woman who had just risen to her feet. She gave her hand a quick squeeze. "He loves you very much."

Sky looked down at her feet for a few seconds before locking eyes with Candy. She nodded. "You're right."

Candy could hear that she didn't mean it. "Take a seat."

They both sat, Sky in a wingback and Candy on the couch directly across from her.

"Don't lecture me." Sky pulled a face. "I'm still feeling a bit depressed but I think that's normal, don't you?"

Candy nodded. "Yeah, but it was your first try. You shouldn't beat yourself up over it."

Normally Sky would clam up and change the subject. Candy was shocked when she continued. "It's so rare for a she-dragon not to become pregnant." She dragged her lower lip between her teeth, her eyes wide. "What if I can't actually get pregnant? I'm so worried." She huffed out a hard breath. Although her eyes filled with tears, she didn't cry.

At least her friend had finally voiced her fears. Ever since finding out that she wasn't pregnant over two months ago, she'd bottled up her feelings and pretended to be fine even though Candy could tell that she wasn't. She didn't mope around all day, but there were subtle signs. Moments when she dropped her walls for a second or two. Candy kept her mouth shut, hoping that Sky would open up a bit more.

She handed the other woman her glass and Sky nodded in thanks before taking a sip. "What if I don't go into heat again? I might not, you know?" She pursed her lips and put her glass back down.

"It won't help to worry about it. You told me that you come into heat once or twice a year like clockwork. It hasn't been long since . . . you know." Sky nodded, but Candy could see that she wasn't convinced. "It's going to happen. You need to try and be positive and keep practicing hard in the meanwhile."

She gave Candy a demure smile. "Lake can't keep his claws off me."

"There you go, he loves you."

"I know but it makes me feel so guilty." She sucked in a breath. Her face turned red and she quickly locked eyes with Candy. "What about you? Still nothing? I feel awful for not asking sooner."

Candy felt a knot twist inside of her. She shook her head. "Nope. Nothing." She hadn't ovulated since arriving on dragon soil almost three months ago. "I'm staying positive. See." She forced a bright smile. "It's not like I'm here with the main purpose of continuing the water dragon royal bloodline or anything."

Sky pulled a face. "That's not the only reason you're here. Silly! Torrent is loopy about you. He can't focus on anything else for longer than ten seconds if you're in the room."

Candy had to smile. It was true. She felt the same way about him. She'd never been happier. He had become her best friend and the sex was ridiculously good. It didn't get any better than that. The only problem was her lack of ovulation. It wasn't like they were actually trying for a baby or anything. Though, she had begun to think that if it finally happened, she might just go for it. In a way, she could relate to Sky. "Torrent is really sweet about it." He kept reassuring her. They'd had a long talk and he'd promised her several times that it didn't matter to him. That she was more important to him than anything else, including being the king. He told her that he would even step down if she couldn't supply the kingdom with an heir. Tide would step in. *If not Tide then Lake.* He joked that there were plenty of royal water princes to continue the line. The thing was, he was excellent at what he did. He was a natural leader. His people respected him. She pretended that she was okay with it, and it mostly was okay. It did sit in the back of her mind though.

"They're so okay with it that it sometimes makes you feel worse doesn't it?" Sky raised her brows.

Candy nodded. "Yup. It does." She leaned forward and touched Sky on the arm. "I understand what you're going through." Candy was exercising and eating healthy, well, mostly. She was also eating more. Ever since coming to live with the dragons, she felt great. More energized and yes, more hungry. So what! She was happy dammit. She'd put on a few pounds and Torrent seemed to love her curvier figure. "It's going to be okay. I know it."

Sky's eyes filled with tears all over again. She blinked a lot but didn't actually cry. "I'm a horrible friend. Here I am whining and carrying on when you've actually missed your heat."

"I've missed several."

"You wouldn't be here if you didn't ovulate at some point when you were being monitored," Sky said.

"Mmmmm. I suppose." She shrugged. "I'm not going to drive myself mad. I'm young. I'm enjoying being with Torrent. I'm sure it will happen again at some point." She smiled.

Sky smiled as well, it reached all the way to her eyes this time. She gave a deep nod. "Yup. I'm going to take your advice. I'm going to relax and enjoy being with Lake instead of worrying." She gave a chuckle and then pushed out a breath. "I feel so much better."

"Me too." She meant it.

"How was your trip into Walton Springs?"

Candy sucked in a breath. "Yeah. It was interesting." She and Torrent had gone to the reading of the will. Charles' will. "He left me everything. His entire estate."

Sky widened her eyes. "Oh wow! That's crazy."

"He left me a small fortune. Charles . . ." she paused as she remembered him. He had been such a softy at heart. "He thanked me for making the last years of his life bearable. He said that I was a good friend." She felt a little emotional. "I'm going to donate most of it to charity. I don't need it."

Sky quirked a brow. "We, the dragon species, are very wealthy."

"Torrent may have mentioned something along those lines but I don't think I would've kept much of it even if I'd never met Torrent."

"You're a good person." Sky smiled.

They continued to chat for about an hour, then the boys came home. They swooped onto the huge balcony, shifted and walked inside, laughing. Both men were wet and naked as the day they were born.

Candy tried not to blush or to look away. This type of nudity was normal amongst the shifters. Sky didn't react at all, except to hand them each a towel.

"Did you see my dive?" Lake was looking at Torrent as he spoke, but he gave Sky a kiss as he took the towel from her.

"Yeah, it was okay."

"Okay?" Lake snorted. "It was a thing of beauty."

"I thought I was a thing of beauty," Sky said, redirecting her mate's attention.

Torrent was already focused on Candy. Her breathing hitched as he looked her way. His pale eyes darkening as they landed on her. He went over to her and kissed the top of her head. Then he brushed his lips across her in an upside down kiss. Water dripped onto her.

She squealed. "You're freezing." She lifted her arms and thread her fingers through his hair. "I'm surprised you don't have icicles on the end of your . . ." She smiled, her mind going straight to the gutter.

He gave her a smile that was just as dirty. "You should probably check on that . . . just to be sure."

Lake murmured something and Sky giggled.

"Are you ready to go?" Torrent was still leaning over the back of the couch. His head right next to hers. She could smell the ocean and his unique scent. An intoxicating scent.

She made a sound of agreement, which turned into a moan as he nibbled on her ear.

Torrent straightened up. She heard him pull on his pants. Sky and Lake broke apart from what looked like a heated kiss.

"We're going to head out," she said, as Sky turned back towards her.

The she-dragon nodded, she rose to her feet as well. "So glad you guys could come over."

"Our place next time?"

"We look forward to it." Sky smiled. "Don't forget about tomorrow though."

Oh yes! Her brain had been in the gutter lately. Love did strange things to people. "Yes, of course. We're meeting at ten?"

Sky nodded. "We're very excited about adopting a pet. We're still struggling about trying to decide between a dog and a cat."

"We're only going to the shelter tomorrow. There's no rush with making a decision. You can always foster first."

Sky grabbed Lake's hand. "You're still available tomorrow, aren't you?"

"I wouldn't miss it for the world. We need to look for a Sky the Second of our very own."

Sky laughed.

Candy groaned. She refrained from stomping her foot but only just. "Her name is Isobel. *Isobel,*" she repeated, this time with more emphasis. It seemed that the original name had stuck. Everyone called the little black female Candy the Second. She caught herself doing it all the time as well, much to Torrent's amusement.

Torrent chuckled.

She gave him a slap on the arm.

"Owww." He pretended she had hurt him and even rubbed his arm. "You're acting just like Candy the Second. Pretending to hate me when in fact"—his voice got all low and husky—"you love me."

"Isobel"—she pronounced the name with infinite care—"couldn't love you more if she tried." She looked at Torrent with googly eyes. Followed him around like a lovesick puppy. "Most women would be jealous."

He nuzzled into her neck. "There is only one female for me."

"You mean the only one for you who only has two

legs?"

"The only one for me, period." He kissed her.

Lake cleared his throat. "Um . . . would you mind taking this elsewhere? I would recommend . . . back to your chamber."

"Sorry." Candy felt her cheeks heat.

They said their good-byes and headed home.

The dogs were excited to see them.

"You do your thing in there." He pointed to the bathroom. "I'll take these two out. Siggie . . . Siggie," he called to the puppy. She had decided to call him Siegfried, which had quickly become Siggie.

There was no reason why she had chosen that name other than it popped into her head and she thought it would be cute. The little guy had grown quite a bit since coming to live with them.

Sensing a potential walk, he bounced up and down around Torrent's feet. Candy the Sec . . . *Isobel,* wagged her tail and looked up at Torrent with such love and adoration in her eyes. "Come on you." He gave her a scratch behind her ears. He hooked her leash onto her collar.

"All set." He walked over and clutched the back of Candy's neck, giving her a lingering kiss. "We'll see you in a few."

She nodded. "Okay."

"And Candy . . ."

"Yeah?" She could hear that he was up to something.

"Don't put pajamas on. Stay naked." He gave her the once over, looking like he was imagining her that way.

Torrent licked his lips, yup, he was definitely picturing her starkers.

"I don't know." She teased. "It's a bit chilly this evening."

He maneuvered her so that her back ended up flush against the wall. "Get dressed at your own peril."

"Is that a threat?" She licked her lips.

"You'd better believe it . . . I know you hate it when I rip your clothes off."

"I liked that dress, and the skirt. I have no more thongs left and I really, really liked those shorts."

"They were tiny." He was breathing hard, his chest almost touching hers. He was leaning down, his cheek right next to hers, talking right into her ear. "I could see your ass when you bent over."

"They were comfortable. My legs looked good in them." She had to hold back a laugh, those shorts had been really tiny. She knew they would drive him wild when she bought them. It wasn't like she planned on wearing them anywhere but at home.

He groaned. "Your legs looked amazing." He squeezed his eyes shut. "Just tell me one thing before I go."

"What's that?" She pulled back just a little so that she could see him better.

His head was still down, his chin almost on his chest. "How much do you like this?" he fisted her top. As he spoke, he lifted his gaze and locked it with hers.

Candy swallowed hard. "I love this top." She lied. "It's one of my favorites."

Torrent gave her a tight smile. "Love, love or love?"

She pulled her shoulders back, trying not to smile. "Love, love. Besides, I need to brush my teeth and"—she slid out from under him—"you"—she walked into the bathroom—"need to . . ."

She stopped short when Torrent marched in behind her, closing the door behind him. She caught his intense stare in the mirror. Teasing him was too easy.

"Fine," he said. "The shirt can stay." He lifted her skirt. Candy braced her hands on the marble counter. "All this talk about your ass." He palmed one of her butt cheeks.

Candy was wearing a pair of cotton briefs. Not very sexy. You wouldn't say so though by looking at the way his eyes had heated. How his jaw had tensed.

He gripped the cotton.

"Wait!" She yelled.

Torrent shook his head, looking stricken. "Please don't make me. I'll be quick . . . I promise."

She laughed and shimmied out of her panties, letting them fall around her ankles. Torrent groaned. Then she pulled her shirt over her head.

He growled, letting his head fall back for a second. She unhooked her bra and her boobs sprang free. As in popped out. It felt good to have that thing off. Her bras had been digging into her lately. Torrent sure as hell wasn't complaining. Not by the way he was eyeballing her.

"Fuck," he mumbled, along with something else that was so garbled that she couldn't understand him. He cleared his throat. "Do you want to watch yourself come?"

His eyes were still glued to her chest, which was reflected in the mirror. Candy dropped her bra on the floor as Torrent pulled her skirt all the way up, bunching it around her hips. It was elasticated, so it stayed right where it was. "Or . . ." he reached around her and found her clit, circling it with one of his fingers.

Candy moaned, she widened her stance and arched her back. Torrent kissed her between her shoulders as he pulled his pants down. "Do you want your ass on that vanity and your legs around my hips?"

She loved how he always checked with her. *Where? What position? Fast? Slow? Harder?*

She moaned louder, closing her eyes and rocking her hips.

"Choose right now or I'll decide for you." He groaned.

She also liked that he could be so damned bossy. Candy giggled. It came out sounding strangled and husky. She arched and thrust some more, catching his gaze in the mirror. His eyes had lightened up. Shit but he was turned on. The muscles on his neck popped. He looked tightly wound. She licked her lips and moaned some more.

"You're such a damn tease but I love it." He chuckled. He glanced down and then gave her ass a squeeze and a hard smack.

Candy yelped. Torrent gripped her hips and pushed himself inside of her. All the way, only stopping when his hips were flush against her.

Candy was panting. She gripped the vanity.

He cursed softly. "I love being inside you," Torrent

rasped. His muscles bulged. His pecs, his neck, his arms all roped and bulged. He was beautiful and masculine and just so goddamned sexy it took her breath away. He grit his teeth as he pulled back and thrust into her . . . hard. His fingers dug into her hips.

It was her turn to curse.

He didn't wait for her to catch her breath, he thrust back into her again, and again, and again. His eyes stayed on hers. Her mouth hung open. She struggled to get enough air into her lungs. Her boobs jerked and shuddered with each hard plunge. She didn't care.

Felt. Too. Good.

Candy had to brace against the counter even though Torrent held her tightly. Her pussy fluttered and he groaned while sucking in his lower lip.

With a devilish smile, he let go of her hip with one hand and pressed it into her . . . *oh hell* . . . *oh damn* . . . self-combustion. Her orgasm ripped through her and she couldn't help but to moan his name.

She loved these heightened senses. Loved. Them. He leaned over her and grunted, his dick swelled as he began to jerk. Then he nipped her neck, just below her ear . . . *oh god. . . . Oh. . . . Oooooh. . . .* Her channel spasmed so hard she wasn't sure she'd ever be the same again. This time she may or may not have screamed. She wasn't sure. He slowed his thrusting and kissed her neck, still grunting each time his cock slid into her.

Torrent's chest heaved. He went from kissing her neck to sticking his tongue into her ear and nipping at her lobe.

She giggled and shivered. His . . . shaft was still hard and deep inside of her. It twitched. "You're insatiable." She panted.

"Do you blame me?" He was out of breath. "You can't blame me." He sucked on her earlobe some more. "You feel so damned good." His big hands slid up her hips before clasping her breasts. "So incredible." He squeezed her flesh gently. Then he moved one of his hands down, rubbing her more rounded belly before rubbing her clit some more.

It was crazy how he could get her off in one second and turned her on in the next. Like her multiple orgasms had never happened.

There was a whining sound, which quickly became two whining noises. This was followed by a scratching noise.

"Oh flip." Torrent pulled out of her. He opened the bathroom door. "I'm sorry, kids." Claws clicked on the tiles and dogs looked up at them with their big brown eyes, leashes still attached to their collars. "You poor babies," he added, before turning to her. "Hold that thought." He brushed a kiss on her temple and handed her a towel.

She smiled at him. "You're terrible. You couldn't even take the dogs out before mauling me."

"You said that like you hated it. Your pussy sang a different song." He grinned.

"You pig."

"It's part of the reason you love me so much. I'm part pig, part dragon." He bobbed his eyebrows.

She choked out a laugh. "You're right." He was about

to walk back to her. "Don't forget about the kids. You already forgot about them once today." She put her hands on her hips and tried to sound stern.

His eyes widened. He'd totally forgotten about them . . . again. "I'll make it up to them"—he looked down—"by taking you out on an extra-long walk." His voice changed as he spoke directly to the dogs.

His eyes moved back to her. "I'll be back. Get into our bed and make sure you're naked." He made a growling noise in the back of his throat. "I'll try and be gentle this time."

"Maybe I can ride you?" She had to talk him into it the first time. Something about shifters needing to be in control, at all times.

His eyes lit up. "Oh god . . . that would be awesome. Will you wear your cowboy hat and boots?" His expression was pinched.

She laughed. That was something else she'd had to talk him into, bedroom props. It only took one time and he was hooked on all counts. "Um . . ." she reached up and kissed him on the side of his mouth. "More like a sports bra. The girls are getting too big. It's all the burgers, pizza . . ."

He kissed her to shut her up. "You love eating those things."

"Yeah, I do."

"I love your curves, fucking love them." He leaned down and sucked on a nipple. "I'll take you any way I can get you. A few pounds heavier or lighter, it makes no difference." It warmed her heart . . . all of her organs, that he meant it.

One of the dogs whined.

"Shit! Stop distracting me." He looked down at Siggie who had jumped up on his leg. "It's your mommy's fault, guys. Blame her." Her heart squeezed as he said it. *Mommy.* Maybe her scent would change tomorrow.

"Hey." She pretended to be mad. "It's your daddy's fault, guys. All him." Another clench. Her mate would make such a good father.

Torrent cupped her cheek. "No sports bra. I'll hold them. I have two hands and a mouth."

Candy laughed, forgetting about her heat, or lack thereof.

CHAPTER 25

Three days later . . .

Candy lay in Torrent's arms. She felt the rise and fall of his chest with each deep breath. It was early yet. She looked toward the big, bay window, the sky was turning. Dark becoming light. Night turning to day. A new start, new beginnings and possibilities.

The sun was still hiding below the horizon, but not for long. The sky slowly bleeding with shades of pink and yellow. The black starting to hint at blue. One or two stars were still visible.

"Hey," Torrent's voice was still thick with sleep. He kissed the top of her head. "You're awake early."

She shrugged. "I couldn't sleep anymore. Look at that sunrise. It's almost a waste to sleep."

"Yeah. It's amazing." His head was higher on the pillow behind hers. He pulled her more firmly against him, her back to his chest. His cock nestled more firmly against her ass. Torrent inhaled deeply, his hips giving a tiny, circling thrust. She didn't think he even knew he had done it.

He buried his head into the back of her neck. "Mmmmm, you scent of heaven."

Was she in heat?

Is that why she smelled differently?

Could it be?

Torrent released his hold on her slightly. "Why did you just tense up?"

Oh shit! What did she say to that? She wasn't completely sure she wanted a baby, and she didn't want him to get his hopes up. She was still young. There was time. She would only be really sure when the time came, when her body finally decided to pop an egg. *Arghhh!* What was wrong with her?

"Is everything okay?" His voice was laced with concern.

"Yeah." She tried to sound relaxed because she was relaxed. Why was she even over thinking this? "Great," she added.

"Mmmmmm." Another deep rumble. "Why don't I believe you?" He pulled away, making space so that she could turn.

He raised his brows as she turned to face him. "Out with it. What's up?"

She shook her head. "It's nothing." *Less than nothing.*

"I can see that something is going on inside that head of yours. I would like it very much if you told me what it was. Even if it is nothing."

She huffed out a breath. "Fine, but it's not a big deal, just something that jumped into my head."

"Okay." He smiled but quickly turned serious.

"I was just wondering just now . . . you know . . ." She paused for a second to gather her thoughts.

"Yeah?" He prompted.

Okay, maybe she paused for longer than one second but who was counting. "I was just wondering when you told me that I scented of heaven if, well, if . . ." Another pause.

"If"—his jaw clenched—"you were in heat." He said, his eyes dipped down and his lashes fanned his cheeks.

She could see by his reaction that he hadn't said it for that reason. "Don't worry about it though. It's not important. It just popped into my mind. You asked why I tensed up." She was talking too much. Talking too quickly. "You asked and I told you, but . . ."

His gaze lifted and her words dried up.

His beautiful pale gaze held hers. "Don't try and pretend it's not important. I can see it is." He cupped her cheek in his big hand. "Don't pretend with me."

"Okay." She pulled a face. "I guess I do care. I don't know why though. We talked about this. I don't even want kids yet . . . I want them"—she quickly added—"just not right now."

His eyes glinted and the corners of his mouth gave a momentary lift. "You're still worried?"

She nodded. "Yes, I guess I am. I *can* ovulate. I *must have* or I wouldn't be here, so what's wrong with me? I want children, more so now that I met you. I want us to be a family one day."

"Firstly, we're already a family and secondly"—he

kissed her—"I want kids too. Lots of them."

"Hey . . ." She gave his chest a small shove. "Don't get ahead of yourself."

He smiled for a beat. "I don't like that this is bugging you. Don't think I haven't noticed." He paused, clearly in thought. "I initially thought that you had dropped it, but then you kept asking me, in different ways, if you were in heat. I've heard you ask Sky as well. You do know that it's considered foreplay if a person sniffs another person, don't you? You keep making her sniff you." He grinned.

"Oh no, really?" No wonder Sky had looked so uncomfortable, every single time.

"Yup." He smiled but it didn't last long. "You do realize that if you were with a human male . . ." His eyes darkened and narrowed. She could see that he hated the thought. "You wouldn't have known whether you were in heat or not. This whole thing wouldn't be an issue."

"I'm not with a human."

"Thank claw." He kissed the tip of her nose. "I did a bit of research on the subject. I googled a human female's cycle to—"

"You did?" *Oh wow!* That was so sweet. Then something occurred to her. "Wait a minute. Are you worried? Is that it?" She sucked in a breath and covered her mouth. "Have you changed your mind about being okay with me if . . . if . . ."

"No," a rasp. "I will never change my mind about anything that doesn't include being with you. We belong together. If giving up my crown in order to keep you makes me selfish then so be it." He looked more deeply into her eyes. "Don't ever worry about my wanting to be with you or our relationship. You don't have to."

She nodded. "Okay. I'm glad."

"The reason I googled it was because it still bugged you and I knew this conversation was coming." He ran a hand through his hair. "A human female ovulates once a month on average. We know this already. There are things that can prevent a female from ovulating. Stress is a big factor. You were abducted and hunted. You and I had a bit of a rocky start. This whole life"—he lifted his eyes for a moment—"here with me is new to you."

"I'm not really that stressed. Maybe I was initially, but not anymore. I'm so happy it's ridiculous. I don't think that's it."

"It could be." He paused. "It could also be"—he sighed—"based on what I researched, that your body is taking a while to get back to it's regular cycle after being on those pills that stop pregnancy."

Candy nodded. She hadn't taken her birth control since coming here.

"I read that it can take months to have an ovulation after stopping." He frowned. "One thing that I found puzzling. You should not have gone into heat in the first place. Not if you were taking the pills."

Candy frowned as she tried to digest what he was saying.

"You were monitored for several months before being chosen to come to us. In that time you had to have gone into heat at least once."

"Mmmmm." Then it occurred to her what it might have been. "I had an ear infection a few months before coming here. My doctor prescribed antibiotics . . . medicine . . ." She added when she realized he didn't know what antibiotics were. "I was warned to take extra precautions during that time because the medicine affected the effectiveness of the pill. I may have ovulated . . . in fact . . ." She racked her brain. "I can't think of anything else. I always took my pills religiously. I always insisted on extra precautions anyway." She stopped what she was saying when Torrent's jaw tightened. "Um . . . yeah." *Awkward!*

"I'm sorry." He brushed a kiss on her lips. "Ignore me, I'm a jealous idiot."

Candy smiled at him. "At least you realize it nowadays."

"If it makes you feel better, maybe we can arrange to go and see a human doctor. They can run some tests."

Candy shook her head. "I'm being silly. It must be the whole stopping the pill thing. It doesn't matter, I'm sure it'll happen soon. If I don't ovulate in the next few months maybe, just to put my mind at rest, we can go and see someone. It wouldn't be because I'm ready to start trying or anything."

He grinned. "Okay, if you say so." She could see that he wasn't buying it.

"I mean it. I'm not ready to have a baby yet."

"Sure thing." His grin only got bigger.

"I'm serious." She gave him another shove.

"So am I." He pulled her towards him. "About making love to you, that is, and right now."

As if on cue, one of the dogs whined. There was a scratching on the side of the bed.

Torrent slumped back down and made a groaning noise. He was still smiling so she could tell that he didn't really mean it.

Using an elbow, she lifted herself so that she could look him in the eyes. "See, even animals are hard work, can you imagine what a small baby would be like?"

His eyes sparkled in the morning light. "Yes, I can." His voice was a tad on the husky side. Was he a little emotional talking about this? "It would be amazing and wonderful and"—he gave a big sigh—"we already have to get up early and sometimes even during the night, so we may as well have a little one while we're at it." That moment of tension, of emotion passed. "A mini you would be amazing."

"Yeah, except I can't have a girl."

He shrugged. "That's okay." He tweaked her nose.

"I'll get up for the dogs." She leaned in and kissed his cheek. "You sleep in a little."

Torrent shook his head. "Nah . . . but I wouldn't mind some company if you feel like coming along?"

"What, and miss out on a morning stroll on a day like this . . . ? Never."

Ten days later . . .

They were grouped on the large balcony that jutted from the main hall. Fifteen males, excluding himself, packed tightly on the landing. They were all big. And powerful. The best fighting males in the water kingdom. Torrent oversaw this team himself. The pinnacle warriors. Their places on the team were all hard earned.

Torrent looked from one warrior to the next, making sure that he locked eyes with each of them. "Today's practice will be about testing stamina. Not strength, or stealth or speed, but stamina. Peak too soon and you will fail. On the other hand,"—he paused—"not pushing hard enough could also result in failure. It's finding the balance that will be most important."

One of his top warriors looked uncomfortable. His whole stance was tense and he shifted his weight from one foot to the other and back again.

"Is there something that you wish to say, Surge?"

The male returned his gaze, unfazed that he had been singled out. He gave a deep nod. "I am questioning how a long, arduous flight would help in battle. Strength, speed and stealth are what counts. Stamina . . ." He shook his head. "You are training us to flee. To succeed at being able to get away even when pursued."

Nonsense. Utter bullshit! It was the first thing that came into his mind. He pursed his lips to keep from saying it. He had always welcomed questions, encouraged his team to speak up. His way was not always necessarily the right way. Well, it was mostly the right way but not every time. "What if our enemy were to flee?"

"That would be different. However . . ." Surge cocked his head. "If we were strong enough, we would defeat them before they could even think of fleeing, there would be no need for stamina."

Torrent had to suppress a laugh. "It would take huge amounts of strength to achieve a feat like that. Unless the opponent was greatly outnumbered, I can't see that being the case though."

"Strength, brute force, that is where our focus should lie."

He could feel Surge's frustration. The male was most often the victor when it came to battles that tested strength. Not so much when it came to stamina. Surge hated to lose. It was important that he make the male understand why stamina was important. He was sure that deep down this warrior knew it already. He just needed a bit of extra convincing.

"It should be both in equal measure. Let me explain it another way." He shrugged. "Battle, in many ways, is like rutting."

This earned him a few sniggers from the males. It certainly got all of their attention. "A big cock will go a long way in ensuring a positive outcome . . ."

There were more sniggers.

"However, a big cock is not, in itself, a guarantee of success. It is important to feel out your enemy. Know their strengths and weaknesses. In the case of a female, know what she wants, what makes her tick. Know what will make her scream. Then it is a case of being able to go the distance to get her there. Stamina is everything. Knowing how, and having the tools, is not always enough." He paused. "We all have our strengths and weaknesses. We are a team. We all have different strengths and weaknesses. Know your team members. Help one another. Work together. Lastly, work on your own weaknesses. It's a pain in the ass but it's a necessary pain."

Surge nodded, then he smiled. It was cocky and arrogant. "Thanks for the analogy. It has helped me to see things more clearly."

Some of the others nodded in agreement.

"Also," Surge continued. "With regards to the whole team work thing, my lord." He quickly added.

Torrent folded him arms.

"Did it extend to the queen? Working as a . . . team to satisfy her . . ."

"No," Torrent growled. He couldn't help but to react.

"One of the human sayings is, sharing is caring." Surge smirked. Torrent could see that he was joking. It still irked him that he dared think of his female, the queen, in that light. It didn't matter that she was sexy and that Surge was justified. The male wasn't, after all, blind.

Torrent wasn't smiling. "Fuck off and fuck you and any male for that . . ." He took a deep breath. "Moving on . . ." The male didn't mean it. No one would dare touch his mate. Of course others looked at her . . . in that way. She was sexy . . . groan worthy. Candy was . . . he cleared his throat. "Let's get going. We only have so many daylight hours."

The males removed their pants and he followed suit. He was just folding the garment when the door to the hall flew open. "Torrent!" Candy yelled.

She sounded afraid. Torrent couldn't see her through the sea of males.

"Your female must have heard our conversation and came running." Surge mumbled and a couple of the males chuckled.

Torrent narrowed his eyes on Surge and growled a warning. The male paled and looked at his feet. "Candy," he called to his mate. He could scent her. Could scent . . . fear.

Why the fuck was she scared?

The males moved to make a path. His female's face was pale. Her eyes were wide. She didn't look at any of the others, she didn't blush or turn away. His female was still shy when dragons were in a state of undress. It was something that he normally found funny. A group of males this large should've had her covering her eyes.

Her lack of reaction scared him more than her pale skin or her trembling hands. Torrent quickly closed distance between them. "What is it? What's wrong? What happened?"

At last she seemed to notice that they were surrounded by an audience. Still no blushing though. "Um . . ." her lip wobbled.

"Surge," he all but snarled. "You take over the

leadership role. The Eiffel Tower is your mark. First male back, wins."

"Thank you, my lord," Surge said. He began to address the team.

Torrent turned his focus back to Candy, back to where it belonged. "Come with me." He put an arm around her. There were a few dragons in the great hall. They nodded their heads.

The scent of her fear and confusion only grew worse. "I've got you." He opened the first door they came across. It led to the great library. There was one male present. "Please, give us some privacy."

The male nodded. "Of course, my lord." He bowed to Candy as he passed them. "My lady." Then he left, closing the door behind him.

Torrent's heart was beating out of his chest. He turned to face Candy, putting his hands on her shoulders. "What's wrong?"

"There's something wrong with me," she blurted.

Torrent ran a hand through his hair. "Wrong? How wrong? Did something happen?"

She nodded. "I'm sick or . . . something . . ." She widened her eyes. "I . . . it can't be . . . it just can't." She tore out of his grip and paced away from him.

"Candy." There was a hint of anguish in the way he said her name. A hint of desperation. It was how he felt right now. "What are you saying? I don't follow." His hands felt clammy. His heart rate picked up even more. So much so, that he put a hand to his chest.

She bit down on her bottom lip. "I felt something inside me. It wasn't normal. It wasn't."

She looked like she was freaking out. What she was saying made zero sense. "What do you mean?" He took in a few deep breaths, trying to calm the fuck down.

"It's just . . . it was . . ." She was breathing deeply, her eyes still wide. "Oh god. It can't be. Either I'm crazy or I'm . . . no way . . . sick. I must be sick." She nodded.

"Stop." He walked over to her and grabbed both her hands in his. "Take a deep breath."

"This is no time for breathing. No time for doing anything other than panicking."

"Panicking won't help." He gave her hands a squeeze. "I love you. We can get through anything. Just for the record"—he calmed right down—"you can't be sick. I don't know how I could've forgotten something so important. Since mating with me, you've become too strong. You couldn't pick up so much as a cold."

"Oh shit! I feel sick." Candy pulled her hands free and went to sit down on a nearby sofa.

Torrent went and sat next to her.

"I'm fine." She nodded. "Everything is going to be okay." She sniffed and turned to look him in the eyes. Then she smiled. It was tense but there was also genuine happiness there.

"What?" He could feel he was frowning.

"I think I'm pregnant." She sucked in a deep breath. "I'm pretty sure I'm pregnant. I can't think of any other reason. Oh god . . ." She covered her mouth, still looking shocked. "My boobs, my weight gain. My lack of ovulation . . . shit! I must be. I don't understand though, I've had my menstruation like clockwork."

"Okay . . . back up." He didn't want to get excited, or to get his hopes up. It couldn't be. Her scent. It hadn't changed. She couldn't be pregnant, could she? "What made you—"

Before he could finish, she interjected. "I felt him kicking. I felt it. Clear as day. At first I was sure that I'd imagined it. That maybe it was gas or something." She giggled. "It wasn't gas. No way it was gas." She smiled. Her eyes were still a tad wide and her face was still pale but she looked much better. "Thing is, I've been getting a lot of gas feelings lately. I didn't think anything of it. My tummy . . ." She stood and lifted her dress. "It's more rounded than . . . I don't know . . . look at it."

"You can't be." He blurted, watching her expression change. From someone excited to one who had just had their hopes dashed. "I'm sorry but you can't be . . ."

Then she lifted her chin and pursed her lips for a moment, seeming to come to a decision. "I know what I felt. It was, it was unlike anything I've ever experienced before. It happened a couple of times and it was kicking."

"You only scent of you. Okay, that's not entirely true, my scent is there as a mate. It would've changed and become more pronounced if you were pregnant with my child. Unless . . ." No! Fuck! "Could it be a human child?"

"Of course it's a human child," she blurted. Then her expression changed to one of anger. "Oh! Human, as in not yours." She put her hands on her hips. Candy licked her lips. "No damned way. I was so careful. I told you that I had only had sex with one person for the longest time and even that was few and far between. We always used a condom. It had been months since we last—you know—before coming here." She lifted her eyes in thought. "I'd say close on three months. You are the only person I've ever had unprotected sex with." She was half yelling at him. "As in ever. The only one."

"Okay." He hooked an arm around her. "I had to ask. We have to . . . get to the bottom of this." She was still tense. "I'm sorry." He cupped her jaw and forced her to look at him. "I'm sorry."

She finally gave a nod. "How do we find out? Can I pee on a stick or something?"

What? He must have heard wrong. "Humans pee on sticks to find out if they are pregnant?" Humans were strange creatures. He wouldn't tell Candy that, of course. He valued his life. "I don't see how peeing on a stick would . . ."

She laughed. "No, silly. Not real sticks. Devices that contain chemicals that change color or, never mind, it's not important."

It was his turn to pace. He ran a hand through his hair and massaged the back of his neck. There was a knot forming. His muscles were wound tight. "I have no clue about any of this. I planned on researching it all when the time came." He huffed out a breath. "Okay. I have a plan."

"Good! What is it?"

"Sky." He already felt better. "There's no one who knows more about pregnancy than her."

"Aside from women who have actually given birth?" She raised her brows. "Not that I have anything against Sky. I love Sky, she's my bestie."

"Let me rephrase that, there's no one who knows more than Sky about pregnancy that we can trust to keep this quiet."

Candy nodded. She worried her bottom lip between her teeth.

It had to be something else. In fact, he was sure that there was a perfectly good explanation. The more he thought about it, the more it made perfect sense. Disappointment welled up in him.

CHAPTER 26

There was no other explanation. None. In fact, now that she finally realized it, she wondered how she could have ever missed the signs.

She'd been peeing often, her back ached as of late. Her boobs were huge and tender. Her belly was rounded. She'd felt movement and if she was honest with herself it wasn't for the first time. Today was the first significant kicking she'd felt though. It was the first time she'd been unable to ignore the obvious.

She was pregnant. It needed to be confirmed, but she was pregnant. Candy felt scared but she also felt excited. No wonder she hadn't ovulated. Flip, she was going to have a little Torrent. Would the baby have his eyes, his smile?

She put her hand to her belly. It was surreal. She rubbed her skin in a circle, feeling so emotional it was all she could do not to cry. She willed the little one to kick again but there was nothing. She was going to be a mom and Torrent was going to get his wish sooner than expected. He was going to be a dad. Parents. They were going to be parents. She smiled past the lump in her throat.

Sky choked out a laugh. "You should see the goofy smile on your face. Then again, you look like you might cry at any second as well."

"What do you think?" She tried to keep her back straight, to stay normal.

"Mmmmm." Sky narrowed her eyes as she examined Candy's belly. "Hard to tell. You have a definite bump but I don't know how you looked before."

"Flat. My female's stomach was flat," Torrent said. His eyes were dark and his arms were folded across his chest.

"You did mention that you've been eating a lot lately." She shrugged. "I suppose that in itself could be a sign of pregnancy. Increased weight, in itself is not a good enough indication though. Dragon females don't get bigger breasts when pregnant. We do not feed our young in this way. Your weight gain in this area is more than likely due to your general increase . . ."

"Sky," Torrent sounded irritated. "Is my mate pregnant? She can't be . . ." He went on, "I would scent it on her. Surely we could scent it."

Sky scrunched her noise up. "Excuse me." She gave Candy a quick sniff, looking distinctly uncomfortable. Then she shook her head. "I only smell human. I mean"—she pulled a face—"I can smell you." She looked at Torrent as she spoke. "You are all over her, but it's not coming from inside her. Her scent hasn't changed other than from being your mate."

"Exactly. I've never known a female not to take the

scent of the male, that special pregnant scent."

"Yeah, but . . ." Sky looked thoughtful for few beats. "There's never been a royal, water dragon before either. Not where the female was a human." She shrugged. "We don't really know what to expect, do we?"

"I guess not. Shit!"

"How do we find out for sure?" He was tense. He kept curling and uncurling his fists. His hair was a mess from grabbing and tugging on it.

At least he was dressed, Sky had tossed him a pair of Lake's pants soon after they arrived at her door. It was for her benefit. Candy couldn't help but to feel weird with her mate naked in a room with another woman.

"Um . . . there should be a heartbeat. If the baby is big enough to kick, it should have a steady heartbeat."

Torrent sucked in a breath. "Why didn't I think of that?"

"Do you think so?" Candy asked.

Torrent smiled. He nodded. "Yeah. Sky is right. When I'm in that area my mind is on other things." He bobbed his eyebrows. "I could have easily missed an extra beat here or there. Especially since my tongue . . ."

"Okay," Candy blurted. "Can you check? Please? I really need to know."

She didn't feel so sure all of a sudden. Maybe it was because she wanted it so badly. She hadn't realized it before but she wanted a baby. She really wanted a little one. Torrent was ready. More than ready. It was only when she didn't ovulate that she realized . . .

Torrent gripped the back of her neck. He looked deeply into her eyes and gave her sweet smile. "I would love for you to be pregnant . . ." He was breathing deeply. He closed his eyes for a second and then kissed her. It was quick and deep. He broke the kiss. "But . . ."

Why did there always have to be a but?

"If you aren't pregnant, please don't be upset. We'll rectify the situation as a matter of urgency. You'll be fine, we'll be fine. Fuck." He put his brow to hers. "I'm saying all the wrong things."

"No, you're not." She said as he moved back.

"I love you." He brushed his lips to hers before dropping to his knees.

She pulled her dress up again, bunching it just under her breasts.

Torrent put his head against her belly and closed his eyes. After what felt like an age, he pulled back. His face was a closed door. He looked tense. He looked . . . different.

He put his hand against her belly and smiled up at her. "My son."

"Oh god," she whispered. "Are you sure?"

Torrent was grinning from ear to ear. "I'm sure. You were right."

Candy squealed as Torrent jumped up in a graceful move, wrapping her up in his arms. "You're pregnant. We're going to have a baby."

She buried her head in his neck. A tear may or may not have fallen. She was just so happy. She was bursting with the emotion.

She looked up in time to see Sky slip away. The she-dragon had tears coursing down her cheeks. Flip!

"I'm so happy." Torrent said as he picked her up and spun her around.

One month later...

"Sit." Torrent motioned to the couch. His mate looked tired. She had rubbed her eyes one too many times for his liking and her feet were swollen. Her belly even more so. She was still as sexy as ever though. All curves. Her cheeks were flushed. Her mouth more kissable than ever.

"I'm fine. I can do it." Using a finger, she swept some hair behind her ear.

He shook his head. "I know you can, but I don't want you to."

"Is it so bad that I want to prepare a meal for the man I love?"

"I don't want you to overtax yourself."

She sighed. "Frying a few steaks is hardly taxing myself." She clutched her lower back. It was aching more and more as his son grew bigger. She tried to downplay it, but he could see it by the way she carried herself, by the way her lips pursed together as she held her back.

"See." He glanced at where her hand was rubbing. "You need to sit. I'll cook if you feel like steaks." By the glint that appeared in her eyes, he could see that she did.

"Mmmmm." She licked her lips. "This meat craving is

nuts."

"Dragons enjoy their protein. It is normal for you to crave meat. I take it that you'd like your steak rare?" He raised his brows.

She licked her lips again. "Yes, please." Then she grimaced, her hand returned to her lower back.

"Sit." He half growled at her, hoping she would listen to him for a change.

"Have I told you lately how bossy you are?"

Torrent had to laugh. "This morning, if memory serves. I insisted on going down on you." He winked at her.

"That wasn't what we argued about. You wouldn't let me return the favor." She smiled, looking so damned beautiful it damn near took his breath away.

"Semantics." He shrugged. "Now sit so that I can give you a back rub."

"I love you so much." She sighed as she sank down onto the sofa.

"Yeah, yeah, more like, you love how good I am with my hands and my mouth and my . . ."

She burst out laughing. "That too."

Using his thumbs, he massaged into the soft tissue on either side of her spine. Candy moaned. "Oh god, yes!" she cried. "There, right there and don't you dare stop."

Torrent chuckled. His female hadn't been this vocal this morning when his face was buried between her legs. She was vocal, but not quite this much. It was funny how things changed.

He was sure to work all of her muscles, paying special

attention to her lower back. After about a half hour, she slumped back against him in an almost boneless state. Exactly how he liked her. Did it matter what methods he used to achieve it? He didn't think so.

Candy sighed.

Torrent put his arms around her and held her distended belly, running his hands up and down it's curve. A feeling of possessiveness wrapped itself around him and he had to fight to keep from holding her more tightly.

The baby gave a soft kick beneath his hand. *His son. His heir. His.*

Torrent buried his head into her hair, breathing in her fruity scent. She sat up and turned to look at him. "Thank you. I feel so much better."

He could see that her eyelids were at half-mast. She spoke slowly.

"You're tired."

She gave a lazy smile and yawned, making a sound of agreement.

"Go and have a nap, I'll wake you when dinner is ready."

She shook her head. "Let me help you."

Torrent raised his brows. "You're already very busy."

"Like hell." She smiled. "Doing what?" She choked out a laugh.

"Growing our baby."

She gave him another lazy smile. "I suppose so." Her eyes were so damned beautiful. The color of the deepest ocean. Her hair was like spun gold. Not for the first time, he longed for a daughter with hair of gold and eyes like the ocean. The feeling soon passed as he pictured his son. The male would have his eyes and hair but her features. He was sure of it. He couldn't wait to meet the little one. It was all he could think about.

Candy gave him a quick kiss and attempted to get up. Her belly really was in the way. Torrent gripped her ass and gave her a push. Yup, in five weeks, six at the most, he was going to be a daddy. Excitement coursed through him.

"I'll wake you, sweetheart. You rest."

She turned and gave him the sweetest smile. The dogs jumped onto the bed and curled up beside her, one on either side. He pretended not to notice. Anything for his mate.

CHAPTER 27

Seven weeks later . . .

Torrent concentrated on putting one foot in front of the other, until he hit the solid wall that marked the end of the hallway, and then he marched back. He turned sharply, yet again, and made his way back. Every muscle was bunched and ready. Adrenaline coursed. He was ready for war. Ready to take on the enemy. Ready to fight. The only problem, his foe wasn't physical.

Torrent picked up his pace.

"Stop that," Tide growled. "We should go. It is customary to wait in the great hall."

Torrent didn't answer. He clenched his jaw tighter and continued to march. Back and forth, back and forth.

The moans started up again. If he didn't know better, he would think that she was being tortured. Skinned alive, broken, battered, bleeding. That she was dying.

No!

Fuck!

He stopped marching for a second and grit his teeth,

trying to drown out the sounds.

"Brother," Tide's voice was softer. "Why are you doing this to yourself? Come with me. We spoke with the healer twenty minutes ago, all is well with your female. You do not have to be here."

Torrent shook his head. "She is human." His voice was thick.

"It does not matter. It is tradition that . . ."

Tide continued to talk but Torrent no longer heard him. He could only hear his mate, his beloved. She was in agony. He could hear how she tried to be quiet. How she tried to hold it in.

Fuck that.

It wasn't right. He knew that she needed him and yet, not once had she called his name. She was trying to be strong. He hated it.

He rushed to the door and barged inside.

"Torrent." Her face was a mask of hurt. Her hair was plastered to her face. Her cheeks red. Her eyes glassy.

"Fuck," he growled as he walked to her. The elderly she-dragon gave him a look of disapproval.

"This would've been over by now if she had been in one of the tidal pools." The healer stated.

"The queen is a human." He took her hand. It was customary for female water dragons to take to the sea within the shelter of the pools. They gave birth there. Candy was not a dragon. "What can I do? I'm so sorry for not coming earlier." His voice mirrored the tension he was feeling. He had been out in that hallway the entire time but it wasn't enough.

Torrent could see that she was fighting her way through a contraction. She was breathing deeply, her belly looked tight. Instead of answering, Candy moaned. It was a guttural sound from deep inside her throat.

After about another minute, she slumped back, completely out of breath.

"I should have come sooner." He cupped her overly warm cheek.

She shook her head, swallowing thickly. Her eyes didn't focus on him properly. This is what thirteen hours of labor looked like. The last four had been hard. Impossible even, but his female wasn't giving up. She had both strength and stamina in spades. She was the greatest warrior he had ever seen.

"You shouldn't be here." The she-dragon chided him.

"I'm so glad you came." His female grabbed ahold of him. "Please don't leave me. Please. I tried to be brave, but I'm scared."

"I'm here now and I'm not going anywhere."

The healer cleared her throat. "My lord, you . . ."

"I'm not going anywhere." His voice was a deep rasp.

"As you wish." The she-dragon didn't sound pleased. She was the opposite of pleased. He couldn't give a shit.

There was a creaking noise as the door closed. Tide had decided to leave him to it. Good. He was the king and if he wanted to be at his mate's side, he would be here. It would take an entire army to remove him and even then, it wouldn't be without casualty.

"Oh god." Candy grit her teeth. "Here comes another one. It's happening more quickly . . ." Her face turned red and she groaned while grabbing her belly.

"What should I do?" He felt desperate.

"Breathe, my lady," the healer said.

Candy began to suck in air, pushing it in and out in hard pants.

The healer looked at him. "There is nothing you can do. The baby will be here soon, we are nearing the end of the birthing process." She peered between Candy's legs.

His female breathed as though her life depended on it. Deep inhalations. Her eyes went from being wide and anguished to tightly shut and back again. She seemed to barely be holding it together. It seemed to last for an age before she slumped back. The shirt she was wearing was damp and clung to her body.

She looked delirious. Her eyelids drooped. His female began to shake. "C-cold," she whispered. "I-I'm really c-cold."

"What's wrong with her?" he tried not to snarl.

"Calm down, my lord. The baby has entered the birthing passage. This too is normal." The she-dragon pointed to a blanket on the sofa. "Put that around her shoulders."

Torrent nodded. He raced to fetch the woolen blanket and draped it around his female's shoulders and upper torso. A few minutes later, Candy began to doze off.

"What's going on?" he asked the healer. "Why has it stopped?"

The she-dragon signaled for him to be quiet. "All is progressing as it should. It is the calm before the storm. Let your mate rest." She shook her head. "It won't last very long."

Not even five minutes later, Candy moaned. Her eyes opened and her face contorted with pain. She gripped her distended belly with both hands. "Oh god!" she groaned. "Oh." She pushed the blanket away. "I'm too hot." She moaned.

"Won't be long now," the elderly female said. "Breathe, my queen." She began to huff and puff.

His mate locked eyes with the she-dragon for a beat and copied her. This went on for about a half a minute. "I want to push," she ground out between pants.

"Not yet, my lady."

"I have to," she ground out. Torrent could tell that she was already bearing down.

"Do it then, but not too hard. Slow and easy."

Candy pushed. She made a grunting sound.

"That's it. Slowly. Keep breathing." The healer glanced from between Candy's legs to his mate's face.

After about another half a minute, she slumped back, breathing hard. She pointed to a glass of water on the side table.

Fuck! He was so damned useless. Torrent scrambled to grab the glass and almost fell on his ass.

Candy smiled as she took the glass from him. He helped her sit up so that she could drink. "Here." He brushed the hair from her face. "You're doing great." He kissed her temple.

She gave him a smile that spoke of exhaustion. "I don't know how much longer I can do this."

"A couple more contractions and the young prince will be born." The healer gave Candy a reassuring smile. "You are doing well, my lady."

Candy clutched Torrent's arm and rested her head against it.

Her break didn't last long. Her contractions were coming fast. It felt like it was happening one after another with barely enough time to catch her breath. Her whole body felt achy. Candy had never felt more tired in her life. It was like she had just run a marathon and was being forced to drop and give one hundred pushups.

There was no backing out. No stopping it. She could feel her belly tighten. Her muscles gripping tighter and tighter. It felt like her entire midsection was being ripped in half. She cried out, gripping her belly. It was so hard. There was a pushing sensation down below. Like she needed the toilet ten times over.

The overwhelming urge to push hit her. There was nothing she could do to stop it. Candy gripped the back of her thighs and pushed. The she-dragon was saying something but she couldn't hear a thing. Pushing brought a strange kind of relief. It still hurt but it also felt . . . good. Although good wasn't the right word. It was like massaging a knot on your back. It hurt to do it but it was a good kind of pain. A relief. After hours and hours, she could finally do something other than hang in there.

She sucked in another deep breath and pushed again, giving it all she had. That feeling of pressure increased.

The contraction finally eased. Torrent whispered words of encouragement. "Do you want some more water?"

She nodded. Her mouth felt dry.

He helped her sit up and held the glass while she drank.

"You should stay sitting, my queen. That way you can use the earth's pull to help birth the child."

Candy shook her head, she lay back down against the pillows in her semi reclining position. There was no way in hell she could sit and push.

All too soon her belly began to tighten and the urge to push took over. It felt like this went on for ages. Contraction after contraction. Rest followed by pushing, followed by more pushing. Her reserves were slowly depleting. Candy kept focusing on her baby boy. She could feel that things were progressing. She knew it wouldn't be long. She needed to stay focused on the prize. Her son. It wouldn't be long before they met him.

Focus on that, Candy.

"I see his head," the she-dragon announced.

With renewed vigor, she gave an almighty push. She normally longed for the moments of rest. This time, when her contraction ended, it felt too soon.

The healer was smiling. "One or two more and he'll be born."

"Can you still see him?" Torrent asked. His eyes were wide with excitement. He glanced back down at her with such love, such pride.

The she-dragon shook her head. "It's normal for the baby to move forwards and backwards once or twice before coming into the world. He is preparing himself."

It took two more contractions before his head crowned. Candy could feel him there. She breathed in deeply and pushed like she'd never pushed before. Her nails dug into the back of her thighs.

"That's it." Torrent continued to whisper words of love and encouragement. She felt so much better with him there. There was something cool on her forehead. He was mopping her brow with a wet cloth.

She felt movement between her legs. The she-dragon was doing something. "His head is out." Her voice was animated. "When the next one comes, you need to push with all you've got, he is about to be born, my queen. You are about to meet your son."

Her heart raced. She made a laughing sobbing noise. Torrent put his forehead to hers, as he pulled back, she could see that his eyes were glinting. His jaw was tense. She realized that he was trying not to cry.

"I love you so much," he murmured as he cupped her chin. He kissed her temple.

She couldn't wait for her next contraction. Couldn't wait to meet their little boy. It didn't take long.

"Alright, my lady. This is it. Give it all you've got." The she-dragon was focused between her legs.

Candy pushed like her life depended on it. It didn't take much. She felt her son emerge from her body. The she-dragon caught him. Her face was filled with joy. Her eyes were bright. Though soon, the joy was replaced with a look of shock. Her eyes widened. She looked . . . distressed.

"What is it?" Candy struggled to sit up.

"It can't be." The healer was looking at her baby. Their baby. By the look on the other woman's face, there was something wrong. Something very wrong.

"Is everything okay?" Torrent's voice shook. "Answer me," he growled.

The baby was squirming and gave a tiny yell. His hands were fisted. He gave another cry, louder this time. He sounded fine. His skin was pink but looks could be deceiving.

"He looks fine," Candy whispered. "Please tell me he's okay." She couldn't see all of him. Her own body was in the way.

The healer shook her head. "You have birthed a daughter."

"What?" Torrent's voice lashed through the silence. "There has to be some sort of mistake." His voice cracked.

The she-dragon shook her head. "No mistake, my lord. I'm sorry."

"Why are you sorry?" Candy could hear the panic in her voice. Her little one mewled and she reached for him . . . her. This was confusing. Surely they could discuss it. She wanted her baby. It didn't matter what sex it was as long as the little one was fine.

The healer lifted her child, holding the baby in both

hands. Her daughter's hair looked wet. "I can scent that . . ." the healer paused, looking down. "I'm sorry, my lord, the baby's scent . . ."

Torrent howled. It was the most anguished sound Candy had ever heard. He turned and left the room. Left.

Candy couldn't help it when a tear slipped out. She had just given birth. This was supposed to be the happiest day of her life. "What's wrong?" She already knew the answer to her question. She knew deep down. "Why did he leave?" she whispered.

"Your daughter is perfect in every way." The older woman put the baby onto her chest. On instinct, she closed her arms around the tiny body. The little one was warm. She squirmed and cried out. Candy felt panicked. Her heart was racing. She was breathing far too quickly. Then she looked down. It was like the world slowed down. Like everything stilled for a moment. She felt a love like nothing she had ever experienced before.

"Hello, baby," she managed to choke out through her tears.

"She is a beautiful girl." The healer gave her a nod. "You did well, child."

"She's human, isn't she?"

The she-dragon nodded. "Yes. Very human and very healthy in every way."

"Can you give us a moment please?" Candy looked down at her daughter as she spoke.

"Yes, but I can't stay away too long. You still need to birth the feeding sac."

Candy nodded. "Thank you." The older woman walked to the door. Candy looked back down at the child in her arms. The healer was right, she was perfect. Her eyes were big and very blue. The little cherub was almost bald with just a few strands of hair on her head. The soft downy tufts were blond.

Her baby stared up at her with what looked like wonder. Her heart squeezed so tightly. She needed to hold it together. Needed to be strong for her daughter. Candy swallowed thickly. "It looks like it's just you and me, kid. We'll be okay though."

"Can I hold her?" Torrent stood at the doorway. He looked stricken. His eyes were dark and anguished. His jaw tight. There were two deep lines on his forehead.

A tear slipped down her cheek. Was this him saying goodbye? Was this Torrent double-checking that her baby was, in fact, human before he turned his back on them or was it . . . She chewed on her lip and nodded once, holding the little one out to him.

He took the baby from her. Holding her like she was the most precious thing in all the world. His eyes were filled with tears, his gaze firmly on her daughter. Seeing the baby in his arms, against his huge frame, made her look even tinier.

Candy could hardly breathe. Her eyes stung and there was a huge lump in her throat.

"I'm sorry I left just now."

"It's okay," she blurted.

"No, it's not." He lifted his gaze from the infant in his

arms and directed it on her. "I scared you, hurt you."

"It's . . . understandable."

"I didn't leave because I'm angry or hurt. I don't blame you for anything. I left because I . . ." He cradled her daughter more firmly against his chest. "The truth is, I was scared, petrified." He paused, his throat working. "I'm not her father." He stumbled on the words.

It hurt her to hear him say it. Her lip trembled and by some miracle she managed to keep from crying all over again.

"I want to be though. I really want to be, Candy. I hope that you'll let me. It doesn't matter to me that she—"

"Yes, of course I want that . . . I want it more than anything . . ." A tear escaped. So sue her, she couldn't help it. "I don't know how it happened. I was always so careful. It must've been that last time, with Charles. The timeframe works." Her mind raced through all that had happened. "I must have arrived here already pregnant. I . . ."

"It doesn't matter. I have a daughter. We have a daughter." He looked down at their baby with adoration in his eyes. "I'm the luckiest male on the planet because I have you. It doesn't matter to me that she is human. Our daughter is a part of you and that makes her a part of me too." He scooted closer and kissed her. Torrent broke the kiss and looked deep into her eyes. He grinned. "Besides, we'll make a little brother for her to play with . . ."

Candy gave him a playful slap on the arm. "Don't you dare talk about the next one. I still have to give birth to a placenta."

He kissed her again. "I will hold my daughter. I might never put her down." His whole face softened as he looked down at her.

Candy laughed. "The scary thing is that I think you mean it."

"Of course I mean it." Then he locked eyes with her. "By the way, I have some news."

She frowned. "What news?"

"I ran into Lake earlier." He grinned. "Sky is pregnant. She is already a few weeks along. After you jinxed them so badly the last time, they decided to wait awhile before telling anyone. I didn't even know that she was in heat."

She had to laugh. "That's amazing news. It makes sense now. Remember, that little vacation they took. We had to look after Maggie." She paused, remembering how well the three dogs had gotten along. "It was because she was in heat." Then she pulled a face. "I didn't jinx them that first time."

"You so did." He nestled into her neck and kissed her just under her ear. Then he looked down at their daughter. "Your mom is a jinxer."

Their daughter made a little noise that sounded like an agreement.

"You tell your dad that he talks through his . . . you know where."

Just at the second, there was a farting noise. The little one had farted. They both looked at one another and laughed.

"You take after your mom," Torrent managed to get

out between chuckles. Then he looked down at the little one and turned serious. He even made a strange noise.

"What's wrong?" She'd had enough surprises for one day.

"Um . . . it's nothing." He gave a small shake of the head. Candy could see that he didn't mean it.

"Tell me and right now." She leaned forward but something inside her spasmed. It felt like the start of a contraction. *Shit!* "I'm about to get seriously cranky."

Torrent licked his lips. "I'm sure I just saw her eyes slit . . . like dragon eyes but that can't be, on account of her being human." He pointed out unnecessarily. "I'm sure I was just seeing things."

"Yeah, you must have been." Torrent was looking intently at the little one. "How would that even be possible? I mean . . ." The contraction worsened and she gripped her belly. " . . . could it be possible?"

"I don't think so." He shook his head.

Candy tried to suppress a groan as the contraction grew worse.

"Should I call the healer?" Torrent looked concerned.

"In a minute. Hypothetically speaking, let's say what you just saw was real."

He nodded.

"How would it be possible?"

"Well." He shifted in his seat, moving the baby to his other arm and snuggling her to his chest. "You've changed in the last few months because of our bond. It's normal after a mating that the human takes on some traits of the male she is mated to."

"My eyes haven't slitted or anything."

"Yeah, but you are a fully grown adult. It might have affected . . . changed her more than you, on account that she was still developing in your womb. She's very much a human, but"—he inhaled deeply—"there might be more to her in some way. Maybe."

Candy grit her teeth and moaned.

"I'm calling the healer. We'll talk about this later."

Candy nodded, her contraction was reaching its peak. Not nearly as bad as the ones she'd experienced earlier, but her body was so bruised and battered that it hurt anyway. Candy made a grunting noise. The baby cried out from Torrent's arms.

Torrent stumbled as he walked towards the door but quickly righted himself. "Oh hell," he growled. "Shit." He chuckled and shook his head before turning back towards her. "I know what I saw this time." He was smiling broadly. "A tiny patch of scales, beneath the little one's skin when you made those noises. She doesn't like that you are in pain." His eyes were wide. "I guess there is a part of me inside her after all. She must've experienced changes because of our mating."

"You're saying your DNA affected her, just as it affected me?"

Torrent nodded. "Although she isn't my biological daughter, there is some of my DNA in her bloodstream. That makes her all the more my child." He was beaming.

She leaned back against the bedding, her contraction

over for now. "I'm not sure what it means exactly but I'm glad." Candy had to smile back at him.

Torrent shook his head in disbelief. "We'll have to wait and see just how much my DNA affected her. She smells of human, yet . . ."

"She's a miracle."

Torrent grinned. "Our little miracle."

Another contraction started up. "Call the healer," Candy moaned. "This thing is coming."

Torrent nodded. "I must inform my family, my people. I must meet with Blaze to discuss what has happened. This could change things for non-humans. We will have to wait and see."

"Call the healer." Candy would have thrown something at him if it weren't for the fact that he had precious cargo onboard.

"I'm sorry, my love. I got carried away. I am filled with excitement."

"I'm filled with something else and it's coming out as we speak. Call the healer." Candy fake growled, she couldn't help but to smile even though it hurt like hell.

"Oh yes." He walked back to her and kissed her. "Fuck, but I love you."

"Go now before you make me a widow."

He grinned wider and finally did what she asked.

AUTHOR'S NOTE

Thank-you for reading the second book in my new series. It is a spin off from my bestselling series The Chosen and The Program.

This book would not have been possible without the assistance of my editor and beta readers. Thank you KR, Aisha and Enid. Also, a big thank you to my ARC readers for your invaluable input and support. Especially those of you that review my books every time without fail. I'm talking about you Judy and Ana . . . there are more of you. Thank you all!!

A big thank you to you . . . my readers. For reading my work and for all your messages and emails. Also, to those of you that take the time to review my books. It means the world to me. You are what keeps me writing on days that I might not feel like it so much.

If you want to be kept updated on new releases please sign up to my Latest Release Newsletter to ensure that you don't miss out http://mad.ly/signups/96708/join. I promise not to spam you or divulge your email address to a third party. I send my mailing list an exclusive sneak peek prior to release. I would love to hear from you so please feel free to drop me a line charlene.hartnady@gmail.com.

Find me on Facebook—

www.facebook.com/authorhartnady

I live on an acre in the country with my gorgeous husband and three sons and an array of pets.

You can usually find me on the computer completely lost in worlds of my making. I believe that it is the small things that truly matter like that feeling you get when you start a new book or a particularly beautiful sunset.

BOOKS BY THIS AUTHOR

The Chosen Series:
Book 1 ~ Chosen by the Vampire Kings
Book 2 ~ Stolen by the Alpha Wolf
Book 3 ~ Unlikely Mates
Book 4 ~ Awakened by the Vampire Prince
Book 5 ~ Mated to the Vampire Kings (Short Novel)
Book 6 ~ Wolf Whisperer (Novella)

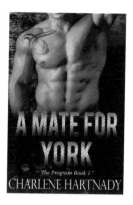

The Program Series (Vampire Novels):

Demon Chaser Series (No cliffhangers):

Excerpt

Chosen
BY THE
VAMPIRE KINGS

The Chosen Series ~ Book 1

Chapter 1

IT HAD BEEN MANY years since he had been in such close proximity of his birth enemy. Zane looked as arrogant and as full of shit as ever. Barking orders at his royal guard like they were his servants instead of trusted subjects. In some cases, those receiving the harsh treatment were probably his best buddies. Then again, the bastard probably didn't have any friends. Shaking his head, Brant turned and surveyed the crowd. He felt sorry for the female that would soon be chosen to become queen to the likes of that ruthless king.

It wasn't his concern though. His own queen was out there. Brant shuddered, praying that the events of one hundred years ago would not repeat themselves. A bloody war between their fathers had been the result of the last choosing. It couldn't happen again, the vampire species would not survive another war at this point.

As his mind returned to thoughts of his own female, he knew that he would not be able to remain sensible where she was concerned. His focus was on protecting his coven, and he would dispatch the other male without hesitation if he so much as looked at what was his. No matter the odds, and the knowledge of Zane's ruthlessness, Brant would allow nothing to harm her. She was too valuable, too precious of a gift to him.

Turning, he surveyed the crowd again. Feeling the electric pulse of her closeness. According to the lores, he would be able to sense her and to tell of their compatibility almost instantly even in a crowd full of females. From the noise projecting from outside, he could tell there were many females present. He hoped his chosen would be willing from the start. The last thing he wanted was to force her, to have to go caveman on her and throw her over his shoulder. The thought did not appeal to him, but the choosing was not something that could be ignored. She would feel it as well, whether she wanted to or not.

"Ready?" his head guard Xavier asked as he moved in next to him. His brother's eyes never faltered as they stared straight into his. Brant knew the reason for the intenseness. Xavier harbored similar feelings of distaste and distrust for their neighboring king. In order to maintain their strenuous hold on the truce between them, it had always been necessary to keep interactions between the two covens to a minimum. This event was no exception.

"Yeah, as ready as I'll ever be," Brant replied while taking a moment to scan the room.

"Your eyes are glowing my lord, maybe you should stop looking in that direction."

Brant looked into Xavier's clear grey eyes. *Always the cool one in a situation.* "My eyes have nothing to do with that bastard at the moment, and everything to do with my female. I can sense her, and the urge to mate is strong. I just hope that she'll be agreeable to a speedy union."

"I told you to take a female, ease your need. Humans are . . . easily broken. We don't want any accidents." Xavier spoke softly, ensuring that no one else would be privy to their conversation.

"I have a plan."

"Please, tell me you at least drank recently," Xavier's eyes narrowed. When Brant didn't reply, his brother's eyes narrowed even more. He made a sound of disbelief and continued, "Brother, should you harm our future—"

"Enough," Brant growled.

Xavier lowered his eyes.

"I said I have a plan. My future queen will come to no harm."

Xavier nodded. "Yes, my lord. It is time."

Brant took a deep breath. He had been raised for this moment. His decision and the events of the next few minutes would determine the future of his coven.

No pressure.

Tanya had seen tabloid pictures of the vampire kings and they really weren't all that attractive, unless you were into the ultra-big, ultra-built and ridiculously bad non-human types.

She so wasn't.

The whole choosing ceremony was so outdated to the point of being down right sexist. Yet, every hundred years, all of the eligible women would assemble to be chosen. A queen for each of the kings. The worst part was that vampires and humans never mixed so there was very little known about them. Their traditions, their ways, their expectations, she shuddered.

For at least the twentieth time, she wished that her best

friend Becky was there with her. The whole thing was a real circus. Tanya hadn't realized how many women there were in Sweetwater between the ages of twenty one and thirty. Aside from age, there had been a long list of requirements. Everything from weight and height to a clean medical exam.

Tanya sighed as a group of giggling women squeezed past her trying to find a spot closer to the podium. Becky was divorced, a complete no-no. It had automatically disqualified her from being allowed to attend the choosing ceremony. Attend, hah, not hardly, the right term would be forced. If all aspects of the criteria were met, it was mandatory to be here. For whatever reason, the human justice system went along with this whole farce once a century. Only those wanting a fast track to jail failed to show up. What scared her the most though was the thought of how many of these women were actually hoping to be chosen today.

Vampire queen.

Tanya cringed at the thought. For once she was thankful for being a little curvy. Most men were into wafer thin model types, so she would be safe.

The whole courtyard vibrated with an excited hum.

The two kings were royalty but they were also vampires. They drank blood for heaven's sake. Had these women lost their freaking minds?

It was early afternoon yet you wouldn't guess it by how some of them were dressed. Little back numbers, low cut tops, sequins and jewelry were the order of the day. The amount of skin on display was obscene. Tanya did a double take as one of the ladies walked by, she was wearing a sheer dress without underwear. Her lady bits on display for all and sundry. With all that exposed skin, she hoped that the woman had used sunblock. The highest possible factor.

Tanya looked down at her jeans and t-shirt. Maybe she should've tried a little harder but then again, she wasn't planning on getting noticed. She had a life to get back to. It wasn't much but she had her little book store. Some might consider it to be boring, but she liked it just fine.

She'd owned The Book Corner for two years now. Reading had always been a major passion, that and coffee. It had been her ultimate dream to own a little coffee shop on the side. That way potential customers could browse through purchases while enjoying a cappuccino and maybe a little pastry. So far she was way behind on those goals. She was supposed to have had half the money she needed already saved in order to do the required renovations. As it stood though, she may not even have a store soon, let alone an additional coffee shop. She couldn't afford to hire someone to fill in for her today. Just the thought of the closed sign on the door, of losing potential customers, had her looking at her watch. Hopefully this would be over soon. The last thing she needed in her life was a man . . . let alone a vampire who would not only uproot her from her goals but from her friends and family as well. She only had one BFF and her aunt, but she loved them both a ton.

It had been a while since she'd dated and her last relationship had ended . . . badly. Sex was overrated anyway. She could just imagine how much worse it would be with a blood sucking vamp. Wishing she was back at the store, she glanced at her watch a second time.

It wasn't like one of the kings would ever think of choosing a plain Jane like her anyways. What a waste of her precious time.

There was silence followed by gasps as two of the biggest, meanest looking men she'd ever seen walked onto the platform. Tanya had expected fanfare. A trumpet call. An announcement at the very least. What she hadn't expected was to be shocked stupid. Pictures she'd seen of the men didn't do them justice.

Tall, *check.*

Built, *check.*

Mean, *check.*

Ridiculously hunkalious, *double check.*

Several women swooned. One woman, closer to the front, fainted. Medics pushed their way through the thick crowd and placed the young women on stretchers.

The king on the left was slightly shorter, from tabloid pictures she'd seen, he had to be Zane. Although short was the wrong description, the big vampire must be at least around six and a half feet. He was meaner looking, with close cropped hair. From this distance she could tell that he had dark, hard eyes. A nervous chill radiated through her body.

King Brant was taller and even though he had a massive chest and bulging arms, he wasn't quite as broad as the scary one. Neither was classically good-looking. Though both radiated raw energy and sex appeal like nothing she'd ever seen before.

"Pick me!" One of the women closer to the platform shouted waving her arms.

The kings ignored her.

A group to the side hoisted a '*Look over here*' sign. *What was it with these freaking women?* For some reason it bothered her that they were so desperate to become one of the next vampire queens that they would do anything to get noticed? And the question of the hour was, *why?*

Turning back to the platform, she noticed that the taller one, Brant, had medium length dark hair, his eyes were dark and his mouth generous. Tanya was certain he would be even more attractive if he smiled.

Both men were tense. They just stood there, hands fisted at their sides. The crowd grew restless. Some women tried to push to the front while others tried to catch the attention of one or both of the men on the elevated platform.

Eventually, Zane stepped forward, his hard eyes were fixed on her. *What the hell?* Adrenaline surged through her blood, but her mind immediately rejected the idea that he was actually looking at her. It had to be some sort of mistake. His eyes seemed to stay on her for a few more seconds. Just as she began to feel the need to look around her for the true object of his fascination, his gaze moved to the back of the crowd. She breathed out in a gush.

"You," his gruff, smoky voice was a low vibration. He pointed somewhere behind Tanya.

An equally big, equally mean looking man came onto the platform from the side. King Zane didn't take his eyes off the female he had set his sights on the entire time he spoke to what had to be his head guard. All of the surrounding men were dressed in full leather. Though, this one wore a silver family crest on his chest.

Tanya shivered, thankful she hadn't been chosen by the likes of him.

Zane continued to shout orders. The head guard, flanked by two vampires, stepped off the platform and stalked through the crowd. Tanya shifted to the side as they approached. They were big bastards. The women surged forward. One dared to touch. The king's head guard paused, without turning to face the culprit, he growled. His top lip curled revealing sharp fangs. The air caught in her lungs. Her pulse quickened.

They were so close, Tanya could smell a musky male scent, could almost feel heat radiate off their huge bodies as they passed.

"You," a deep growl sounded through the crowd.

"No," a feminine wail responded. "Let go of me!"

Tanya was too afraid to turn. So close to the action, she was fearful of being noticed.

Another wail, louder this time.

"Put me down!" the woman shrieked. It seemed Tanya was not the only one there that didn't want to be chosen.

Tanya moved with the crowd as the guards passed, the woman was slung over the shoulder of the head guard. She kicked and screamed. The big vampire didn't seem to notice though. Tanya caught the look of sheer terror on the young woman's face.

This wasn't right.

How could this be allowed to happen? Tanya looked around her at the multitude of willing ladies. Women that were practically throwing themselves at the vampire kings. *Why did the SOB have to go and pick one of the few that wasn't interested?*

Tanya took a few steps in the direction of the platform. *Not happening.* She stopped. She didn't want to get involved. Couldn't afford to. She didn't even know the girl. It wasn't like she could change the situation even if she tried. This ritual had been going on for hundreds, possibly thousands, of years.

A large group of women at the front screamed to Zane that he pick them instead. One of the young ladies even lifted her top.

The king didn't take his eyes off his chosen woman the entire time that his guard maneuvered through the crowd. They narrowed though as they got closer. The girl screamed louder.

"Please don't do this. Please, I beg you." The screams had turned to sobs at this point.

Tanya couldn't bear to hear them. Each word struck a nerve.

Zane nodded in the direction of the waiting SUVs.

"Oh God, please no," she was sobbing in earnest.

The nerve quickly rubbed raw until Tanya couldn't take it anymore. "Stop!" She marched in the direction of the vampire king. "Stop that at once. Let her go."

Neither king took any notice. Maybe some of the others in the crowd were feeling the same way as she did because the women parted to let her through. "What you are doing is nothing short of barbaric."

The crowd hushed.

"She doesn't want to go with you. Let her go right now." Tanya projected, sounding more confident than she felt.

Zane glanced her way before turning in the direction of the waiting vehicles.

"This is a sexist, disgusting tradition that needs to be put to an end. Why can't you choose someone that's actually interested in going with you? Why does it have to be her?"

He turned back, his dark eyes zoning in on her. Her breathing hitched. Her heart rate increased, a whole damn lot. *I just had to get involved. Couldn't leave it alone.*

"This woman has been chosen as my mate. What is done cannot be undone." He turned and made for the waiting vehicles. Like that was a reasonable explanation. *So not.*

"Bastard! Leave her alone!" She must have completely lost her mind because she walked after him and straight into the massive chest of one of the guards. There was only one thing to do in a situation like this, she beat against the chest in her way while screaming obscenities at the retreating back of the bastard king.

"Easy," a low rumble that had her insides vibrating.

Tanya looked up into a set of dark, penetrating eyes. She froze. It was Brant. The second vampire king.

"What would you like me to do with her?" asked a voice to the right of the king.

His eyes stayed on hers. His nostrils flared and his body tightened. It was then that she realized that her hands were flattened on his chest. She snatched them away.

"Lord Brant?" the voice enquired.

"She's coming with me." He took her hand and strode towards the remaining vehicles. She wanted to pull away, to dig her heels in the ground, but her traitorous feet kept on moving in time with his. It was only when they reached the waiting SUV and Brant opened the door and gestured for her to enter, that she finally snapped out of it. Part of her didn't want to believe this was happening. As ridiculous as it seemed, King Brant had chosen her.

No. Surely not.

"Wait."

His eyes snapped to hers. Dark, fathomless, deadly.

Chosen by the Vampire Kings (Ménage)—available now

Printed in Great Britain
by Amazon